SCARY
KISSES

SCARY

KISSES

BRAD GOOCH

G. P. PUTNAM'S SONS
NEW YORK

The author gratefully acknowledges permission for the use of lyrics from "Hungry Heart" by Bruce Springsteen. Copyright © 1980 by Bruce Springsteen.

G. P. Putnam's Sons
Publishers Since 1838
200 Madison Avenue
New York, NY 10016

Library of Congress Cataloging-in-Publication Data
Gooch, Brad, date.
  Scary kisses.
  I. Title.
PS3557.0478S24   1988   813'.54   88-11440
ISBN 0-399-13410-7

Design by the Sarabande Press

Printed in the United States of America
1 2 3 4 5 6 7 8 9 10

FOR HOWARD BROOKNER

Special thanks to my editor, Janis Vallely,
and to my agent, Joy Harris.

TIME:

LATE SEVENTIES,

EARLY EIGHTIES

NEW YORK

TODD GETS OFF ON HIMSELF

Clumsily.

Todd gets up. The leftover smoke from last night's cigarettes stuffed in his throat like cotton. His cabin room is dark and anonymous and breezy. Sun registers on the pulled-down orange shade (litmus paper). He rolls apart from the sheets, one hairy leg hanging off the double-thickness mattress onto the floor, the other leg scissored up, one palm on scratchy chest, the other cupping matted sac of balls.

He sleepwalks through a shuffle on the floor of loose glossy magazine pages and rough newspaper sheets into the main room of the cabin. Pulls on some white chinos. Stands there. Twenty-four. Six feet. Brown wavy hair stuck in place from salt water. Skin dark from lying on the beach all week by himself. Cats eyes: transparent splotches of green, brown, blue, red, gray. Makes a half-smile to no one.

(It's not true that older men and women are any more likely to have spirits waking them up, or following them, than teenagers and young people. Twenty-four is a magic age.)

Todd makes a path through bullrushlike reeds, pinprick spears of grass. Over tracks brushed in the sand the night before by migrating snakes. The whites of his toenails and fingernails look ivory in contrast.

No one is around on the Skunk Hollow Beach, an illegal beach on lower Long Island with condemned shanty shacks, condemned so the area can be turned into a state park. In the meantime a few squatters take advantage.

Todd stretches in front of the in-full-blast ocean. The noisy birds in the stinkwood trees around the cabin can't be heard. He touches his toes. Bends from side to side. Then unzips his zipper and wriggles out of his white parchment pants. Lies down using his discarded pants as a beach blanket, but an irregular one, so he feels random scratches of sand and nicky rocks on his back and the backs of his legs. He starts rubbing himself.

Todd lathers his dick in pH-balanced spit from his mouth. His mouth is a pond, full of algae. The ocean sounds like a highway. Todd's fist is a funnel, or a hot-dog bun, going up and down. Soon the tube releases its sputter of falling stars in the daytime.

Then quiet. The sun grows hotter and bigger faster, a Beethoven symphony finally getting rolling. Todd stays indolent like a splayed starfish on this, his last beach day.

Todd: (mumbling out loud, but making no sense, to a helicopter flying overhead) Drop a bomb on me. It won't matter. I'm a bone.

Later in the afternoon he catches a wooden ferry home.

"DON'T TREAD ON ME"

Blah.

The office the next week is filled with blah. No matter how many insect phones ring. No matter how many stories the workers tell each other in the basement offices of The Student Galaxy of Travel Options (S.G.T.O.) across from the United Nations.

Todd is talking to a guy sitting next to him at a flat teak work table where they are both writing out plane tickets. Todd's face is still burnished. He has on black cuff trousers and a white button-down shirt with ink stains above the pocket line, like storm clouds over a butte. Deep cranberry Weejuns, used. His impassive paleface friend is dressed in a blue cotton suit.

Todd keeps next to him a small book of the flags of all the nations. It's open to his favorite, the Don't Tread on Me, with an emblem of a coiled snake that looks more like an angry Tibetan spirit than anything colonial American. He rips out the flag's page and Scotch-tapes it to the wall in front of him. Palms it flat with a pound.

Todd: (to adjacent ticket-writer) The best part was the only other squatter. Every night at sunset he'd come and sit on his second-story roof. Right on the shingles. With no clothes. Just his gray naked flabby body. And he had this gray beard and long hippie hair. He looked like that publisher of *Screw*.

Adjacent Ticket-writer: (to Erica, who just walked up) The highlight of Todd's vacation was a flasher.

Todd: (correcting) A sixties person.

Erica, though, is not bounced off course. She is small, pale, as pale as a porcelain old dish. But now her blue veins are showing in her chestnut-contoured big forehead, her thin brown hair pulled back with a rubber band. Erica is a friend. She even got

Todd his job. (They went to college together, where Todd met Lucy.) But Todd is messing up, and when he messes up, Erica receives a buzz (shock) on her intercom from her boss. So she is standing there in her light plaid jumper that flares up to a top that snaps around the back of the neck and covers over much of a blouse, as water is always covering over some land, and she is chewing at him.

Erica: I'm angry at you. And so are the three students stranded in Paris because you wrote "Paris" on their return tickets and not "Amsterdam." They missed their plane. (straining each word) It . . . costs . . . us.

Todd: (staring ahead at the coiled snake, but mild-mannered in his voice) You don't say "us" like you mean it. If you're going to say the words, mean them, or don't say them.

Erica: You're not being obedient. I'm the manager and I'm being obedient.

Todd: That's why you're the manager. Here. Read this. Out loud. Just to get a grip.

Todd takes an index card out of his top shirt pocket on which he has written down in pencil a paragraph from a novel he's been reading.

Erica: (dutifully reading out loud) "She lifted her minidress over her head and stripped it off. She wasn't wearing a bra. Her bikini briefs were white nylon. There was a single word 'Saturday' in blue embroidery on them."

When she stops, she looks around and sees nearby desk workers watching her. They look screwy, or they are looking at her in a way to make her know they see her as screwy. She hands Todd his index card back. Realizes that he has tricked her.

Erica: (imperatively) Don't slink.

Todd: (stopping smiling, pulleying up some feeling) What I mean is you're not really angry with me. You're pretending. So level with me. I'm not saying that I don't know I put those three losers through a wash cycle. I do know that.

Erica: (feeling apologized to) Thank you. Now I feel better.

All about the big noisy room are lots of other desks. At one a fat young woman is talking about her late night at the clubs in the East Village. She is all mouth right now. ("They used my table like it was their equipment.") At another a thin guy is reading a *Batman* comic. At still another an Irish green-carder is talking on the phone to the friend she married to get it. He was beat up on the street last night for his wallet. ("Go to a jaw doctor.")

PICK-UP

As soon as Todd gets out at five, Happy Hour, he speedwalks to a corner bar with an Austrian Tyrolean green-wood motif and drinks down green bottles of beer. He glugs the emerald liquid. Some of his unhappiness subsides, and some happiness surges in. He leans, standing, letting the curve of the bar push into his numb cotton-covered thigh muscle.

Then he takes the shuttle, and then the downtown Seventh Avenue IRT, and disembarks at the Fourteenth Street stop, the Twelfth Street exit, marked by a white building with wave motifs and porthole windows, looking more like a marina than the hospital it is. He is walking south, whistling some unmelodic notes, toward Perry Street, to his apartment building that is only a block away from the dirty muscular powerful Hudson River on its way somewhere, out to sea.

Just this morning, walking the same route in the opposite direction, Todd had been picked up. A woman had been trailing him for a block of Seventh Avenue, walking speedily off the curb, right onto the street, bikes veering off to miss her. She had striking auburn-red hair, probably dyed, the same color as the prostitute dancers on the cardboard posters of Toulouse-Lautrec. Gravlax-colored hair.

She stuck a silver card for a modeling agency where she works, Zebra, into his hand. The card featured a raised silhouette of a zebra that blended in with the silver of the background, except for its black diagonal stripes. She put her palm on top of Todd's hand. "Call me." Then she turned back into the street and saluted a yellow cab.

Now Todd feels for his wallet. He opens it, and out from among the green bills, some dirty, some clean, he retrieves the silver card. He slips the card into his shirt pocket, and the wallet back into his pants.

Todd turns on Perry. Walks to his apartment building. Up to his fifth-floor studio past the flat metal mailboxes that have been jimmied open, past the door of a woman and her two wheezing dogs, past the door of the Polack late-teenager who usually wears a black T-shirt and often stares with drooping eyes.

Todd's apartment is a shoebox: a long rectangle of a room painted off-white. The floor is imitation gray marble linoleum. Its two windows are the glassy eyes of a whale. A counter breaks up the room's relentless right-between-the-eyes vanishing perspective. There's a glassed-in movie poster on the wall for *Les Valseuses*, with Gerard Depardieu as a moto-head, a prototype of the surf Nazi. An open bottle of framboise on a low bookcase gives off an ether smell. When Todd opens one window a crack to atomize the place, the white sheets on his unmade mattress on the floor ripple.

Todd steps out of his shoes, pants, shirt, letting them pyramid on the floor. Left only in white T-shirt, boxer shorts, gray socks, he slips down under one sheet on the mattress. Fumbles at a half-smoked Chesterfield extinguished in a metal ashtray—its inside a painted map of Florida. Lights up. The more he smokes, the more nervous he feels. As he thinks, he stares through the two pastel (tinted now by sky) windows at all the different apartment buildings and warehouses and factories at different heights that block out whatever horizon there may be. The rectangle of twilight sky visible in his window has the same value, and depth, as the buildings. It's one shape among many, changing from light lilac to dark maroon. In many of the lit buildings people are moving around in a yellow, or blue, or white haze.

Todd picks up his powerful binos and begins to swoon over the landscape, looking for some action.

Just then the phone rings. Todd is glad the machine will pick up. His message comes on—a friend made it for him—simulated Rocky and Bullwinkle voices do the talking.

Lucy: Todd. Are you there? (her singsong voice rising into a more upset treble) Where are you? We were supposed to get Chinese food. I'm hungry.

Todd thumbs his cigarette out in the ashtray as if he is pushing down on a button. Then he scrambles over to the low wooden shelves and pulls out one big black scrapbook from a whole shelf-full of big black scrapbooks. In a studio that's otherwise as disheveled as the inside of an appliance carton filled with packing confetti and litter, the scrapbooks are ordered and immaculate. Todd returns to his mattress and opens the oversized book out on his lap. Takes the Don't Tread on Me snake out of his shirt pocket. He had ripped the flag page off the wall before he left work and cut the snake out from the rest. So he pastes it in one big blank page. Then takes the silver Zebra card out of the same shirt pocket and pastes that underneath.

Looks intent.

Todd has been keeping scrapbooks since he was a kid. At first they were just columns of headlines on current events. Assassinations. Space Maneuvers. Papal Visits. Then, as a teen, his scrapbooks became more personal, biographical. He pasted in a 45 of Chuck Berry's "Reelin' and Rockin'." One used rubber. Polaroids of the disastrous insides of his parents' two-story house that was washed off its foundations during a big flood in northeastern Pennsylvania.

Since Todd has arrived in New York the pages are more Islamic and abstract. The cutting and pasting is virtuosic. On one page he stuck tickets to BAM to see Laurie Anderson. (A first New York date with Lucy.) But also on the page are silver cutout silhouettes of Dead Kennedys–style band members that Todd sketched then scissored then stitched in. He hammered the black-and-blue orchid down flat (not a memento, but bought at a nearby flower store expressly to be pressed in). Up at top, a full-length newspaper-grainy *Post* photograph of Fidel Castro, with beard and mustache and hair all hand-colored Marxist red.

When the phone rings this time, he answers. It's his friend, Lee, the actor. Lee's voice booms from Todd's receiver. Lee is a commercial TV actor, in a series. They met at dinner after work one night; he was the friend of a friend. Todd became all interested in acting. Strasberg. Now they're phone buddies. Todd tells him about Zebra.

Lee gets excited. He is sure that Todd can do it. He offers to call his friend, Louis, a big fashion photographer. So he quickly hangs up, and calls back five minutes later, having set up an appointment for Todd to go by Louis's place in two days.

Lee: I'm going out to my spiritualist church in Brooklyn this Sunday. Do you want to come?

Todd: You know I just get jealous of everybody when they feel the spirit. I have to get off now.

All at once Todd wants Lucy. He misses her so much that it burns. He dials his clunky rotary black film-noir telephone. His finger makes its circles over the phone's face, like the circles he used to make when he swirled his own spit on his high school's stone steps. Lucy's machine message is just a beep. No nonsense.

Todd: (lying back with head on mattress, body stretched out on cool floor) I'm sorry I missed your call baby. I'm sorry I missed our Chinese dinner. I just had to be a zombie for a while on my own. You wouldn't have liked me anyway. But if you're looking for a man who knows how to stir your taffy the way you like it . . . if you're dying for a tongue to separate those soft hairs of your you-know-what . . . if you want to be properly felt up . . . pleeeaze call me back.

Todd clicks down. At the same time he raises one eyebrow and whistles out. He knows he just did something hot.

LUCY'S MATTRESS

Same time, next evening.

Lucy's lying like an odalisque on her mattress. She has medium-length black hair. Not the kind that looks dark, the kind that looks bright. Face as white as a whippet's. Copper-brown eyes, cool and see-through. No lipstick on lips. Is dressed in a white wrinkled blouse, black corduroy skirt, black stockings. Lots of shapes to her body, not flat. She twitches around a bit. Would look good in a girl band.

Her mattress is on the floor of her place on the top floor of an illegal building on the corner of Bleecker Street and Bowery. Across the street is CBGB's and the Amato Opera. Down the street is the deli where Lucy buys her coffee in the morning and her sandwiches in the afternoon.

(Behind the counter of the deli usually stands a tall teenager whose face is splotches of pink and red and orange from the night when a crazy bum came in the place and threw acid at him. Lucy was there, stunned. The red revolving light on top of the ambulance was particularly lopsided the night of the tragedy—a tragedy that persists every time this guy is looked at by strangers as a goon.)

Todd is lying curled up next to Lucy's mattress on the raggedy fuchsia shag rug. Has on the same black-and-white clothes as yesterday. Came straight from work. Is resting his head on the side of the mattress, neck cricked, like a broken toy. There's a hole in the brown brick wall opposite him the last tenant made with a pickax while angel-dusted one night. Lucy's apartment is really two apartments—formerly Chinese sewing factories— joined by this one hole. A faint smell of gas leaks from the stove burners.

Lucy: (stretching one leg brushingly over Todd's shirted abs) And then what happened?

Todd: I dunno. So Lee called his friend Louis and I'm going by to see him tomorrow. If he thinks I'm any good he'll do a few snaps.

Lucy: (twinges, withdraws leg, lights a long Benson & Hedges Light) Why did you use that word "snaps"? That's not one of your words. Where did you pick it up?

Todd: (stopped short) It's Louis's word. He's English and he used the word "snaps." And Lee used it when he was mimicking him to me. . . . It's not a fuck word.

Lucy: (mellowing, brushing him with her leg again) Oh. He's English. . . . But when did all this start, hon? It seems like just yesterday.

Todd: (kissing the tops of her hands) It was just yesterday. And nothing's happened yet. (dismissively) What should we do?

To snap out of it, Lucy kicks Todd once in the crotch. He doubles over in a hernia howl. This kick is a signal between them. Lucy wets her bottom lip. Todd comes at her, putting his one hand up under her dress, while rubbing his other palm on her corduroy behind. He has her in a grip. She wriggles away, her spine vibrating as if it were just tapped. He moves on her. They laugh a lot and start rolling around. Like two people slow-dancing, but this time horizontally rather than vertically.

But it's a fizzle. The two never get past the heaving part. And so in a few more minutes fade themselves out by napping. Soon it is black outside, the depressing light of the streetlamp blurred by plastic tarps that cover the windows to keep heat in in winter. Lucy never untacked the sheets during the summer.

Todd: (waking up first, tasting sleep in his mouth) I've gotta go. I've gotta Woolite my underwear for tomorrow.

Lucy: (surprised) You never have clean underwear. You always have yellow stains.

Todd: This is different.

Lucy: (feeling hollow) Did you eat?

Todd: (wanting to move on) Let's go to the Chinese place and each take our own takeouts.

Lucy is massaging the back of Todd's neck, and making revving-up motor sounds. Some pains in her hands and fingers. The wind is whooshing the plastic sheets around. Lucy feels at a loss tonight. Maybe because fall is starting up with its dark chill breezes.

A CAMERA IS A KIND OF MIRROR

Todd gets out of work early the next day to make it to Louis's penthouse while the sun is still usable. It's about four on a late September afternoon. The penthouse turns out to be a studio apartment on a top floor with a reprieve of terrace.

No black-white clothes today. Rather tight light blue jeans with white paint stains, a lucent green rugby shirt a friend mailed him from Laguna, and white basketball sneakers with red racing stripes. He trudges as he walks in. Not sure which way is up.

Louis: (with English accent) In Italy at this time you would get the most golden gorgeous light. In New York it's more—high-tech. (laughs at his own joke in the direction of a wall)

Louis is about forty, looks twenty-seven. He had once been a model in Europe. And somehow is preserved at the same age today, with blond hair, and magazine-paper skin. He acts a tad snotty. But actually his soft-candy core can be tasted all the time. His English assistant, littler, younger, but older-looking, is already outside on the terrace, fiddling with silver reflectors, silent, obsequious, and proud.

Louis directs Todd onto the wraparound stone terrace. They try out different positions, sometimes using the building with the ziggurat clock tower on Twenty-third Street that looks like an architect's idea of a building circa Hammurabi as a backdrop.

Todd's thick hair stays in place in the blustery wind, although the reflector warps and cracks and swirls out-of-hand. Louis talks to Todd a bit during the camera work.

Louis: (disinterestedly) Why do you want to be a model?

Todd: This woman gave me her card.

Assistant: (furious) That attitude will end you up on the road to perdition faster than you can bat those pretty eyelashes.

Louis smiles maturely at his sorcerer's apprentice. Todd bites down on the inside of his cheeks.

Every few seconds a light flashes. Whenever possible, between flashes, Todd looks away to clear the dot from his eyes, and to scan the windows of nearby apartment buildings for people, maybe walking around nude, maybe eating, maybe watching TV, maybe jacking off. Then suddenly he starts talking.

Todd: (in a streak) My girlfriend called me this morning. She read me this article, well part of it, about Amish people who won't let their pictures be taken because they think it will steal their souls. Thanks a lot I said to her. . . . But it's true. I'm just a target for that bazooka you've got there. And the more I concentrate on my body, the more I'm having an out-of-body experience. It's weird as shit. Weirder than shit. . . .

Assistant: Shut your moving mouth and stand dead as a doornail.

Louis: He's right. I'm using a slow exposure. Dead. But with lots of life.

Todd, stopped mid-sentence, feels like a projector flapping sillily at the end of a reel.

The phone inside chortles. The assistant hurries to answer, brings the phone back out to Louis, then turns toward the reflector, the glare of its silver lining making him look like a tin man.

Todd moves just inside the sliding glass door and flips through a copy of GQ left open on a short pillar. A big smiling guy in a cinnamon-colored sweater is twirling a basketball on one handsome finger. A darker fellow in a blue parachute outfit has another smaller fellow in a necklock, both with big grins. A red-haired girl is kneeling next to a melancholy brunette lunk who's lounging on a pastel beach chair—her face as available as a drugged doe's.

Louis calls Todd back to finish the roll.

Louis: (flashing away, as clouds make last shreds of the sun, and the air turns purple-gray) I hope you like to read.

Todd: Yeah. I like to read. I also make scrapbooks.

Louis: (ignoring the scrapbook part) Well you'll be able to read on shoots. Most of the time you just sit around waiting to get your picture taken.

Assistant: (ever angry) They sit around all day in a mist, half of them, petulant as hell, and you have to soothe their feathers . . . with cola . . . and with loud music.

Louis: (claps hands) That's it. I think we've got it. Ring me in a few days and you can come by to see the contacts.

Todd: Thanks Louis.

Louis: Don't worry. You'll loosen up.

SIXTY DOLLARS

While Todd is posing, Lucy is out spending sixty dollars.

In her short blue navy peacoat, the same length as the skirt underneath, black stockings, black flat shoes, an imitation crocodile-skin bag hanging from a chain strap slung over her shoulder, she walks out the front door of her tan brick building.

She walks on a diagonal across Bowery, into a day that is orange-tinted and windy and loud. Then down the street of the Men's Detention Center. None of its scuffed men whistle at her or make comments. Because of their poverty and potential for violence they have this subliminal dignity.

Lucy finally emerges at Second Avenue, the boulevard of this low-lying neighborhood. She is standing at a corner, looking north toward a wedding cake of a clock tower, then south toward a fire raging in a rusty old tin can. Is stiff. Struggles to cross northeast through traffic that is flowing south, then arrives thirty seconds later on the far side. Stops in at a corner pizza store.

Lucy orders a slice with anchovies, and a sugary iced orange soda. Next to her is a thin rakish young woman dressed for nightclubs in the middle of the day. Lucy can tell by her Soviet-style black lamb's-wool overcoat that she is no stranger to fashion.

Lucy: (talking to the stranger) I have this sixty dollars that I just have to spend. It's burning in me. I won't be happy until I spend it and I'm poor again.

Lucy pays the man in the fingerprinted apron with money loose in her bag, then holds up a fifty-dollar bill to the fashion victim, or victimizer, doesn't know which.

Lucy: Do you have any ideas? I thought of an antique fur coat. But I'm tired of those. I'm tired of screening that aesthetic to the whole world.

Stranger: (annoyed, gnawing on a stub of crust) I'm thinking. I'm thinking.

Lucy gives up on her. Walks out. Turns right. Strolls stallingly past a gray stone church with bullet-proof-glass front doors. Then past a Czechoslovakian pharmacy, Freipac's. Across the street a guy and girl sit in the back of a garnet-colored convertible, he slumped, smoking away in sunglasses and suede jacket, she propped on back hood in black leather jacket, their friend leaning outside, his hair a brown hedge on his scalp, his ratty jacket purple velvet, his muddy black boots somehow casting a shadow in the shape of Daffy Duck. A blue-vanilla Greek-coffee-shop coffee cup rests on the hood of the car. Whole scene looks like a poster for a tough movie.

Then Lucy snaps one finger. Obviously has a quick conclusion. Cricks her head. Turns around to retrace her steps. This time makes a left at the pizza corner. Walks down a few doors. Into a head shop.

The narrow boutique is popping. Customers two thick trying

to buy this and that from one Pakistani behind plastic shield. Lucy keeps brushing her hair in different directions as she looks, as if she were her own wind. Mostly they're buying newspapers, cigarettes, lottery tickets.

Not Lucy. She points with her finger at items she wants. A hookah pipe. A little tin weighing scale, with balancing trays like the scales of justice in old marble statues. A pocketknife. Bambú papers. A black plastic–encased magnifying lens. A lighter in the guise of a gun: you pull the trigger and a flame shoots out its muzzle. One copy of the most recent issue of *Soldier of Fortune* magazine.

Lucy: (explaining to thin fiftyish brown-paper-bag-skinned attendant in dirty white surgeon's shirt) I love the mercenaries' clothes.

Then she stares down into the aquarium of a glass case for dildos, whips, chains, handcuffs, aphrodisiacs, creams. Points to an aphrodisiac vaginal cream called Try that comes in a green-and-white-striped tube.

Lucy: (busy paying the incommunicative clerk) Can you believe this tiny bag of stuff is fifty dollars?

She exits. Crosses Second Avenue. Waits on the far side for a tree-green municipal bus, which arrives in three minutes.

Lucy: (to Asian driver) Will this drop me near Confucius Plaza?

He nods. Lucy doesn't care so much about visiting Confucius Plaza. It's just a landmark. She likes to drift away from home sometimes for a few hours. Get lost. Just ride on a bus. Especially through Chinatown with its inscrutable signs.

Lucy is sitting at the far end of the last seat at the back of the bus, her head nodding in a patch of lemon-yellow sun, breathing through her nose, eyes closed, rocking with the motion of the bus, humming something from Kraftwerk.

INSOMNIAC

A week later there's a knock at Todd's door. He has just finished showering five minutes ago. Is wrapped in a long blue-and-white Japanese kimono robe made from cotten. Not wearing any underwear. The cloth clings to parts of his body. Opens the door without asking who's there.

It's Lucy. She has on black jeans, a plush black velour sweat-shirt, and soft black shoes.

Lucy: (doesn't miss a beat) You're all wet. (tosses him a brown paper bag) Look! I got us two beautiful sandwiches from the takeout.

Todd: On Hudson? New? Gourmet?

Lucy: (declaratively) The expensive one. I got us roast beef with Russian dressing and condiments. (pushing past) Let me in.

Lucy has a knack for making the normal abnormal. She takes Todd's red-and-white checkered bedsheet to spread out as a pic-nic blanket on the floor. Lights tall red ruby-red candles with pictures of Jesus etched on front and Spanish prayers etched on the sides; they smell fruity stringent. Plops the sandwiches on paper napkins. Fills paper cups with Gallo.

The two sit twisted on the floor, classical music broadcasting over the radio.

Todd: You know this Mozart sounds just like Muzak to me. What's the big diff?

Lucy: You never know how Muzak will sound in the future. It might age. Like red wine.

The thin phosphorescent glow of the radio dial illuminates a patch of the room.

Todd: (a voice from a phosphorescent body, like a talking moon rock) I have a job for Bloomingdale's tomorrow with Louis. I think it pays seven hundred.

Louis has just called that afternoon. Asked him to meet the van in Central Park at nine.

Lucy: (suddenly sparked, like a lightning rod in a storm) I'm trying to learn to do the bossa nova, that dance from south of the border. So I found in a sixties record shop an album with a sheet of cutout feet that you put on your floor to mark where your feet go while the music plays. Today I took the feet . . .

Todd: (winded) You couldn't have heard me.

Lucy: I heard you sweetmeat. But you finished your news. And besides you're just talking about work and money. I'm talking about fun. (ticks concepts off on her fingers) South America. Dance Music. Love.

Todd stares at her as distantly as if she were a map of a state whose capital he was trying to locate.

Todd: (in a *j'accuse* tone) You must be jealous.

Lucy: (standing) Sto-o-o-op. I'm sure if I wanted to do Eminence underwear ads I could.

Todd: (standing up) You're being an ostrich again. Your head is in the sounds, not in the sense.

Lucy sits on a stool and starts ripping the pages of Todd's yellow message pad. She rips a page at a time, each page only once, and lets the debris accumulate around the bottom of the stool.

Todd: (roaring) Clean up! I have to be up at seven. (as a dig) I need my beauty sleep.

Lucy winces her eyes together, making them into slits.

Lucy starts putting away the dinner plates. But with lots of banging and noise. Todd stacks dirty dishes and bright orange plastic dishes in the deep sink with extra clatter. Every time Lucy closes the aqua fridge door she slams it. Todd turns the hot-water faucet on full force and blasts the glasses and clayware stuck at the bottom of this whooshing waterfall.

But the slapstick of their own anger finally begins to amuse them. And imperceptibly the storm passes. Speeded up by Lucy who reaches into her bag for the tube of Try, which she holds up like a find. Then Lucy kneels on Todd's floor mattress, holding the tube in one fist as she rests forward on her elbows, her back sloping down rather than arching up, her behind trumpeting toward the messy white stucco wall. When Todd sees her contorted his robe falls from him like Icarus's waxy skin melting in the sun. He walks toward her so his stick fits right in her mouth, a key in an ignition catch. His hands on the front of his hips, he keeps his head bowed looking down at her moaning for him.

Lucy: (drawing back for air) I need to be myself.

She means that she wants to take off her jeans. So she stands up, sheds her jeans and sweatshirt, pulls down on her flesh-colored panties with her two thumbs. She hands the tube to Todd, then lies down on her back and throws her legs high over her head like a gymnast warming up. Todd moves in, kneelingly, casually rubs the jelly into the temperate zone of Lucy's insides, then relaxes his stick in the prepared area. As he pushes, she pulls.

Todd: (getting close) I wanna work for you forever.

Lucy: (has no words) Shhhhhh.

They both feel their hearts turning like windmills made out of playing cards and the thin fit-together poles of Tinkertoys. Then the wind dies down. Then they make dying-down de-plugged machine noises.

Lucy: (curling inside a rolling wave of blue turning into black) I love the center of you.

Todd: (noticing a police helicopter flashing by in the dynamo of the outside) You do?

Lucy turns soon into a sleeping lump. Todd, though, has drunk too many cups of coffee. He spends most of the night awake, insomniac, drenched lying on top of the sheets, feeling he wants to crawl out of his skin. Even gets out of bed, curls on top of two brown pillows piled on top of each other next to the window. Hangs on while the world revolves at top speed. Finally the hypodermic needle of the sun pops a few veins of purple in the black skin of the sky. Truck traffic starts up on Greenwich Avenue.

Todd feels relieved. He walks over stealthily and draws the glowing white sheet off Lucy, wrapping it around himself like a cape. Lucy is still heaving up and down steadily. Her hair pasted over her face. Although she is on her back, flat, she has her two legs crossed over to one side, like that abdominal exercise where both legs are crossed over one way, then baaaaack over to the other side, or like Christ on the cross, with his knees both knocked over to one side, and flattened out by his tormentors. Lucy continues to rise and fall undisturbedly. Todd feels a moment of tenderness. His heart cracks ever so slightly. Like an egg in boiling water, when the yellow stuff begins to pus out. It is tenderness, globs of tenderness.

Then he shuffles into the bathroom, turns on the electric light, closes the door so as not to alter the dawn light in which Lucy is making baby sucking noises. He still has the sheet wrapped around him. Picks up a mildewy purple-crimson bath towel, flaps it over his head, like pharaoh hair, and stands staring in the mirror with his arms X-ed over his tanned sandpapery chest.

FRANK

Frank is hanging from a thick tree branch in Central Park, his big feet barely scraping the earth. He is tall, 6'1", with longish blondish hair. Dressed all in his white street clothes—white pullover, white loose soft cottony pants, white fancy basketball sneakers. His skin a blend of pinks and tans. Neck thick. Hands gripping strong.

Frank produces a big grin as he hangs there, effortlessly, confidently. Then.

Frank: (swinging back and forth, yelling out Tarzan yodel) Yo-oooo-oooo.

Louis and Kathy titter. Louis is looking through his one-eyed camera on tripod, framing scenes. Kathy, checking out Frank, feels a whirlpool in her lower tummy. She's the Bloomingdale's rep, short and chubby, with page-boy brown hair, a recent grad from a community college in the Bronx.

Kathy: (loud and gutsy, a young Ethel Merman) Frank's such an animal. How could those wimps at dinner last night say that models are no good sex?

Louis: (inscrutably) Models have the knack to be dead in life. They save their life for their work.

Frank: (dropping from tree as Louis's assistant follows him with a light meter) What's the beef?

Todd is bumping into blocks of light. He is nearby in the field. Walking barefoot in the prickly grass. Wrapped in a red silk robe waiting to be dressed for his set. But he is as direction-less as a metal ball in a pinball machine. He hasn't talked yet to Frank. But something about Frank, this new kind of animal, half-human, half-image, and about the shoot, makes him panic.

He walks several yards through some slicing bushes filled with purple berries. Finds a tall brown scaly tree to pee on. The yellow spray, like water from a lawn sprinkler, splashes dead twigs, little black ants, hapless dandelions, broken stems of lime grass.

"ADMIRATION"

The next shot scheduled is a double. Frank and Todd. The entire crew travels down a pebble path through a tunnel of trees to the next location, a sizzling green field, talking in squibs along the way.

Kathy: (complaining to Frank) So every day she walks into the office like she doesn't own the place. If it were mine, I'd walk into it like I owned it.

Louis's Assistant: (lugging golden reflectors) It's almost photographic high noon. When every face looks like a shoot-out on Main Street.

Todd: (pipes up) I don't get it.

Assistant: (condescendingly) Shadows.

When they arrive Kathy claps a hand on Todd's shoulder. He looks too far into her. She tenses. She takes him past a hospital screen and dresses him for the next shot.

Kathy: (flat out) You're not with an agency. Are you a sex favor?

Todd: (shocked, getting even) I heard this joke. "Why did God invent alcohol? So fat women could get fucked."

Todd reemerges dressed in pricky, starched goofy clothes that he would never wear. Bright patterned shirt. Wool gray trousers.

Frank lopes around the field, waiting, as restlessly at ease as a sidelines football player. When Todd approaches Frank gives him a smile that's only in his eyes. Kind of sarcastic, and seductive. He lets Todd size him up.

Frank: (yells) Kathy, I need the other shoes. Do your job.

Kathy and her assistants hurry over, cherry blossoms blown by a gust of wind. Frank, however, doesn't loosen his tie shoes. So they have to get down and undo them. Then he slips into a pair of beige bucks, with their help. When he finally shifts the balance by starting to talk to Todd, Kathy skulks away like a lengthening shadow.

Frank: So what agency you with?

Todd: (flattered) I'm not. Louis just took some pictures. And now this.

Frank: (squeezes Todd once on the shoulder) Listen to me, kid.

Todd: (critically) How old are you?

Frank: (aggressively) Twenty-six. Why? (then evens out) Listen. You gotta be tough with these people. They love it if you treat them like dirt. Don't carry any bags. Be rude. They love it. I've been watching this circus for two years now. And I know what they like. You be the star. And let them be the fans.

35

Todd: (finding it hard to work himself into such a frenzy) How did you get started?

Frank: I was just on the beach in North Carolina for the summer. I was working as a carpenter. On summers from school. And then I got discovered by this big photographer. It all happened real easy and right away. I wanna go back to college and be a lawyer. Cause you don't use this (points into his own skull). Most of the people you meet in the business are scumbags, they don't know shit. You gotta make it work for you. Understand?

Frank sits on the edge of an axed-down tree limb, his knees wide apart, the soles of his bucks touching each other flat. He is pressing his knuckles together (isometric exercise) and jittering calmly.

Louis is no fool. He has been watching Todd and Frank together. The picture he invents is a head fuck. He poses Todd holding down a low-hanging branch with one arm, while Frank is up front smiling. Todd is in profile looking over placidly at Frank who is looking straightforward at Louis. If Louis were Fragonard and he wanted to devise a painting of the allegory "Admiration," this would be it. Which Louis knows. He is clever, and was in art school in London. He has a maliciously precise (malicious only because so precise) sense of what's up.

Since no lights are popping this time, it doesn't seem as if any pictures are being taken. There is no line between life and non-life. The only cue is when Louis says "Ready," or when the camera makes its lift-off sounds. Then the two freeze. It's an adult version of "Statues."

After the shoot Todd and Frank walk slowly up the hill. When Frank talks, he every so often smacks the back of his hand for emphasis against Todd's arm. He is expansive with his gestures. Seems oblivious, though, to concerns that eat away from the inside. Todd is stimulated by all his attention.

Frank: (out of breath) I just got a new bike. A ten-speed, white. It helps to live above a bike store. So I ride around to all my go-sees. Screw the subways. A lot of us guys have bikes. Not that I hang out with models much. In a way. Except for at Soupy's, my agent's. Sometimes he has weekend parties in his cabin in the country. So we go wild—canoeing, playing peewee football. You oughta come Todd.

Todd: What are you doing tonight?

Frank: My girlfriend's home making pasta. I'm just gonna lie low. Go with me.

Todd: I've got a girlfriend, too.

Frank: Four's kind of a crowd. You know. Too boy-girl-boy-girl. I start feeling like I'm in an *Archie* comics or something. Plus she's a girlfriend from before, right?

Todd: Before what?

They are now riding in the van, Frank and Todd in the back, Louis's assistant on the hump. Kathy is glum silent in the "suicide seat"—the one on the right up front. She is wary of Frank's palling around with Todd.

Frank: Get ready. You could take off any day. One thing. If you wanna make it in this business, you've gotta go with the flow. Is your thing with this girl still hot?

Todd: We've known each other for a couple years.

Frank: I don't hear what I wanna hear.

Todd: (accusingly) What about you and your girl?

Frank: (smacks palm against wood panel on front of bench) I'm not you. I'm a whole other personality type. Can't you tell that?

Todd: (undercut by hearing the simple truth from his riled-up new friend) You're right, Frank.

Frank: I don't wanna get heavy, man, but (lowering voice almost down to a whisper) you spend a lot of effort pretending that what's going on isn't going on. But it's written all over your face.

Outside the gray buildings of downtown Manhattan are starting to whir past. It's after five. People are lurching every way to get to their next stop. The weather has just changed so there is an eerie fear that seeps, like radioactivity, into the skin.

Even though they are walking horizontally, these pedestrians might as well be falling vertically: a girl whose hair is too tight for her head; a marine tapping some car keys impatiently against his shins, obviously waiting on that furtive corner for a date who is late; a red-haired male midget; a tall fancy lady whose glossy copy of a business magazine slips from her hand; he whose denim jacket advertises that a reggae Jesus is his savior; the fortyish woman exiting Macy's with a piece of ticker tape sticking to her Persian fur collar on her cloth coat; the group of messengers telling social jokes, invented in prison, back and forth in front of a street-window shop; the lone homeless who has just left a Vespers mass at the St. Francis Church and is on his way to an AA meeting.

Frank: (shouts) Yo. Let us two off at the corner of Seventh Avenue and Twenty-second Street.

Kathy's eyes flinch as she twists to stare accusingly, without really being able to see a thing, into the back of the van that is now suffused in a gray shadowy fog.

THREEWAY

Frank lives on a side street. Top floor of a four-story gray brick building. He keeps his bike strapped outside one window with belts and chains.

Todd and Frank are sitting in the near-dark living room. Sharon, standing in the gray tile kitchen, is tossing back her blond bangs, while busily stirring spaghetti in a deep metal pot. On another burner a bottled tomato-and-meat sauce is bubbling. Sharon is about 5'8". Is dressed in pink button-down blouse, short pastel-blue corduroy shorts, no shoes. Her legs are curvy. She walks in a circle around the pantry, casting her legs out exaggeratedly, while listening to Top Ten music on the countertop transistor. Having a good time. Sharon is an earth daughter, and is at her best when racing down a Connecticut hill with a couple of her family's rusty red Irish setters. Works by day as an assistant at a law office. Is twenty-two.

Todd and Frank are sitting, drinking beers, in a blue TV light that makes the living room into an orgone box—the man-sized cabinet invented by Wilhelm Reich to cure people of cancer who sat long enough inside its bluish ozone.

Frank is stretched out on the couch, pointing his clicker to switch the channels—he does this nonstop. Then he pretends the clicker is a .45 and shoots at Todd who's rocking in a cane rocking chair by the window. Todd cricks his neck, hit. But Frank doesn't catch this reaction shot. He's already back staring at a boxing match on a sports channel that Todd can only see from a sideways curious perspective.

Frank: (legs over couch) You like boxing?

Todd: (studying Frank's reflection in the nighttime window next to him as if he were watching an actor on TV) I think I like bullfights better than boxing.

Frank: Not the big fights. They're rigged. But the little amateur fights. The Golden Gloves at the Felt Forum. Then you get to sit down close with the boxers' families and their girlfriends.

Todd: (sarcastic) All blood-splattered?

Frank: (defending) I like boxing cause boxers get back what they dish out. They get hit. Maybe you walk too much on the mild side.

Todd stands up and paces, hands in pockets. Every time he strays into the path of the TV beam, Frank makes a fly-swatting gesture with the clicker to warn him off course.

Todd: (ticked off) I'm not so sure you know what you're talking about.

Frank: I'm not so sure you're not just the latest pretty towel boy.

Todd: (sitting on front edge of rocker so it tilts steadily forward) Kathy said I was a sex favor. Is that what you're saying?

Frank: I don't even wanna talk like this. (scratching top of his head, cracks a half-smile, then shouts into Sharon) Sharon you got a ciggy-butt for Todd?

Sharon: (coming out from the tinny-sound-filled pantry) What hon?

Frank: (above the screams of a Crazy Eddie commercial) You got a Pall Mall for Todd?

Sharon: Sure thing. Oh now I know what you said. You said "ciggy-butt." (she lifts up one of the seat cushions on the sofa and offers Todd one cylinder from the squashed pack) I put them there to keep from smoking so many.

Todd: Thanks Sharon. What do you do?

Sharon: I'll tell you when we sit down to eat. (then) I work in a legal firm. (flicks a high-shooting flame with her lighter to get Todd's cigarette started) I just realized *Dance Fever* might be on then. Which is no time to talk. (Sharon looks over to Frank who is nodding with his whole body, anxious for *Dance Fever*.)

Frank: (loudly stretches, then to Sharon) I was the pivot of the shoot today. I got to do all the solos. And the big shot, full page, for the *Times* will be me. That oughta get my face around.

Sharon: Greeeat.

Sharon walks back in the kitchen. Frank mutes the TV sound. Much quieter.

Frank: (to Todd) Did you come down from the day yet?

Todd: (letting go) No. I've still got all this buzzing in my head. So many hills and valleys.

Frank: Listen to your buddy Frank. Take off all your clothes. And lie down on the floor.

Todd: (not getting it) What? (laughing) You and Sharon gonna rape me?

Frank: Ease into that floor. It's a relaxation exercise.

Todd follows Frank's orders. He undresses slowly, glancing every so often at Sharon in the kitchen. Then lies down flat on his back on the hard, hemp-covered floor. At first he feels completely other. Can't get most of his back, buckling up like damp wood, to settle in. But slowly the jolts even out. And he begins to feel the tensions of the day unkink.

Frank: (coaching) Breathe deep in and out five times.

Todd does. Then groans, and stretches out in a mess on the floor. He breathes in blue oxygen, and breathes out yellow carbon dioxide. The nerve freeways that were so lit up are dimming. Whatever's left is tingling in the soles of his feet, pouring out through the bottoms. He feels as if he's bobbing on a lake like the dark velvet lake from *A Place in the Sun* where Montgomery Clift murdered Shelley Winters. A murder which supposedly took place during the 1920s on Harveys Lake near Todd's hometown. Todd feels himself in a canoe on that treacherously wide natural-water lake about to tip over any minute into sleep. His eyes and nose and mouth and ears are gradually filling up with inky purple lake water.

Todd is alerted by the whistling as Frank strips off his clothes in the adjoining bedroom. So he half-wakes. Watches Frank blearily through the ajar balsa-wood door. Frank is as nude as a classical statue, his clothes in a pile next to his left foot. He shimmies into a pair of yellow Jockey shorts, his loose hairy balls hanging out the bottom vents, slips into thick rubber thongs. Sharon's white cupped bra is hanging by its strap from the knob of the opened closet door, reflected in its full-length mirror, as is Todd's askew head.

Frank walks loudly past Todd's ears into the kitchen. Walks right into Sharon. No words. Dives his head into her clavicle area. Holds her around and rubs his hands over the behinds of her thighs. Sharon leans back into the steam, turning the volume down to zero on the transistor, adding to the growing quiet. Todd can overhear them talking as they disentangle.

Sharon: Todd seems like a nice guy. Nicer than most of those models.

Frank: (drawing back, exaggeratedly) You saying I'm not nice? Is that what you mean?

Sharon: I wouldn't think of you as nice exactly. Would you?

You're more . . . more . . . magnetic. You've got undertow, Frank. (pushing back his long hair, revealing a rocky forehead) He's more on the nice side. Nice eyes. Nice buns.

While Sharon is fussing with Frank's hair, he is unbuttoning her pink blouse, letting it flutter to the floor, then unsnapping her shorts, which she squeezes out of. Only in white panties, Sharon is as ruddy and fit as an Aryan girl. Frank has his hands all over her healthy skin, skin she rubs abrasively with oatmeal paste every morning.

Frank: (mouth in her neck flesh) Let's initiate him.

They amble, arms around hips, out into the darkened living room. Todd feels uncomfortable. It's been a hard day. He's been listening attentively to their far-out dialogue. Maybe it's a put-on. Maybe he is keeping them from going all the way. Is intrigued. But decides to make a break anyway. So Todd stands up, creakingly, his face puffy, and his eyes' whites turned pink from his brief nap. By now the two are right there, staring at him like an uncaptioned photo from a swingers' magazine.

Todd: (clearing out his throat from way down deep) Look. I'd love to hang with you guys and watch *Dance Fever*. But, you know, (squinting) I just woke up and couldn't remember where I was. So I think I'd better walk home.

Sharon: (trying) No dinner?

Frank and Sharon both walk Todd, dressed again, back to the door, each with a hand resting on a different side of his back. When Todd turns around at the door, they back off a bit. All three feel momentarily drunk.

Todd: (stumbling in a bog of no words) Thanks.

Sharon squeezes him around the top of his chest. Frank all of a sudden realizes that they are parting. He only met this guy a few hours back. But he already vaguely needs him.

Frank: (scratching his balls through his yellow Brooks Brothers briefs) Don't be a stranger now.

THE FILE OF LUCY'S WORST FEARS AND
DISTRUSTS IS CALLED UP ON THE SCREEN
OF HER HEART

Todd is making his way down Seventh Avenue, hands in jeans pockets, arms tight against his side. He is shuffling as if to some unheard funky music. As smugly wrapped up in himself as the green-yellow leaves are wrapped in the hairnet of the curbside trees' crisscrossing branches.

Then suddenly he sees Lucy and Erica walking toward him. Lucy runs up and puts her arms around him. Erica stands there fanning herself with a party invitation. It's a hot September night, the sky plum-colored.

Lucy: What synchronicity!

Todd: I'm too beat to be synchronized tonight.

Erica: What happened on your job? Was it worth the sick day?

Todd: (hiply) Is one sick day worth seven bills?

All of a sudden Lucy puts her hands down and looks out wide-eyed, not moving, not talking. Erica shakes her.

Erica: What gives? What gives?

Lucy refuses to budge. Erica glances accusingly at Todd.

Todd: (even-voiced) I didn't do it. She just decided to be that way like (snaps fingers) that.

Lucy shakes her own head, then starts loosening up her body and grabs Todd by both shoulders, feeling into his bare bones with her insistent fingers.

Lucy: (penitent) I'm soooorry. (squeezes eyes shut) Here I'm supposed to be the person closest to you in the whole world and I didn't even remember—for a split second—that today was this big day for you. Your big day. I'm sooorry.

Todd: Don't be.

Lucy: (relaxing hands down to her sides) How did it go? (sighs out the words) How did it go?

Erica: (gaping at this action) That's what your seizure was about? I don't believe it. We see our friends one way. Then we see them with their lovers and they're a whole new way. (hands her fan to Lucy) Look. You guys go to the party.

Lucy protests. Erica splits after warning Todd to be level-headed enough to show up at work in the morning and not count his chickens. Lucy takes Todd's hand and starts to lead him in the direction of The Ritz, off Third Avenue, the site of the party.

Lucy: Tell me about it. Now that it's quieter.

Todd: I don't really want to go to this club. I haven't really eaten. And it's been long. And I have to go to work at the office tomorrow. And what else?

Lucy: (recalcitrant) You tell me.

Todd knows what he has to do. He stops and leans back into a lamppost. He folds his hands in front of him, rubs the side of his cheek against his own shoulder, feeling the soft cotton of his light-blue sweatshirt, then rubs his palms against his denimed thighs, then just looks at Lucy.

Todd: (in a calming voice, the kind used on crazies) Let's go across the street now and eat some raw fish.

Lucy: (same demure) Okay.

Todd: Good. Now kiss me here. (he points to the side of his cheek) What do you feel?

Lucy: (after her lips graze Todd's cheek) Stubble.

Todd: Right.

Todd looks hard at Lucy in the Loony Tune light. She suddenly looks a bit different to him. He never noticed her pointy ears poking through her black hairs, like a black hamster's. But he quickly shakes the spooked unfamiliarity. Restores normal relations. Takes Lucy's hand and leads her across the street against the red light.

Once inside the restaurant they drink brown Japanese beer,

as thick as ale, that comes in tall cylindrical glasses. As Todd tells the story of his workday.

Lucy: (quietly stirring her soy sauce in saucer with one wooden chopstick) It is fascinating.

Todd: (repeating himself) But then this guy Frank for instance. I had him psyched for one of those shark types. He was cool, but almost too cool. You know?

Lucy nods forcedly.

Todd: Then he turned out to be this warm friendly . . .

Lucy: (irritated) You've mentioned him so many times already . . . (covering up) . . . that I can't wait to meet and get to know him and his girlfriend.

Todd: (finally getting rid of his secret in a cruel blurt, not able to hold the news in any longer, a weighty medicine ball) That would be great except he doesn't seem to want to meet and get to know you at all.

A ding! goes off inside Lucy, a dissonant ding! The file of her worst fears and distrusts is called up on the screen of her heart. She pretends the message of misfortune isn't there. But for the rest of the meal she is frazzled.

Out on the side street they walk through the multicolored pastel light that is cast through the restaurant's high horizontal windows onto the dirty sidewalk in parallelograms. They are heading southeast toward The Ritz. Along the way Todd pays an excessive amount of attention to architectural details, pointing out carved angels on doors, the white wood of window frames, this month's violet lighting of the Empire State Building tower. But Lucy doesn't even pretend to look.

Lucy: (finally) Why did you say before that Frank doesn't want to see me?

Todd: (lightly) I just got that impression. I mean I tried to get you invited along tonight and he nixed that. And then just from different things he said.

Lucy: (her stomach hollowing out like a dumped wastebasket) And you're going to accept that?

Todd: (playing dumb) Why not?

Lucy slows down her steps as they approach the barren stretch that is Fifth Avenue in the low twenties after nine at night. When Todd doesn't slow his steps down to stay in sync, she quickens up again to catch up.

Lucy: (in a higher-pitched voice, not her own) You think he wants to get into your pants?

Todd: Nope. Definitely not Frank.

Lucy: (scratching) What could it be?

Todd: (more tenderly) I don't know. I get the feeling that it's a whole other world they're in. Things don't mean the same things. You know?

Lucy: (emphatically) No.

RAINY DAY

It's a rainy Saturday. Lucy is watching the thin lines of rain through the opaque plastic sheets over her windows. She is pacing while talking to Erica on her long-corded phone.

Lucy: The thing is that he seems really calm and placid. But under it all he's even more of a mess than I am. He's a screamer with strips of cotton stuffed down his throat and into his lungs. I mean I might be strong but I'm not that strong. And then I start feeling like an actress in a movie or something, a really teary one, like Meryl Streep. I'm beginning to feel soaked. . . . I don't want to get into therapy. I think that therapy is voodoo. . . . No I don't want to get into voodoo. You think that because I compared therapy to voodoo, that that means that I'm favorable to voodoo? Girl, get a grip. . . . The rain hasn't let up all day. All day. It's like it's falling all the way from Mars or somewhere. I remember when I was a girl I always thought that the harder and longer the rain was falling it meant that it was coming from farther away. . . . Why aren't there any jokes that put down young good-looking men in their twenties? Tell me a joke, Erica, pleeeaze, I love jokes. To death.

ZEBRA

Todd files his test shots from Louis in the plastic pages of a Lamston's portfolio and breezes into Zebra on his lunch hour. He had phoned Sandy, who handed him the card, and she set up an appointment to meet Dom, a short bland full-faced Italian man, with a black clipped mustache and a black shadow, early thirties, who inspects new men.

Zebra is located in a brownstone in the east fifties. Todd walks down into its *Town and Country* main waiting room. Big armchairs, chrome-and-glass tables, abstract wall paintings. Dom is sitting at the main desk. The interview takes place right there, in the waiting room, while models traipse in and out, talking jolly talk. A tall Swedish guy is busy calling long-distance to an entire atlas of countries on the desk phone the whole time Dom and Todd are doing business.

Dom turns through the pages of Todd's clunky big black portfolio filled only with pictures taken by Louis.

Dom: You seem to have bad skin in these pictures. But I don't see any acne on your face.

Todd looks at the upside-down face—his—to try to see what Dom is calling acne.

Sandy walks in, ignoring Todd, leading by the wrist a girl, around seventeen, with light-green Chartresque stained-glass eyes and a wolverine head. The young woman has on a dress that looks like just an apron.

Sandy is wearing an imitation African leopardskin dress, with a single tied leather cord as a belt. She is an animal trainer dressed in animal skins.

Sandy: (to Dom) Don't you think she could lose some weight in the face?

Dom: You said it.

Sandy: (starts twirling her belt and strapping her own thigh with it) Yeah. Dom. Come on. We've got to whip these kids into shape.

The girl model raises her clear eyes at Todd, trying to make an alliance, a pact, to balance the odds. Todd won't go along. He is staring at Sandy waiting for her to recognize him.

Dom: This is your Todd.

Sandy: (theatrically slaps her own forehead, then goes over and kisses Todd on his forehead) I'm too sorry. (to Dom) You know on the street I can see them. But in here all the models, especially the guys, they just whoosh together.

Sandy goes back, twirls the girl around by the shoulder, and leads her down the hall to the women's division, telling her, laughing the whole way, the story of Todd.

Dom: (closing the portfolio with great finality) I'm afraid you're too catalog for us. Zebra specializes in a high-fashion European editorial look. Try us again in a year if you work.

Todd: (pissed at Dom's dictums) You think I can change from one look to another in a year? And what does working have to do with looking?

Dom lights a little cigar, ignoring what he interprets as hostile questions. Todd is angry at himself for liking the acrid smell of Dom's thick Puerto Rican cigar. For wanting to stay there in the chair and just smell it.

A TUNNEL, A WINDY TUNNEL

Lucy has a diary. She has it open to write in, lying on the mattress on the floor, but is stumped. Is sucking on the lead in the pencil. Then scrawls in big block letters, "I AM A NYMPHO-MANIAC," and slams the book shut.

She lies on the mattress on her back, starts rubbing in the crotch of her black chinos. Then rubs up where her breasts poke into her scratchy pink shirt. Lucy is feeling as horny as all nature. Her skin is prickly. And she is moaning out loud.

Lucy: (feeling the rounds of her butt) I hate it. (then makes clucking sounds) I hate it! (screams) *I hate it!*

She stands up to find matches. Lights her cigarette. Draws the abrasive smoke in deeply in a reverse whistle. Then there is a thud thud thud at the door. Lucy makes her way through the hole in the brick wall to the gray steel door in the next room. Opens.

Todd and Frank are framed in the rectangle. They are both covered with damp spots. It's raining again, an unforecast storm. Their hairs are glistening slick. Todd has on a loosened tie over his pinstriped shirt, open, showing neck, tan cords, brown tie shoes, and is toting the black portfolio left over from his lunchtime Zebra appointment. Frank is wearing a T-shirt with Hawaiian motif (a sunset, palm trees), blue jeans, padded white sneaks. He rests his elbow on Todd's shoulder. They look like a couple of chums.

Todd: This is Frank, Lucy. I ran into him on my way home. They didn't take me at Zebra. But he's going to do me a favor.

When Lucy looks at Frank the first time she feels as if she is a tunnel, a windy tunnel. But she doesn't show this. She doesn't say a word. Just walks away leaving Todd to push the closing door open. Frank carefully watches Lucy disappear through the hole in the wall.

Todd: (anxiously shuttling between Lucy and Frank, wanting them to get along, as he leads Frank through the hole) He's going to call his agency for me.

Frank: (sitting down on the mattress on the floor, spreading his legs out, and positioning the phone in the cleared V field) Here let me get this over with.

Lucy doesn't go along with the chumminess. She sits at the kitchen counter in front of a little round set-up collapsible mirror and cleans her face. Puts on a light-blue lipstick. Leaves her lip imprint on a Kleenex. Walks over and hands the smeared Kleenex to Frank who is just clicking down.

Frank: (passing a series of puffs of air through his almost-closed lips) What's this for?

Lucy laughs at the confusion she has created, without giving a clue. Frank rests his chin in a cradle of fingers and watches her laugh. Then she goes off to fix drinks.

While Lucy is a few yards away making the three black scotches, Frank puts his arm around Todd's neck in some kind of lock, and forces his head down into the mattress in a twisted bend. Todd is yelping and heaving laughing at the same time. Frank is shouting, "Say uncle, say uncle." Lucy, fascinated by the two playing this boy's game, walks back, sits down on the bed next to writhing Todd, and watches. She's like a cat that shakes its aloofness the minute its mistress and a cab-driver visitor start having anonymous sex on a water bed, and comes over to prowl, or just sits above them like a little black sphinx in the natural shade of night. When Todd finally pleads the word "uncle," and bobs up scarlet-faced, embarrassed, Lucy loses interest, returns to fetch the black metal tray with the red rose painted on it (looking much like the little painting on the rosebud sled in *Citizen Kane),* and loads it with three drinks.

Todd drinks his scotch while still breathing hard from the wrestling. Frank lays back and lets the brown liquor flow down into his mouth like wine from a goatskin. Lucy on the stool keeps the tray balanced on her knees and chain-sips.

Lucy: (as an opener) I heard this psychiatrist on TV yesterday, and she was claiming that if your heart is going pit-pat for someone, that means that they're probably going pit-pat for you. Now is that garbage or what?

Frank: Do you have mice? I thought I heard scratching in those boxes over there.

Lucy: Yes, I do have mice.

Todd: (picking up on Lucy's topic) I think it's garbage. Because then it means things are the way anyone feels they are. But when I go pit-pat for Deborah Harry . . . I'm a fly on an insect candle, and she's like a comet or a meteor.

Frank: You two talk funny when you're together. But I can bulldoze in anywhere. Something I always wondered, almost the same thing, is how if you jerk off thinking about someone that's supposed to wake them up. But what about Marilyn Monroe? If she woke up every time someone jerked off on her, then that's why she's dead.

Lucy: I know what you mean. It's so romantic. It has to be true.

Todd: (getting angry) Lucy! Now you're not talking right. What's making you do that?

Frank: (grunting as he gets up to a goalie squat, leaning his palm on Lucy's knee for support) I think you've got something there Luce. (now standing) I'm outta here.

Todd: Let me get you that book.

Todd disappears through the hole and returns with a *Captain America* comic. He hands the colored magazine to Frank who slaps him on the back of his neck with the rolled-up paper, bad-dog style. Todd feels embarrassed again, in front of Lucy.

All three say good-bye a few times, almost to no one in particular. As Frank exits through the hole, Lucy notices that his back, which was up against the wall, has the only remaining damp rain spot, or maybe that irregular darker patch on his Hawaiian T-shirt is just new sweat.

Lucy returns to the main room, collects the rusty-looking glasses distractedly, carries them on the tray to the sink, starts washing them. The window is opened up halfway, rainfall sounding like a cheap shower.

She is staring out at the back windows of the youth detention center on the other side of the airwell. A young thin man is lying facedown on a bed of white sheets, no blanket, his blue square old-fashioned suitcase opened up on a chair, a tiny tape-player with separable tinier speakers on a table playing who knows what. The delinquent in white boxers, nothing else, acne all over his back, is prostrate twitching to the music.

Lucy: Todd, I think if you have that interview tomorrow you'll need time at home tonight, to center.

Todd: Are you suggesting that we spend a night each alone? That's a switch.

Lucy: (making a soapfall from the yellow sponge into one single glass receptacle, as surprised as Todd) It is a switch.

SCRAPBOOK

Todd uses the rest of the night to catch up at home on his scrapbook. He has on lots of candles, plus, next to his mattress, a gimmicky lamp that looks like a movie projector with a bulb. On his ghetto blaster he is playing Marvin Gaye's "What's Goin' On" over and over, singing along in falsetto with the backer-uppers, sitting cross-legged on his mattress in his white guinea Ts and briefs.

Todd has the current scrapbook open. Is cutting out pictures of himself and Lucy from a group photo of friends playing volleyball on a Hamptons beach that summer. She is on one side of the net, he on the other, so it's easy to cut them out separately. He cuts himself in a circle. Lucy in a diamond. Then he takes the composite he swiped from Frank's book at Lucy's that afternoon and cuts out a head of Frank, leaving behind his tennis-playing body. Frank's shape is a square. He glues them on the black page. Todd to the left, Lucy to the right, Frank bottom center.

Then he draws renditions in white pencil of different tattoos (mostly love tattoos) he has seen on arms or backs or even just walls. The name "Peg" with two female symbols (crosses hanging from circles) linked together. The word "Revenge" with a pair of hands in handcuffs underneath. "Mom" in a bulging heart. "Hector + Rita 4 Ever." He adds in some of the traditional iconography of chivalrous love: a heart with an arrow through it, Xs, lips, a crescent moon, a dagger, chains. He paints in the lips with a pale strawberry lipstick Lucy left in his bathroom cabinet.

Later that night, before falling asleep, Todd calls up Lucy. She is busily watching a television program about a woman in Maine who refuses to sell her land to a nuclear power plant.

Todd describes the page to Lucy.

Lucy: (saying it with plenty of diphthong) Suuuper. . . . (then, more quietly) I missed you tonight bobcat. But I'm glad you got inspired. I never get inspired by nobody nothing noway. I'm just a housewife without a house. And all I've got of the lifestyle accessories is this TV. Not even bonbons.

Todd: You're a wild card.

Then Todd makes a dozen or so little kisses, almost noiseless, onto the phone, feeling the percolation of the receiver holes against his lips. Lucy makes the same kisses back.

AT THE AGENCY

When it's Todd's turn, he makes his way around some bends, the hallway walls dotted with magazine covers from yesteryear featuring Roxanne, former top model and now agency owner, looking like Audrey Hepburn.

He finds the doorway into the men's booking room where he stands for a minute, lost. It looks like Operation Central for a marathon television fund-raising. Four young women sit plugging into a giant switchboard, talking times and prices. ("Beer models get thirty-five hundred a day, bottom.") All flavors of male models stand around, rubbing themselves, making dates with the bookers at the switchboard, feeling each other out to try to find leads for jobs or reports on the flesh markets in Europe or Asia. The bookers, mostly in their mid-twenties, mostly plain, earning low wages, enjoy having the models hanging all over them, and they enjoy sometimes talking dirty. ("What's the dessert gonna be? Whipped cream on your stick?") It's not so much perfect features—blow-dried hair, ivory cuticles, veined biceps. These guys all have body halos, or auras. They literally shine. Todd is struck by these flashes of bioenergetic light.

Soupy pushes open the accordion door to his office. Though only in his early forties, he already has silver hair that sticks out in shocks from his head, mad-scientist style. He's dressed sloppily in a flannel-design shirt, tan pants, Hush Puppies. Though he's homely, his manner is irresistible. Blue oval eyes keep clicking off to the side.

Soupy is always popping. He could easily be a television personality. (That's why the models gave him his Soupy Sales nickname.) He's a talker. A second-rate joke-teller always elbowing for a response. He invites Todd into his cubicle, sits down then shoots up then sits down again then slumps his long lanky body down deeper then heaves up again a few times before he finally settles in his plush pumpkin-colored leather swivel chair.

Soupy: (pushing a crimson button on the intercom) Jackie. Hold my calls. Especially close calls.

Todd is sitting in a white folding director's chair, not dressed in his travel-bureau clothes but in more comfortable black chinos, white sweatshirt with hood out over yellow canvas jacket, Bass Weejuns worn over thick soft gray socks. He looks around the tiny office feeling comfortable because the walls are Scotch-taped with lots of cutouts. Just like the wall in front of him at the agency. But these are mostly photographs of guys. Biggest is the poster-sized picture of Soupy running in a marathon.

Todd: Are these all in your agency?

Soupy: Some yes. Some no. Some were. Or they're guys I'm interested in. In getting in here. But why did you ask the first question? Before me?

Todd feels punched. But knows he has to keep up. Soupy keeps baiting him.

Soupy: You seem kind of nervous. Nervous and blasé at the same time. Are you?

Soupy stands up and opens the accordion door.

Soupy: Jackie. How many more are out there?

Soupy returns to his desk chair.

Soupy: You want to try some pictures on me?

Todd hands over his black book. Without a word. Palms damp. Soupy is flipping through the book, the pages slapping smackily as he does.

Jackie comes to the door. She's short, chubby, has dyed blond hair with roots showing, a squeaky voice, is wearing a tight brown felt dress, and black gauze stockings with seams up the backs.

Jackie: Four more. But there could be more.

As she walks away her skirt keeps rising up on her curve, riding bronco.

Todd slouches down in the chair, and crosses one leg up on the other knee, in a cool fashion.

Soupy: (picking up) Don't you know how to get into a comfortable position?

Todd: I hope so. Why?

Soupy: Because it comes through in the pictures. Sometimes in these pictures you don't look all there.

Todd: (without guile) What can I do about that?

Soupy puts down the book open to a shot with Todd, hair wetted down, in boxer shorts, standing in a tiled room, probably a bathroom, which is all blurred. Todd has his hairy legs spread out and a steely dreamy look in his face.

Soupy: This is a great picture. The rest I don't get anything from.

Soupy doesn't say anything for a while. He's in one of his rare patches of quiet. Then he decides.

Soupy: (flatly) I think you have potential.

Todd: (tempting the sadistic comedian in Soupy) You think I have potential?

Soupy: (ignoring the nervous response, stands up) Let's put you in the TV lounge. Do you have time? Then we can talk again later. To the end.

Soupy walks Todd around different bends to a lounge off a hallway. Some guys and girls are in there watching a soap on TV. Including Trixie with the yellowish long hair who came up from junior to young sophisticate in the women's division. And Paul, short, his height adjusted by cowboy boots, with broad chest, and a Cajun accent. And others. Soupy doesn't just drop Todd off. He sits down and starts to take part. Todd sits, too, unintroduced, on a Naugahyde auburn couch.

Soon Jackie comes to the door, hands-on-hips angry, like a sixties television housewife or maid.

Jackie: Soupy! You've got all these hopefuls waiting. What are you doing in here?

Soupy: Wait. I have to see if she's pregnant.

Jackie: How long will that take?

Soupy: Nine months.

The members of the lounge group start shaking and laughing as if he has said something funny. Todd makes a few breathy sounds just to fit in. Soupy sits on the arm of the couch, starts rubbing into Todd's shoulders. Paul picks up on this oblique intro and so talks to Todd. That done, Soupy drops out to do some work for a few minutes.

Paul tells his story, buoyantly.

Paul: Now I'm living out in Westchester, we have a place, my girlfriend came up with me, I couldn't take living in Manhattan. I hate the subways. I need more wide-open spaces. You know I was a real cowboy. Like a Marlboro man. Except I didn't smoke. People have all these fantasies about cowboys, and it's none of it true. Did you ever talk to a farmer?

Todd: Nope.

Paul: There's one in the agency, Sal. He says the milking of cows is done now in pneumatic tubes with hoses and shit. I used to do hog-busting, the old-fashioned way, in the swamps of Louisiana. You flush the hogs out of the swamps with these vicious little dogs. Then we cowboys come down and cut their balls out and their penises off. To castrate them. The castrated hogs go back into the swamp and just grow fatter and fatter for the kill.

Todd: (almost seeing and smelling and feeling the thick dense conflict) You've held loose hogballs in your hands?

Paul: (unstoppable now) You slit the sacs and you just pull out the testicles, snip it in the goo.

As Paul's tale goes on, the rest of the TV watchers leave. They have vouchers to deposit, phone calls to make, Cokes to drink. Eventually Paul is depleted of gore.

Soupy is leaning wryly against the door frame, scratching his ass through his tan pants. He says—"if you have any appetite left"—that he ordered Chinese food for the two of them to finish their meeting. Paul saunters off to catch the train home. Todd snorts as he notices that Paul walking down the hall is actually bowlegged. Then he and Soupy walk the labyrinth back to the little office and resume their seats.

While the bookers finish up and leave for the day, Soupy spreads open the fresh Chinese boxes filled with gooey foods in similar red and yellow sauces. The two eat out of the same containers, Soupy using fork and spoon, Todd chopsticks. Soupy slots a cassette into a tape player on a nearby yellow plastic filing cabinet. It's a men's choir singing big old German Protestant hymns.

Soupy: I have a brother who's a priest.

Todd takes off his white sweatshirt with hood for the first time today. He's wearing a sepia T-shirt that fits to the form of his trapeziuses, his natural padding.

Soupy: Do you have a girlfriend? Or a boyfriend?

Todd: (slurping loud in his cup of scalding green tea so that he burns the inside of his mouth) Well I have my girlfriend, Lucy. We've been together since college.

A pulsar goes off in Soupy's eyes.

Soupy: And Frank? Where does he fit in?

Todd: He has a girlfriend too. A neat one. Do you know her?

Soupy: Of course. Everybody knows everybody. But that's not what I asked. (leaning back) Do you want to go to bed with Frank?

Todd feels that the record has just been changed in speed from 33 ⅓ to 16, as if the robust German choir were suddenly chanting the Tantric chants of Tibetan monks, the chants that affect dogs like ultrasonic whistles and raise the dead.

Todd: (steeling shut) I wouldn't know what to do.

Soupy: Don't go on the blink on me now. It's just that people in this business are always going to be trying to find out what denomination you are. Sexual denomination. I was just testing you.

Soupy leans back and hands over to Todd a big calendar titled *Pin Downs,* in which every month is a different model, most on gym mats or by pools or on top of lifeguard towers.

Todd: (turning through) But every month in here looks like summer. (puts it down, annoyed)

Soupy then explains to Todd that he has a European look. Brown hair, dark skin, sensitive smart face. When Jean, the agent from Milan, visits in a few weeks, Soupy will set up a meeting. If it works, Todd will go for starters to Milan.

After pulling his sweatshirt back on, Todd stands up to leave. He and Soupy lock eyes.

Soupy: I like you. You don't suck up to me.

Todd: (feeling a fluorescent tube of strength light up inside him) What's your real name anyway?

Soupy: Earl. Earl Velch.

Todd walks through the door of the booking room to connect to the hallway that links to the reception area. He feels that his day has been a trick Chinese box containing smaller and smaller boxes within it. Open one, it leads to another. The farther in he goes, the farther it opens out.

FEMINIST DRUG DEALER

Lucy's day is a box that keeps closing in on her. She stays put but invites the pressure to build. It is a shrinking box.

Lucy has been working as a feminist drug dealer. (She only buys from women, only sells to women.) Today is her day to stay home and sell ounces to her visitors. She puts on her oversized Fabian-face T-shirt the minute she wakes. Her smallish foot bottoms throb from the cold of the wood floor.

She looks in the mirror. Reflected in there is the rest of the room looking even longer than it already is. For a few minutes Lucy can't remember what's up. She knows she's Lucy. She recognizes the room, especially the metal gooseneck lamp at the far end. She remembers Todd. But can't put it all together. Like waking up in the middle of the night, especially after having traveled recently to many cities, and not being able to place yourself, especially within the moonlight blaring in the window, and so not having a self, other than an abstract one.

Lucy spreads cold cream all over her face so it's thick white and cold. Then she swipes a Benson & Hedges Light from its pale pack, lights, and lies on the mattress smoothing her palm over the luxurious silk of the apricot panties she's wearing. She feels better now. Simulating the feel of the lifestyle of the court women in old imperial Japan.

Lucy likes to refer to the days she sells as "receiving." Today's the day she receives other ladies. She got this idea from a novel. The way it goes is they shout up her name from down on the street below; Lucy swings open the plastic-covered door-sized window that opens onto a rusty wide fire escape and shouts back, "Be right down"; she clobbers the wood steps on her way down from the fourth-floor apartment; lets them in; returns to a chemistry lab–looking still life of strainers, plastic bags, a scale, joints, all laid out on a stool set up within the halo of the gooseneck lamp. Lucy wears a green lucent poker visor while she dices the herbs.

The first call of the day is a coincidence, or more correctly a surprise, though every surprise is surprising because of some coincidentalness. But. In a surprise, one party is surprised, and in a coincidence, both parties are surprised.

Brrrrriiiiing.

Lucy: Ullo.

Sharon: Lucy. I've been meaning to call you. My name's Sharon. I live with Frank Yastremski, the (a question in her lilt) model? I heard about your business from Todd. You're so enterprising I can't stand it.

Lucy: (freezes for a sec at the mention of Frank) Do you want to buy something?

Sharon: Yes. (voice goes down) I'm at work in a law office right now. But I'd love it if I could come down after work which, I know the address, would be five-thirty, quarter of six.

Lucy: It will be dark then.

Sharon: What should I do?

Lucy: Yell up "Lucy."

Sharon: Will Todd be there?

Lucy: (the question reminds her that she's lonely but she hides it) Probably not.

Sharon: I've really been wanting to meet you and talk to you.

By the time Sharon shouts up, Lucy has already had a long day. She has smoked many crinkled joints with her customers. Comes down dressed in a brown dress with beads she bought at an antique-clothing store on Second Avenue. A Charleston dancer's dress. Sharon is dressed more mainstream, in a red office dress, a black cashmere coat over. Not the kind of black cashmere coat you buy at an antique-clothing store, but the unfrazzled kind. No unmade-bed look in those shoulders; no cracked buttons.

Sharon and Lucy climb back upstairs and sit around the stool. Lucy chops fine and weighs precise.

Sharon: You have the most beautiful brown eyes. They just swim in this light.

Lucy: I almost never hear that. Not about brown eyes for some reason. People are prejudiced against brown ones. I'm sure you hear that all the time about your light blues.

Sharon: Not even Todd? Doesn't he compliment your eyes? (noticing the mound of green powder Lucy has made) I just want a half an ounce. That's all we can afford.

Lucy: (getting annoyed at Sharon's too-insistent dependence on boy-girl couple talk, especially today) We?

Sharon: Well Frank and I are going dutch on this treat. (laughs at her own joke) Frank described you in a really strong way to me.

Lucy: Did that worry you?

Sharon: (grimaces with nose, too young and too optimistic for a question like that) No.

Lucy: (chopping seeds and greenery with a sharp tool) Oh.

Sharon: What do you like best about Todd?

Lucy feels pierced, as if a miniature screwdriver were turning and turning a hole in her aorta. Every time she hears or thinks about Todd today she feels this loneliness.

Lucy: (feeling each word) I like the way he mumbles sometimes.

Sharon: I think he's special too. What do you like about Frank?

Lucy: I like his . . . (censoring herself) aggressiveness. Doggy aggressiveness.

Sharon: That's a great way to put it.

Lucy: (getting upset at what feels to her like chitchat) Level with me Sharon. No. That'll never work. So I'll level with you. I feel like this modeling might take Todd away from me. It cracks me up.

Sharon: You'll get over that when it doesn't happen. (then) I hope he and Frank become friends, I think he could keep Frank from getting too hotheaded, or swelled-headed. Frank can get real difficult if he starts getting attention, if he's at the center of attention. I don't know if you've even been at a models' party? (Lucy shakes her head that she hasn't.) But the most successful guys are just followed around by junior guys who feed on their success. It's weird. Like in high school with the star athletes. And I see that's already happening with Frank.

Lucy: (strident) So you've got storm clouds too. You've got problems. I'm not an old driven hag. Unstrung.

Sharon: No. Except I'm not afraid of losing Frank. I'm the marrying kind so I'm sure we'll get married and have kids. I can almost feel them in me already.

Lucy: You sound old-fashioned.

Sharon: (ignoring the slur) You're not secure with Todd. That's too bad.

Lucy moves over to the mattress and motions for Sharon to sit down next to her. They both lounge, lying sideways, heads facing in different directions, fitting into the semicircle of the other's legs and tummy area. They make their own yin-yang design.

Sharon leans over and touches Lucy's warm pointy breasts

through her floozy dress top. Looks up for a reaction. Lucy, returning the favor, then reaches out to do the same to Sharon's fuller nippled cups padded by her red flannel dress. They giggle, their eyes alight with frontier sensations. Just a light flirt. Then they return, businesslike, to their topic as if nothing had transpired.

Lucy: Todd said, too, that Frank wasn't interested in meeting me. That hurt me.

Sharon: But when Frank met you then he changed, right? He was just being bossy.

Lucy: (much louder) How can you know all these awful things about Frank's personality and still be so faithful and so devoted? Something's gotta give.

Lucy rests her head on her elbowed-up palm, perplexed.

Sharon: That's just the way I am.

Lucy: Is Frank good in bed?

Sharon doesn't answer. She stands up, unraveling the mystical tapestry. Pulls her wallet from the inside pocket of her coat. Unsnaps its bronze thingamajigs, opens the long thin turquoise-colored rubber wallet.

Lucy: (up, too, now, with a Jiffy bag of grass in her hand) No don't pay. It's my gift.

Sharon: (strong and vertical) Absolutely not! Here is thirty-five dollars and I'm not being polite. There's no way I'll take a gift from you. It goes against my Connecticut blood. Absolutely not!

Lucy: Okay. Okay. You're every bit as weird and messed up as me. Just in a whole other way.

Sharon smiles agreeably.

Sharon: Call me anytime. You'll be my first friend in the city. Frank's all I know so far.

Lucy: Good.

Lucy gives Sharon a fake punch as a vow of friendship, and to undo what she feels is a syrupy sentimentality that Sharon shouldn't get away with.

LATE-NIGHT CALL

Now Todd is in bed. He is crashing. As soon as he returned from Roxanne's he pulled a green-and-red Mondrian-design winter comforter over his fidgeting body. If he had a TV he would have watched it all night.

Instead he makes phone calls. He calls a line called "Confession," where criminals leave messages anonymously confessing the hows and whys of their crimes. Todd listens to a series of serial killers. Then he calls a sex tape and listens to a sex kitten named Molly (she says it rhymes with "jollies") reveal how her hubby would put her in a different motel room every Friday night and then go out to a nearby bar to find new men to come back to plow her while he watched. She says how relieved the men were when they walked in to see she didn't weigh three hundred pounds or look like the Hunchback of Notre Dame. Then he calls "Passion Phone," a personal-ad service where swingers leave pleas for sexual favors. Finally, though, Todd gets tired of listening to strangers' voices. He feels as if he's eaten too much fast food. Nods off for an hour or so.

Todd wakes up around two in the morning. The steam heat is on for one of the first nights this season making its racket of white noise. He stares out through one tall window (a bit steamed, or is it just dirty?) at a powdered purple sky. Leans over and pushes the buttons for Information without thinking anymore. Asks for a number for Frank Yastremski on Seventh Avenue. Holds the numbers in his head as he dials Frank's listed number. The wind is forcing smoky clouds to pass at highest speeds across the visible sky leaving locomotive steam trails.

Frank: (voice inconvenienced and phlegmy) What?

Todd: It's Todd.

Frank: What the fuck?

Todd: I'm sorry if I woke you.

Frank: (stretching out while calming Sharon back down into sleep with one arm) This better be good.

Todd: It is good. I mean. It's not good. It's just that I felt like I had to call you up. I hadn't told you what happened today with Soupy or anything. When I get butterflies that means I have to do it, whatever it is.

Frank: I don't care about that. Where do you get off? What am I getting out of this? Where's your girlfriend? Cause I was asleep junior. And I haven't heard anything yet to make me happy you woke me up. Huh?

Todd: (emboldened by Frank's half-asleep condition, carries on as if they were both in a dream with no consequences for tomorrow) I know it's impolite and everything. That I'm completely in the red as far as this is concerned. But I wanted to tell you that things went well today. And thanks.

These words said just in the right order and in the right tone of voice soothe Frank. He is no longer all bristles. Peace spreads out from his ears through his arms to his hands and through his legs to his feet. It's rare for him to be so accepting. Even in bed.

Frank: Buddy. I appreciate the sentiments. Let's talk tomorrow okay?

Todd: Okay.

Frank clicks down the phone and lies back. He feels fine. And he just goes on hearing Todd's voice like a sleep-teaching machine under his pillow.

Todd is less easy. What has he done? So he gets up, puts on the kimono robe, and sits by the window again smoking a cigarette. The more of the titillating tobacco he sucks in the less likely he will ever sleep tonight. He's lucky if he gets three or four hours. Now he is rustling in a metal box where he keeps scraps of paper with friends' numbers written down. He would like to make another call.

Phone rings. It rings three times. One for every hour. Todd uncradles it.

Todd: Hello? Hello?

Frank: (standing by the kitchen wall phone, dressed in pajama pants, feet on cold floor) It's me.

Todd: Uh. (exasperated) Look I'm sorry. It won't happen again. Just don't hound me about it.

Frank: So I just remembered I'm in this little fashion show at Saks on Friday at seven and I wanted to know if you wanted to go watch me as my personal guest.

Todd: (exclamatory) I'm working that show too. As a tuxedo waiter.

Frank: (almost disappointed) So you'll see me anyway.

Todd: You'll see me too. In a penguin suit.

Frank: Bark like a penguin.

Todd: No.

Frank: Okay. I'm drained. Look for me. And steal me a bottle of champagne.

Todd: I surely will Frank. I can't believe you called me back.

Frank: Well don't get any wrong ideas. I just felt we had some unfinished business.

Todd: (poetically) I always get wrong ideas.

The music is an Australian version of "Walking in the Rain" sung by a David Bowie soundalike.

Todd is standing behind a long bar table decorated with a carved ice swan. His tuxedo has a thin velvet collar so that it doesn't look identical to those of most of the other waiters. He looks elegant and punk at the same time, like the young Fred Astaire. He and his bloated, middle-aged partner, Clay, are wearing white gloves like those worn by the policemen in Japanese sci-fi movies who impassively direct panicked citizens to drive on.

They are in a men's-suit department on an upper floor of Saks. Rows of racks of soft gray suits are split apart by a balsa-wood ramp set up for the fashion show. Frank is the first out. In a dulled-gray suit, the texture of expensive toilet paper. He walks up to the end of the ramp and then back. As casually as if he were walking down the street. Not even bothering to look at the audience crammed among the polished silver trays weighed down with orchid glasses filled with yellow champagne supported mostly by young handsome models, actors, singers, dancers, students, hustlers, making extra bucks.

There is a siren in the music. Frank scratches his butt as he disappears into a black drape.

Todd: (to his bloated middle-aged partner, Clay) That guy's a friend of mine. He makes thousands of dollars just to walk up and down like that.

Clay gives Todd the middle finger. Todd didn't know that Clay, now as ruddy and splotchy and overweight as the Friar in Chaucer, was one of the first big male models, back when the profession was invented in the mid-sixties, when he was a dead ringer for George Harrison, with long hair, and so did all the Carnaby Street ads, until the style changed, but by then Clay had already spent all his money shopping.

NUDE SHOTS

Today Soupy has Todd booked for test shots. At the studio of one of the eccentrics in the business: an independent stockbroker named Wheelock whose hobby is taking pictures of amateur male models. Wheelock doesn't like men after they've turned professional. He prefers to capture them as dumb deer.

Wheelock's studio is actually a friend's loft. He rents it for the day. (His own home is an expensive Sutton Place apartment where he lives with his wife and kids.) The loft is way downtown and looks out on an aluminum-foil Hudson River one way, on hulks of older Wall Street buildings the other way. Whee-lock likes to have his guys stand on the rusty fire escape so the stripes of the bars make jail shadows on their faces.

Wheelock is about forty. Has a paunch. And a walrusy mus-tache, the same silver tint as the rest of his long straight hair. He is dressed all in soft, gray clothes: turtleneck, cotton pants, soft sneakers from Italy.

Todd, arriving carrying a garment bag, is stiff and his stiffness is making him feel tired. Especially along his spinal cord in the back. He is on the defensive today, though not sure why. Whee-lock tries to put Todd at ease by guiding him first to the win-dows at the far end of the loft to point out the different New Jersey buildings on this clear-because-windy afternoon, the smoke of a freighter pulling its weight draggingly to a cove on the other side. Then, walking back toward the bed under track lights in the dead center of the mostly empty space, Wheelock reaches into his shoulder bag and pulls out a fistful of already-rolled joints.

Wheelock: (handing over one joint, which Todd smoothly sticks in his back jeans pocket for later) What did you bring to wear?

Todd: (jaunty) Everything in my closet. Which means not much.

Wheelock unzips, then looks through the garment bag of clothes. It's mostly dress-up: suits, trousers, ties, shoes. Some of the suits are spiffy retros: a fifties sharkskin, a sixties red velvet, a seventies Tony Manero white jacket over a black silk shirt. But Todd's collection doesn't interest Wheelock.

Wheelock: (disappointed, flaming alive the bronze tip of a joint) Here. Smoke this. I think I'll just shoot you in the sweater you have.

Todd: (surprised) This leftover?

The sweater is white cashmere. Todd's jeans are soft light blue. His boots pointed, with bronze tips. Todd starts to smoke grudgingly, Wheelock gustily. Wheelock's lips are muscles that draw in the cigarette puckeringly, without the use of his fingers.

Todd: (after the joint) No offense. But you're looking like a vampire with ashtray skin.

Wheelock: (grinning) Don't forget who's got the camera.

Wheelock takes his Leica camera out of its pack and starts making pictures. Todd stands against a wall that is bleached in white sunlight. Has trouble with his eyes: they water, squint shut. Wheelock orders him into different positions: one foot on other, head tilted, head straight. Tells him to take off his white sweater. Shoots him on his side in his purple-brown undershirt, legs drawn up to chest, on a bed covered with a leopard skin.

Todd: Now I know how it feels to get shot.

Wheelock: (annoyed) What?

Todd: (undoing the pose, moving to sit on the front of the bed) I feel gummed up.

Wheelock: (cloyingly) You know working with young models is like dating virgins. And I have the same advice. Breathe deep! Clear your head!

Todd: (sincerely interested) How strange am I acting? Less strange or more strange than the others?

Wheelock: (lying) Definitely more strange.

Todd: How?

Wheelock: Because you're resisting me. But it's getting better. You just need to get nude. That'll cure you.

Soupy told Todd this morning that if Wheelock wanted to take nude shots, it would be okay. He has shots of all the top models in New York in the buff and his files are completely top-secret. But Todd felt confused by this advice.

Wheelock: I'll show you.

Wheelock pulls a manila envelope out of his camera pack. Tosses it to Todd. Inside are dozens of contact sheets of recognizable cigarette or beer models with no clothes on. The poses are all arty. The men's penises hidden, like modern Adams, behind hands or horses or swords or dune vegetation.

Wheelock: (softly) Take off your clothes.

Todd: You gonna show my pictures around like these?

Wheelock: (insistent) Take off your clothes.

Todd does. Then, surprisingly, begins to enjoy himself. Nude except for an open dress shirt sitting in a director's chair, the shirt brushing gently against his lower hairs. Stop. Hazel eyes as alert as a bald eagle's as the camera brushes past his face while he lies on his back on the animal skin. Stop. An erection showing through the white cotton towel wrapped around his hips as he exits a steamy white shower stall, his defined torso covered in jewels of splashed water. Stop.

Wheelock is whistling Dvořák as Todd starts to dress again an hour or so later. Sun in its lazier, pinker, getting-off-work phase. While Todd is shimmying into his starched Calvin Klein briefs, Wheelock proffers a tip.

Wheelock: (one bushy eyebrow drooping upward) Working with beginners I can always tell who's going to make it and who isn't. You know the best test? Models who don't wear underwear go on to be the biggest successes.

Todd: (pulling on the tight white short shorts anyway) That's cool. Now men are sex objects too.

YELLOW STAIRWELL LIGHT

It's full spring. Winter came and went. Todd did meet with Jean from Milan, and will be flying there tomorrow to start work.

He is walking down Bleecker Street on his way to say good-bye to Lucy. Pink bulbs are sticking out from the few stick trees curbside. Bums are sunning on the sidewalk. Across the way he watches a woman who always reminds him of the old woman arsonist in the attic in *Jane Eyre*. This woman's hair is teased out, gray; clothes wretched; fat. She lives on a ground floor. Her companion is a young man, fetchingly handsome, one of those bums in his early twenties. When she goes for a walk the young man follows behind her at two paces. When she stops, he stops. Always.

Todd yells up. Has on green fatigues, L.L. Bean brown low hiking boots, no socks, green thermal T-shirt under partly unbuttoned gray cotton workshirt. He's not afraid to let his voice be heard. But no Lucy. He didn't call ahead. As suddenly as Todd realizes that she's not up there, his mood changes to anxious.

To wait, he heads across the dusty Bowery over many blocks to Tompkins Square Park where dogs pee indiscriminately on concrete walls, grassy mounds and wood benches alike. Todd sits up on one of the splintered benches, feeling the hard stripe of wood under his lower butt. It's dusk so his Army pants look almost lime in the in-between light, his gray workshirt silver, his boots cooper.

On his way over Todd stopped in a liquor store—with bulletproof glass protecting its clerks—to buy a pocket bottle of clear gin. Now he sits there drinking the hot stuff straight from the little bottle, letting circles of wet from the top of the glass burn on his lips. It's getting darker and darker. A passing green-brown-skinned teen with lots of necklaces around his skinny neck says "yo" only because of the mellow mood of the moment. He's not selling anything right now. It's almost dark enough that a movie in a drive-in could begin to be visible. The more Todd drinks the foggier his heart, the drier his mouth, the scratchier his eyes.

Next stop: CBGB's. After yelling up to check that Lucy is still not there. CBGB's is a rock club. By now he is walking pretty outrageously. He angles in (an early night, punk-rock band) and orders another burning gin straight up with a water chaser. He likes the feel of the many-sided gin glass in his hand. The band is playing noise. Up close to the stage guys are heaving into each other. Toward the back are some girls, one or two with shaved heads, wearing monster-movie makeup.

Half an hour into the show, or two glasses later, Todd meanders to the wall phone to call Lucy again.

Lucy: Lo.

Todd: (his heart a puddle) Where have you been?

Lucy: Out. Where you?

Todd hangs up. His insides are turning around like taffy. He feels so bad. So he leaves and crosses the street with all its contradictory beams of light and yells up. This time his voice cracks, like Stanley Kowalski yelling "Stella" in *Streetcar*. He leans against a big old hearse that some joker in the neighborhood has converted into his personal station wagon.

Lucy runs down to let him in. She looks great in the doorway, letting her hair down, like an aria singer in an opera. But she looks sad, too. Has on a yellow T-shirt (inside out), white jeans, red beat-up pumps. When something is wrong Lucy doesn't wear black.

Todd: I feel sick.

Lucy: I smell a dragon. Come upstairs.

Todd: I think I have to throw up.

Lucy: Go ahead. But wait till we get to the bathroom, okay?

Todd is in the narrow bathroom with a toilet flushed by pulling down on a hanging chain. He starts to heave into the porcelain bowl. Purple, orange, brown, white flecks in one whoosh. Then again. Fireworks of upchuck. Settling into a green swamp below.

Todd: (loud) It's disgusting. It's disgusting.

Lucy: (standing in the bathroom doorway) I can't believe you're taking it so hard. Even I know it's not so bad.

Todd: It is bad. It is bad. I'm a bad person.

Lucy: Why?

Todd: Because I'm leaving you.

Lucy: (walking back across the long room, lighting a Benson & Hedges) I have to just keep moving around the room. Walking around. Do you care?

Todd: (rushing out of the lav while a torrent of toilet-bowl water roars) Who in the world talks like I'm talking now? Or acts this way? What's wrong with me? I'm under some heavy curse.

Lucy: (angry) You're not.

Lucy sits Todd down on the mattress. She takes his two hands in hers, stroking their tops the way you stroke the tops of a dog's paws.

Todd: Hands are private parts, too.

Then she leans sideways and lights the kerosene lamp next to the mattress. It gives off an amber glow.

Lucy: You're just getting used to it. The life we see around us is as pretty as a postcard. But felt life is a monster movie.

Todd looks at Lucy but doesn't really get what she's saying.

Lucy: How long will you be in Europe?

Todd: About three months or so.

Lucy: I'm going to come visit you sometime in there. Okay?

Todd: You have to ask? But how are you gonna pay for it?

Lucy: Dealing I guess. And I can write porn novels for a Mafia publisher I know.

Lucy walks Todd over the uneven floor to her door. He's still breathing alcohol, and feeling a brouhaha in his chest and stomach area.

They clasp each other around their torsos and kiss on the cheeks like two European politicians at an airport. Then they kiss on the lips. Good-bye.

About an hour later, on a hunch, Lucy gets out of bed. She inches to her front door, opens it, and looks down the rickety steps at Todd asleep making mouth-gurgling sounds on a landing down a floor. Lucy descends dressed only in the white panties she sleeps in, her stomach an oval, and pushes at his shoulder to force him up. Having to budge Todd doesn't seem out of the ordinary to her as she's still sort of asleep.

Lucy: Why you here? Want to sleep upstairs?

Todd: (roused, caught, ashamed) No. I have to go. My plane ticket's at Perry Street.

Todd leans on a banister and bangs down the steps, without any formal good-bye this time. He looks awful to Lucy in that yellow stairwell light.

MILAN

Milan is the Pittsburgh of Europe.

It doesn't have any smelly cats reflected in canals, or snotty starched white buildings, or cracked ruins where people walk around all night. Few movies and few postcards are shot here. Visitors visit the mud-drip Duomo Cathedral, the fading da Vinci *Last Supper* mural, the Trump Tower–like Galleria, and they're gone.

But Todd doesn't know this. And neither does Paul, the agency cowboy. The two are now standing in front of the tiny glass Milan airport building, about the size of a car-rental port at Kennedy. Through the wire fence on the perimeter of its front

yard they can see red-tile roofs and bushy green trees with scarlet flecks.

Todd is dressed in a tan suit, white shirt, black Tony Lama
boots. His big brown canvas bag is his home now, as he sublet
his Perry Street studio to an illegal alien. Todd looks more like
a cowboy today than Paul, who is wearing a striped violet-red-
black rugby shirt, green cords, darker olive-green tie oxfords
with argyle socks, all his belongings folded in a standard gray
patent-leather suitcase.

Todd: (about a billboard, off over a field) Look how much
swarthier they are than American milk families.

Paul: Rule Number One. Don't jump to conclusions.

Finally a pale white taxi comes round the circular drive. Todd
studies a nearby soldier leaning against a wall in a gray uniform
(ropes slung around one shoulder) whose machine gun is casually pointed at Todd's crotch. Then they pile in.

Todd: Corso Magenta Number Forty. Top Model. That's the
first stop. Then he's going on. To Star.

Driver: *Cosa?*

Todd had taken it for granted that the driver knew English,
thinking of him as an Italian-American.

Todd: Corso Magenta. Forty. (then makes four finger flashes)

Driver: *Quaranta.*

They are on their way. Past industrial stacks, shiny brick
factories, glossy billboards. Under crisscrossing metal wires
zinging with little flit birds. As they close in on the city (through
tunnely underpasses) the road gets squeezed in. Older heavy
gray buildings bottom out.

Paul: (smugly scratching his balls, and drawling) I think they
have a hero-worshiping attitude towards Americans over here.
Because of World War II.

Todd: (in a you-jerk tone) My uncle bombed the Italians in
World War II.

The taxi edges by a big city block of a department store with
its mannequins posed inside silver and amber-tinted display windows, dressed in geometric clothes, red triangular dresses, gray

square-shoulder suits, sitting on ultra-tectonic chairs and Miró-shaped sofas among a conniption fit of televised video images. Long cardinal-red Communist banners hang from the store's upper windows, and lots of yellow and brown people stand around outside in clumps yelling and fisting the air.

Taxi Driver: (explaining) *Sciopero.*

Todd and Paul look at each other blankly like two halves of a doppelgänger.

Soon it's time for Todd to get out in front of palazzo number 40. Paul travels on to his own agency. Todd lugs his brown duffel bag through iron gates. Stops for a minute in a secret-garden courtyard filled with green shadows, old working stone fountains, tall cypresses. He feels as if he's been dropped here. Hardly wants to dispel the fuzzy fictional feeling by budging up the few steps, but does. Pushes little gold button, ancient door snaps open automatically, walks in.

Inside is the opposite of outside. The dusty Renaissance cube is filled with plastic furniture, electrical gadgets, neon lights and rock music. Todd's entrance is monitored in the quick eyes of the guy and girl models lounging on stone benches in the hallways. No hellos. They might as well be gazelles. Then he turns a corner into the booking room. Can see, hear, feel the pressure here. Again models are scattered around, on the edges, cruising, checking out one another's head shots on the walls.

A large central buzzing rectangle is where the business is. Four people are sitting at its corners doing a work ballet. Jean, the head booker, is an oddly beautiful black Brazilian around thirty-five, wearing a short-sleeve Qiana silk shirt patterned with palm trees, airplanes and hotels. Diagonally across from Jean is Luigi, a curly-blond-haired Italian with beginning bald spot and receding hairline, dressed in bright Fiorucci clothes that don't look quite right on him. Across from Luigi is Beatrice, a short sweet young woman with brown hair tied back, Mona Lisa smile, wearing slacks. Diagonal to her is Susanna, an awkward cool dark young woman who doesn't mix smoothly with either the bookers or the models. She spends her weekends on yachts.

Jean: (not getting up) I remember you. Lucky for you.

Todd: (friendly) I've been on a long flight. I don't feel like myself.

Jean: (has a mean streak) Well that's fine because we don't need you. Soupy made a mistake.

Todd: (low) Just explain to me what you're talking about.

Jean: (his voice going higher to counteract Todd's mumble) I mean that Soupy sent you at the wrong time completely and he'll pay for this we won't.

Todd: (feeling some worry) You mean there's no work?

Jean: (to Luigi) Luigi is there not work? (pause, while Luigi looks up but won't play along) Is there work in Milan?

A Tall Blond German Woman Model: (making epileptic body twitch) No!

Luigi walks over, wanting to find out who Todd is. Puts his hand on Todd's shoulder.

Luigi: You have pictures? Can I see your book?

Todd unzips his bag and tugs out a new tan portfolio with a stuck-on postcard on its cover of an English punk guy and girl with auburn-and-black-dyed hairdos spiked to the skies and tie-dyed shirts as radiantly bloodshot as industrial sunsets. Luigi sits down at the table and turns through the plastic portfolio pages. The book is inconsistent, with one series of black-whites of Todd looking more like a forties movie idol than a current stud.

Luigi: *Stupendo.* . . . Susanna. Where do we have Todd staying?

Susanna: Medici.

Luigi: Pensione Medici? Todd, if you like, I come by tonight and we get something to eat, very simple, and I show you around Milano. You like? If not, I understand.

Todd: (glad for company) That'd be super. Do you know where I live? I don't.

Luigi laughs and laughs but doesn't bother to answer.

Beatrice: (walking over to Todd, sweetly) There is a truth to what Jean is saying to you. Not that there is no work . . . at all?

. . . but that this weekend in Italy . . . how do you say? . . .
facciamo il ponte.

Jean: (shouting from phone) To make a bridge.

Beatrice: Is a holiday. And so we make a bridge from tonight
until Monday. No work. The agency is closed.

Todd: (feeling tossed about like a volleyball) But I left New
York in this big rush. I could still be with my girlfriend.

Luigi: (warming up to the girlfriend part) You need to relax.
To learn to enjoy Milano. Everything is for the best. So I come
by at eight. I write down your hotel for you, for the taxi.

Todd takes the folded-over pink paper and spastically drags
his bag back along the floor back to the front doors. An American girl around seventeen, looking a bit like Sharon, Frank's
girlfriend, jumps over to open the door for him.

Girl: (in informant tones) You're lucky you're in the Medici
and not in the Lucinda. An American model was killed in the
Pensione Lucinda. He was taking a shower and the owner left
the gas on or something in the water boiler and it exploded. He
was one of us, and he got gassed.

Todd can almost smell the bitter deadly fumes as he exits
through the held-open door.

PENSIONE

Todd is barefoot in his room in Pensione Medici. The room
is very small, very narrow. There is a single bed along one wall
with a plastic imitation-wood bookshelf as headboard. A sink in
one corner with a metal tube circling above with a curtain attached that can be pulled around the sink area. A plastic bidet
stashed under the sink. A folding table and one wood chair. Big
armoire. The only lights are an overhead bulb and a little lamp
with orange shade on a bookcase by the bed. A copy of a Bron-

zino painting of Neptune hangs on one wall. Two doors lead out to a balcony.

Whenever Todd passes by the chipped mirror over the sink he checks himself out.

Todd: (out loud) Wild thing. You make my heart sing.

It is starting to get dark now. Todd has both lights turned on though some light is still coming in from outside. And some breezes. Todd takes his clothes, all rumpled, transfers them to hangers in the armoire. They look darker and dirtier and weirder here than in New York: more like costumes, say of a Renaissance highwayman. Takes his bag of toiletries and empties contents onto shelf over the sink—Head & Shoulders, Ban, VO5, Colgate, Listerine, One-A-Day.

At the bottom of the canvas bag is a new blank scrapbook that he shimmies up into the workings under his mattress.

Then he tips the bag in several directions so that articles left inside clatter against each other. Takes out a loud-tick portable wind-up alarm clock that he puts over his bed. Some current plastic cassettes. A classical tape of Tchaikovsky. Arranges the tapes like books on the bookshelf case.

From the pocket of his carry-on bag he takes a paperback, Ernest Hemingway's *A Farewell to Arms*. Someone recommended the novel because it's set in Milan. There's a still life of a white cup of espresso with a smoking cigarette on the lip of its saucer on the book's cover. Todd puts it on the shelf next to the cassettes but it slides down flat. Then tunes in his transistor. Settles on a male crooner singing the soft-rock love songs so popular around the moody Mediterranean.

Music playing. Todd now walks out onto his balcony, which stretches along the entire front of the third floor of the *pensione*. Four rooms face out, their sections separated by little waist-high wire fences partly concealed by tie-on flowers and growing plants. One guy and two girl models live to one side. Todd already met the guy, a tall basketball player from Michigan, who had explained how the one girl had been his girlfriend in college, but now the other was. So the old girlfriend sleeps in the single.

At the far end of the balcony, to the right of Todd as he faces the street, a man and a woman, she fat he thin, maybe from Tunisia, are sitting watching an Italian cowboy movie on a little black-white TV placed on the same kind of folding table as in Todd's room.

Across the street is a more modern apartment building. Todd watches a thick Italian woman, middle-aged, working on supper. She is boiling water, cutting up red peppers and lettuce and tomatoes, making some kind of pasta on a wood board. She looks over, sees Todd staring, goes back nonchalantly to her colorful work. Her long-haired boy is undressing in the next room. He stands there naked and thin, looking like a wolf, with no clothes on.

Todd needs a cigarette so badly he can't stand it. He slaps down the hall, knocks on a door he saw a slant-hipped blond girl, must be a model too, go into earlier. He waits, she comes out, and he pops the question. She fidgets for a cigarette, obviously wanting him away. He finds out she's Australian not American. Todd takes the one cigarette back into his boycave. Lights it, strips down to his underwear, lies back and starts sucking in the gray smoke. As he manufactures a smoke cloud, he has his usual anxious inspired response. Stands up as if at attention. Throws on shirt and trous.

Is onto something. Doesn't ride the one-person elevator. Runs downstairs regularly, the soles of his feet blackening.

The first floor is mostly a doily-dotted living room where guests can sit and suitcases can be left. There's where the tossed books are piled, including lots of Harold Robbins novels. The owner's family is sitting in a tiny kitchen eating and cooking and smoking and yelling. In the hallway next to an even tinier office is a framed cheap illustration of the Virgin Mary with roses sprouting about her. Todd smacks his palm down on an old-fashioned metal reception alarm, a self-service bell tower, releasing its ting.

Todd: I have to call America. Quick!

Padrone: *Aspetta. Aspetta. Dove? Scrivi!*

The owner, dressed in an old David Copperfield vest and dress pants, overweight, puffing on any of a few mutilated cigarettes, hands Todd a paper to write on. Todd writes Lucy's number. The owner calls the operator to put the call through.

Padrone: *Aspetta!*

Todd paces around the sitting room, every so often rubbing its lace curtains between his sweaty fingers. The phone rings and rings, not for him. Until twenty minutes later.

Todd: (rushing out to grab the old-fashioned black receiver of a style Al Capone must have talked on) Lucy?

No. It's still the operator. Then after some beeps and scratches, the telephone sound, Lucy is connected.

Todd: Lucy?

Lucy: Todd. I can't believe it's you. What time is it there?

Todd: I dunno exactly. Why?

Lucy: Well it's earlier here. I looked it up. But I forget how many hours. How expensive is it to call here?

Todd: I dunno. (more insistent) Why?

Lucy: I miss your face.

Todd: (fishing) Do you have any plans? What are you doing now that I'm not there?

Lucy: Actually your friend Frank called and we're going out to eat this week. To console each other over losing you.

Todd: (blurts) I don't want you to.

Lucy: (brushes over) How is it being an international fashion model? Do they love you?

Todd: Stop talking that way. Are you baiting me?

Lucy: (coming down heavily on the name, the way she does when she wants to derail him) Todd . . .

Todd: (hearing that tone, immediately changes for the better) Yeah. It's great. The agency is really fancy. It's in a palace. Next to a church where *The Last Supper* is by Leonardo da Vinci. You've gotta see it. And one of the bookers is taking me out to dinner tonight. They don't do that to everybody. And I miss you, a lot.

Lucy: That's sweet. I miss you too. It's so gray here today. The sky is as dirty as the street. And it's cold. It's May and it's cold. What am I gonna do without you?

Todd: Ask Frank.

Lucy: (again) Todd . . .

Todd: (voice goes down as Padrone comes in to theatrically check the little meter that is clocking Todd's call, clicking every few seconds) I don't want to get off. I'll get lonely. You know where I feel the loneliness most? In my feet.

They buzz off. When Todd turns around he sees Luigi, who's been leaning in the door during the finale of the phone call. Luigi's dressed in fancy Italian designer clothes: a striped blue-yellow jacket, pants that are a shimmering weave of black and silver and white threads, pointy black shoes, silk shirt open at the neck.

Todd: (remembering) I'm late.

Luigi: No. Come.

Todd: I can't go like this can I? (points scowling at his own blue denims, yellow T-shirt with VENICE BEACH written in pink lipstick print)

Luigi: Yes. We just go to a Communist restaurant down the street. That way you'll see other models who are in the same way as you.

By "Communist" Luigi means inexpensive.

Todd: Okay. Let me just run upstairs and run a comb through my hair.

Luigi: But your hair stays in place without a comb. It is a bush.

Todd does run upstairs, slips on tennis shoes, but he doesn't own a comb. Instead douses head under faucet, wetting hair, dries off, then pushes his fingers through. Slams through the door without looking back at an intruder tabby cat slowly scratching its back up and down on his black cowboy boots.

SUMMER CAMP

Luigi is leading Todd down Via Torino. The front windows of different restaurants light up parts of the sidewalk. Luigi is the Spirit of Fun. He is trying to jostle Todd to fully arrive.

The restaurant he leads him into is one big room jammed with tables for four. Lots of customers. The room is narrow at front, larger in the rear, with kitchens in the back. Is a cheap Italian workers' restaurant with a 500-lire fixed menu of pasta, meat and a quarter liter of wine. Fat, friendly owner with capped teeth, thick glasses, dirty white apron is sitting at a stool in front of the cash drawer. He is arguing with his wife, also in apron, who in turn is yelling at a young Italian boy making coffees at the bar whose other job is to deliver carafes of water and wine to the tables.

Luigi, looking like an aristocrat in his weaves, grabs one of the waiters, Sandro, by the shoulder. Sandro is absorbed with a bunch of his friends in a Rolling Stones pinball machine. When a player scores, the machine plays different Stones hits in melodic beeps. Sandro has an earring in one of his ears, dirty hands; he's a Milanese version of a hood. When he recognizes Luigi, though, he turns friendly and pink. He points Luigi out to his buddies and they all kiss and hug and smack hands. Then they close back in on the glowing toy. Except Sandro, whom Luigi has roped in as his private waiter for the night. The two talk in rapid Italian as they move through the crowded middle of the restaurant, Luigi gesturing every so often to Todd.

Sandro shows them to the only two available seats at a table with two rough older men and three younger ones, also hood variety, bunched at one end.

Sandro: (to table in general) *Un americano.*

Man: (looking like a diesel truck driver) *Come si chiama?*

Todd: Todd.

Other Man: New York.

Todd: (surprised) Yeah. *Si.*

The men laugh to each other. One of the boys holds out to Todd the back of his hand tattooed with an American eagle. Luigi and Sandro murmur away. Pretty soon the Italians get interested in each other again, and Todd and Luigi are left alone.

Todd: (referring to a table of male models a few away) Those guys look just like me. I mean compared to everyone else.

Then five young women models make noise getting to their table at the back. One waves to Luigi. One looks at Todd. He's been close to Lucy since college. But realizes in the look of the fox-faced teenage girl that he is on his own. Thoughts start to cross his mind. Thoughts, those shadows of feelings. A click goes off in Todd's head. Not like the click of a gun, threatening. More like the click that occurs at rare times at the bottom of the spine during sex. Todd kicks out his one leg involuntarily as he sits back at an angle with his spine straight, not fitting into the chair, in an alert slump.

He looks over at the table where she sits. The five are all making food jokes looking at the menu. At the height of the anorexia craze. His favorite is waving her fingers with azure-painted fingernails to show a ring to her friend. A girl with an emerald ring compares hers. He can overhear photographers' names—Olivieri Toscanni, Fabrizio Ferri—dropped like the names of high school English teachers in cafeteria gossip. The girls' hands are all over themselves, especially over their own legs and hips and asses.

Todd: (hands going wild, on one of his tangents) It's not what I thought it would be like. It's like summer camp. All these American kids lost in Europe, eating spaghetti every night, not knowing the language. Just trying to get laid and get paid. And then not wanting to go back home to Kansas and Nebraska anymore. Flesh slaves for life.

Luigi: (bored) *Basta!*

Sandro returns with some noodles on a green plastic dish with thin tomato sauce on top. He pours Todd and Luigi glasses of the strong red wine from a carafe. Shakes cheese on the pasta from a spoon. Teases Luigi by feeling the bald spot on the back of his head.

Luigi: (to Sandro) *Puttano.*

During dinner Todd tells Luigi the plot of the latest *Superman* movie in detail. "Margot Kidder is a piece of work." Luigi explains which designers and models in Milan are gay, and which are straight.

Luigi: (handing Todd a wrapped-up piece of paper) Go into the bathroom and take it up your nose.

Todd: (protesting) I just ate.

PRIMADONNA

Todd did do the coke. When he walks in the doorway at Primadonna its ticket window seems scintillated, filled with dots of baby-blue light, like a Seurat. One ticket costs as much as ten meals at the Communist restaurant.

Todd and Luigi descend the long, steep, rubber-covered steps to the basement discotheque. Neon-tube lighting turns pinker and oranger the lower they go. Luigi, stoned, leaves Todd the minute they touch bottom, as emphasized a feeling as touching the bottom of a filled swimming pool.

Luigi: I have to work now. (breaking with too big a smile into American slang) Work it.

Todd: (mocking him) Gotta go disco.

Todd rolls through there like a moving camera on a track. He checks out the carpeted bleachers where lots of the same models who were in the agency this afternoon are yakking and posing—sucking in cheeks, tilting heads, looking more like rock formations than advanced biochemical organisms.

It's an office party. The bar is almost one hundred percent

models, designers, photographers, agents, magazine editors, clients. Todd spots Beatrice and Susanna from the agency dancing together on the dance floor in the next big room, its sound waves trebled. The two women dance with their arms on the small of each other's backs. The music is classics: Rolling Stones, Diana Ross, Michael Jackson.

The deejay is a wild frizzy-haired Italian with spectacles wearing a Primadonna T-shirt and shouting often into his microphone to the dancers from his partly-enclosed-by-yellow-Plexiglas booth.

Deejay: (speed-talking, like a radio announcer) *Buona sera buona sera buona sera. Ciao bellissimi.* Welcome to Primadonna. The first lady number-one nightclub of Milano. *Ciao carissimi.* Premier. *Uno. Prima.* Number one. *Molto Star.*

The chiseled guys dance mostly from side to side, their hips locked, in tight pants and muscle shirts, or silk shirts, buttons open down to the navels. The girls try not to drink and so keep themselves fenced in, a strain that shows in their wraparound minisarongs. Paul pushes up in his old Western duds with a short girl with curly black hair, a younger Anna Magnani, though probably American-Jewish. Paul wraps Todd around in a strong squeeze, too noisy to introduce his partner, but gives Todd a complicitous smile about her.

Todd: (shouting) Back in the saddle.

But Paul doesn't hear, or doesn't get it, and they head off into a tangerine haze.

Luigi's back. Grabs Todd on the backs of his shoulders and steers him around and back into the men's room. White porcelain, lime light. Luigi stands in front of a urinal, fly not opened, looks around, then puts powder from the little wrapped-up origami piece of paper on the back of his hand, and sniffs it up. Todd, adjacent, does the same. In comes a dark, short woman, around thirty, in black cocktail dress, dyed blond hair, high heels, lots of gaudy jewels. Luigi screams when he sees her.

Luigi: Rosalina! Rosalina!

Rosalina screams back.

Rosalina: *Cattivi ragazzi.*

She squeezes between them at the urinals.

Luigi: (kidding) *Solo per uomini.*

Rosalina laughs, mouthing along with "I'm Coming Out" while Luigi draws a line across the back of her hand.

Rosalina lives on inherited money. She spends her year moving from one resort to another, meeting young men. She gets no satisfaction, but is always in the early stages of love, the worst. Has her fortune read nearly every week by a different tarot card reader.

After she finishes the blow, Rosalina looks instantly older. Her lines crack, her brown eye-circles turn black.

Todd: (spuming air out of his mouth to release tension) Too many people. I can't keep them straight anymore.

Rosalina: (putting her hand around his skull and kissing the side of his head) No no. Go on to dance with me.

Todd, not having slept since the plane, can't do much. But he holds her tight with his palms on her behind, and breathes in the strong smell of a forsythia perfume that is rising from a little puff down in her breasts. She is pleased to feel that he is hard in his pants. He does lick her skin on the exposed part of her chest, the sweat mixed with the chemical tang of some toilet water.

Rosalina: (sincerely) *Ti amo.* (then moaning it, less sincerely) *Ti amo.*

Luigi slips his arm around Todd's waist as he is escorting Rosalina from the photoelectric cell of a dance floor. He cleaves them and steers Todd over to introduce him to Rex, the assistant to Milan's most famous men's fashion designer, Ferrati. Rex is short, with short dark brown haircut, flannel shirt open on a sprouting of curly brown hairs, post-spinach Popeye hairs, tight black jeans that make a canvas relief map of his crotch, and sandals he bought on Fire Island last summer. About the same age as Todd, he acts older, is more wasted, balancing a straight vodka, cigarette and bottle of poppers all at once.

Rex: (to Todd, in a heavy accent, hardly understandable) What scene are you?

Todd: (Luigi had explained Rex's connection to Ferrati on the way over, so he's playing along) Scene or sign?

Rex grabs Todd around his head and squeezes him in so he can smell his body odor.

Rex: (European disciplinarian tone) Luigi brings you now to a party at my house. What sex are you?

Todd: (wrestling) Guess.

The party at Rex's is a mumbo-jumbo. His apartment is one cathedral-ceilinged room with a loft above. The tape playing is "Funky Town." Some leather straps and chains hang down under the wood of Rex's loft. He is nude now, with a motorcycle cap on, snorting a little amber bottle of amyl nitrite with a bright yellow label and passing it to a bunch of visitor friends of his from Los Angeles. One nude guy with a brown goatee is kissing a calendar picture of a muscleman porn star who is dressed like a gladiator in a movie.

Most of the models at this party—all young guys—are lounging on the floor where lines of coke are passed round and round on a hand mirror as regularly as the second hand of a clock. Silently. Todd, feeling insulated, watches as the faces of projected innocence maintain a healthy look even as the eyes go pink and lips dry out. The guys, in their jeans and khakis, are a collage sculpture, like a John Chamberlain crush—legs interlocked, making a cats' cradle of glances, armpits showing as plainly as traffic signals.

Todd senses a warm mouth on his cock, but because of the medication it stays more muscular than skeletal, feels like a fish in a pond.

Then Todd hears a distant muffled tower bell. Feels nudged, as in a tale, to flee. Stands up and walks straight past the noise of talking voices. Out on the street is lifted for a minute by the clarity of the silver wind. Then Luigi catches up, puts hand on the round top of his head, flattening his hair.

Luigi: I show you one more candy shop of Milano.

Todd: (his last words for a while) I'm ready now to go to Niagara Falls on a honeymoon.

The next stop is the Residenza Clothilde. The most Alpine and upscale of the hotels frequented by models. Even has room service. The party is given by a bunch of the more successful women. Lots of black-leopard and silver-tiger vehicles are pulled up in the circular driveway out front. These are the rides of the playboys, a thriving Milanese type always on the make for a new woman model to kidnap onto a yacht, or to ply with black diamonds, or to introduce into Roman films, especially Barbarella ballads.

The apartment is decorated like a Miami condo—white shag rugs, round pink Formica tables lit by hanging mosquito lamps. It's crammed with women actually wearing leopardskin tights or see-through plastic tops, and men whose black hair is actually slicked back or whose neck chains are actually gold.

Todd sits, though can't sit still long, on a folding chair at a folding card table. They're all in a cloud of smoking. A white-haired Sean Connery in a white suit has his arm around a young intelligent-looking brunette woman who is listening to him lecture about his yacht's mission.

Playboy: I believe I have found the lost city of Atlantis. Our depth chargers can detect gold. The government is afraid of any hint of extraterrestrial garbage, but they are willing to fund us if we should bring back a fountain or a piece of loose palace.

Woman: (helpfully) I read that *The Iliad* may have been written on Atlantis.

Playboy: (thrilled) Exactly put.

Todd is soon enough alone, humming "Everybody's Talking," his sneakered steps echoing as he crosses the wide stone moon reflector of a square in front of the Duomo on his way back to the *pensione*.

Milan at night. The Duomo Square on one side, neon Times Square signs on the other. Inside of the Galleria with boys skateboarding on the waxy stone pavement. Closed subway stations with corrugated men shooting up heroin. Jukebox at punk club. Rigolo restaurant with customers ordering different lush desserts from a tray. Drinking coffee at Tabac. Drinking drinks on a terrace. Castello Sforzesco. Giardini Pubblici. The Leonardo da Vinci canals. Tram driving through the pillar ruins on Via Torino. Malpensa Airport with plane flying in. A desk clerk. Empty brutal streets seen from fast-moving car past police with machine guns and insect helmets.

STILETTO HEELS

Todd is lying in bed in his *pensione* room. His heart is beating double and his veins and arteries are tingling. He is licking his tongue over the fronts of his teeth, comparing back a few hours when they were completely numb. Streetlight breaking sketchily through the closed shutters. Clock ticking. Tape player playing the Tchaikovsky tape, a little uneven in sound quality. Tape clicks off.

Todd is irked by the periodic sound of high heels clattering up and down the stairs, or through the hall, followed by loud door slamming. He gets up and looks through his toiletry pouch for Unisoms, his favorite brand of sleeping pill, but must not have packed them. Rocks himself, sweaty, on the mattress repeating the words "horse tranquilizer" over and over again.

Suddenly there is a loud pounding noise. Todd rolls out. Puts on his Japanese bathrobe and unlaced sneaks. Spies into the dim hallway. Sees an obvious female prostitute, painted face, stiletto heels, tight vinyl dress, leading a client into a room. She looks disapprovingly at Todd before slamming her door. Todd wants to know more about these noises. Slam slam. Click click. Plus he can't sleep anyway.

Todd pads downstairs. He's passed on the stairs by three policemen with lots of heavy weapons. Feels naked in his kimono. Feels they must be after the whore in heels. But when he gets down to the lobby he sees a fourth policeman with pale jowls leaning against a wall next to the corny print of the Virgin Mary with palms stuck behind it, combing his thick mustache with his fingers, while the *padrone* takes money from another painted lady, lit by the dim desk lamp. Todd can't put two and two together. The *padrone* is not happy to see Todd there.

Padrone: *Cosa fai?*

Todd: I can't sleep. (then louder and more desperately) I can't sleep.

Padrone: (looks apologetically toward the woman) *Per piacere, signore. Silenzio.*

The three policemen come back down, not with the disappearing prostitute, but with a blond American boy Todd had seen earlier that night at Rex's. Todd is angry and confused at what he feels has to be an injustice. The model's arms are held behind him by one indifferent cop.

Cop: (stern) *Passaporto. Subito.*

Padrone: (produces the little blue book) *Eccolo.*

While the police and *padrone* chatter among themselves, hazed in by the thick smoke of the prostitute's cigarette, Todd and the model talk evenly and quietly.

Todd: What did you do?

Model: I couldn't pay my rent this month. They found me in my friend's room. They had a warrant. I was in the closet.

Todd: Who are you with?

Model: Star.

Todd: (relieved) I'm with Top Model.

Model: Same thing. You have to pay the rent somehow.

Todd: But isn't there work?

Model: When did you get here?

Todd: Yesterday.

Model: My advice is to go to Switzerland to do catalog.

Todd: Where you sleeping tonight?

Model: I dunno. Clothilde.

Todd: (getting the picture) I'm afraid of running out of money. I don't have that much.

Todd doesn't follow every grunt and gesture, but pretty soon the officers and the oddly resigned model are all gone.

Todd: (flatly) *Telefono*.

Padrone: (suspicious) *Come?*

Todd: America.

Todd writes out the phone number on the pad, the *padrone* contacts the operator, and Todd waits. The *padrone* emerges in his red silk robe to answer the return ring twenty minutes later.

Todd: Mom?

Elaine: Todd? What's the matter?

Todd: Nothing. I just wanted to let you know I was here. What time is it there?

Elaine: Nine o'clock.

Todd's mom always talks in a slowed-down way, as if she's on Valium, though she isn't. Todd has no brothers or sisters.

Elaine: Your father is at work. We went to the bank today to clip coupons on our bonds. You know how you hear about old people clipping their bonds? (she laughs)

Todd: Why did it take so long?

Elaine: Well he likes to clip bonds for a whole year ahead and then keep them at the office until it's time to turn them in. So it was three o'clock when we got out of the vault. Then we stopped at Arby's to get a roast beef sandwich. Maybe when he gets home we'll go out to get something else, small.

Todd: Your birthday and Father's Day fall on the same day this year.

Elaine: Yes. We had free tickets we won at a raffle for discounts at a list of restaurants. We picked out one we hadn't been to yet, in an old train parked in the square, and went there to eat. But we didn't eat much. Because the next day your father had to take out a man he was interviewing for a vice president's job and his family. They had been looking at high schools. They're from Wyoming. And their son is on the debating team in high school. So they had to look for a school with a debating team. The only one is a private Catholic school.

Todd: Are they Catholic?

Elaine: I guess. But Dad was out there all weekend clipping the bushes. I think that he should pay someone to do that.

The talk ends soon.

Todd: I can't hear you, you're echoing, you're being bounced off a satellite.

Elaine: I just thought we had a bad connection.

Todd feels like the astronaut in 2001 talking to his mom and pop back on distant earth.

Todd: I love you.

Elaine: Be a good boy. (titters) I shouldn't call you a boy. (titters) Be careful.

They get off. She didn't ask him about Milan. Maybe she doesn't want to admit he's there. Todd goes to bed and wraps himself up in his white sheet like a mummy. Luckily the next day is the holiday. Whatever holiday it is.

LUCY AND FRANK

That night Lucy shows up at Frank's door for their get-together. She is dressed in a less homemade way than usual. White dress with gray pinstripes. Blue canvas shoes. Black hair sweeping all around her like a disturbance of black bees. She is shifting from foot to foot as if the door were staring her down uncomfortably.

When Frank opens it the tension drifts off. He's wearing soft gray pants, a light-gray T-shirt stitched with the badge of a college, black moccasins.

Frank: (all there, radiating something) Come in for a while first. (as soon as Lucy gets through the front door) Sharon's away at her family's house for the week.

Lucy: (as if defending her) I like Sharon. I think she's fresh.

Frank sits down on the couch and settles his chin in his palms that are the radar saucers on the antennae of his arms. Lucy rocks back and forth rapidly in the splintering rocking chair.

Lucy: (formal chat) I talked to Todd. He sounded down.

Frank stretches out full length on the couch, lights up a blip on the TV monitor then darkens it, moves around fitfully, then lands on the floor as energetically as a gymnast completing a flip, and heads over to the rosy square window.

Frank: (studying the outside) My bike needs a good cleaning.

Lucy: (insisting) Have you heard from Todd?

Frank: No. But I'm in Milan next week. I'm sure he'll be riding my coattails there, like here.

Lucy: (put off course) You shocker. I thought we were going to get together to say nice things about Todd.

Frank: It's not my nature. My nature is to, uh, steal you away from him. (walking over and looming above her, monstrously) To fill my belly. To make the shit hit the fan.

Lucy: You have Sharon.

Frank: Better yet.

Lucy: (rocking faster and faster, laughing hectically) I'm so glad to be with someone I can talk crazy to.

Frank feels easier now. As a joke he moves backward without looking until he fits into the frame of the window. Lucy laughs at his joke.

Frank: You want me to take something to him in Milan for you? A piece of your underwear?

Lucy: You have a real thing about underwear? (going over to join Frank in the window) You're too much. You're a devil's egg.

Frank: It's deviled egg.

Lucy: Why? What does that mean?

Frank holds his palm on the back of Lucy's neck and draws her in to look through the window up toward a violet-blue evening sky. There's even a sliver of butterscotch moon. And breezes are causing the tan burlap curtains to swing and sway.

Frank: (tenderly) Let's walk as far as the river.

Frank puts on his black nylon jacket, and he and Lucy walk out of the yellow-brick Chelsea apartment building, down Eighth Avenue, over toward the Hudson River by way of tiny West Village streets that connect like the forked lines of a busy palm.

They stop at a small fruit market run by Koreans on a corner. The fruits look almost waxed—so shiny, so colorful.

Lucy: I want to buy you something to eat. What'll it be?

Frank: You can get me a candy bar if you want. One of those Swiss ones there, with cherries inside.

Frank points at a European torte packaged cleverly for the American market to suggest candy bar, a delicacy concept commercialized in 1923 by Minnesota candymakers Frank and Ethel Mars who made the first Milky Way bar. Their family's many billions of dollars is now one of the biggest fortunes in the United States.

Lucy picks one up. Then reaches into the refrigerator and pulls out a small container of fresh-squeezed orange juice. Holding the door open she breathes into the refrigerated shelves to make a puff of white breath.

Lucy: I feel like it's winter when I do that.

She pays, they leave, and walk west toward the river. Soon enough they arrive at iron railings at the water's edge. Stroll a promenade that is lit by disturbingly bright crime-protection lanterns overhead.

They've hit at an unusual time. A procession is winding down to the river's edge. The procession is made up of men and women who have just left a ceremony unveiling a statue to American soldiers killed in Vietnam. The statue is in a nearby Village square. They carry candles, garlands of flowers, and cardboard names of friends who died in the war Magic Markered. The candlelit crowd gets to the railing and they one by one throw their flowers into the choppy waters. The wavering tapered light shows faces flushed with feeling. Not many people are crying out loud, or sobbing. But they almost all seem filled with tears, their souls melting along with the wax of the stubby candles. Some toss their candles in high catapults that smash down in a fizzle in the dark waters—waters where so many bodies wearing cement pajamas have been dredged up by the police.

Frank: It takes you down a peg.

Lucy: Have you ever seen footage of Hindu funerals on the shores of the Ganges where they burn the body and throw the ashes in the river? It reminded me of that.

Frank: (making a no head) Uh-uh.

The two go back to Frank's apartment by way of an ice-cream store on Seventh Avenue. Frank gets chocolate, Lucy strawberry Tofutti. They carry the cold little hills home to eat, where they sit facing each other, boxed by the same windowsill, their legs alternating in each other's.

Frank: To answer your question, I'm an underwear freak because it's like touching someone's clit.

Lucy: (accusingly) I thought your mood had changed so much. That you were so moved.

Frank: It did. I was. I didn't answer your question before and now I am.

Lucy: Oh. (thoughtful and quiet for as long as it takes the traffic light at the corner to change from red to green, and the cars to start moving again) Well. My Joan of Arc voice is telling me to leave now. Before any other questions are answered. Or anything else happens.

Frank: (stroking her throat) That's fine by me.

They are soon standing at the door.

Frank: Say good-night to me.

Lucy does. She stretches up on her toes and kisses him on his cheek, actually his cheekbone, near the same spot of physiognomy where she had kissed Todd that night under the lamp-post on Seventh Avenue, the night of the day he had met Frank.

ROMEOS

Todd is standing with about twenty-five other guys in the dank basement of *Vogue* studios. At ten in the morning. Racks of clothes are angled all over. Screens partition the room into different sections. Spotlights shine here and there. Looks like registration at a college: polo shirts, neat haircuts, khaki pants, white teeth.

Less spiffy than most of the models, but more striking, is Michelangelo (real name: Mike). He was a Times Square fashion billboard—his wavy black hair was as tall and textured as a cypress tree, his cheeks as caved in as a canyon. The only picture in his portfolio is a shot of this billboard. Yet he's been working every day.

Michelangelo sits, one leg up, on top of a deserted oak desk, talking to no one, muscles bulging from a tight black T-shirt, dressed in green Army fatigues, cap with brim, and reflector sunglasses. Todd feels the fashion soldier staring at him through the glasses, either disdainfully, or just zonked, but steadily and with no apparent expression. Since Michelangelo's the most famous model in the room, the other models talk about him.

One Texan Model: (to Todd) I hear he's got a heroin habit. If he steals one more camera on a shoot, Jean's gonna boot him out of town.

Todd: (honored by Michelangelo's inattentive attention) I don't believe it.

One Long Island Model: (later to be terminated at Zebra when his nude photos appear in *Blueboy*) He has a wife and two kids in America, but some agent found him in a hustler bar.

The go-see is for a two-hour reshooting that afternoon of a single page of editorial, minimum pay. Two women parade in, murmuring to each other in low Italian, asking for cards from the models. They're local types. Since they live in fashionable Milan they wear round black metal earrings. If they lived in Calabria they'd be wearing black kerchiefs. Todd hands over a black-white Xerox of Louis's shower picture. His card isn't ready yet.

The women bow to Michelangelo, who is obviously the winner of the quick-bucks job. He doesn't offer a card, they don't demand one. Instead they ask him—a black prince—to stay behind. The rest—the courtiers—are dismissed.

Todd walks up the steps with two instant pals, just listening.

Model #1: Can you believe it? A cattle call for one *facocta* page in a magazine?

Model #2: At least I've got my real estate business to go back to.

Todd walks to the nearest underground, then escalators down into a sleek red and gray metro station where he deposits coin tokens into a curved yellow plastic telephone machine that resembles an espresso maker.

Todd: (to Jean) How do you think work is in the Soviet Union?

Jean: (rapidly) All you American boys think about is Russia. Seriously. There is a client here who wants to see you this afternoon. You must come by the agency at three.

Todd strolls in the strong sunlight down Via Torino toward his *pensione.* He has a few hours. Stops at the takeout food store across the street. Buys a *Herald-Tribune,* a plastic container of strawberries, a carton of milk. Dodges much tram and automobile traffic crossing.

In the cool of his shadowy room, Todd shimmies into a loose black swimsuit. Then spreads down a towel on the terrace and lies there in the oven-warm sun, reading the tissuey newspaper, eating tangy strawberries. Stretches out flat on his back to let the sun solve his problems for him. Licks his own hot lips. Rubs his own tummy. Feels as if the atmosphere is giving him an invisible massage.

Thoroughly warmed, Todd fetches his scrapbook, then lays the blank book out on a terrace table, puts on GI green-tint sunglasses, reminiscent of Michelangelo's, and works. The first page he leaves empty. Flips over. On first left page he pastes on a snippet of a map of Milan from his *La Mia Guida,* cut with jagged edges. On the facing page he draws a silver-pencil rendition of Edvard Munch's *The Scream.* Below that pastes in part of a title from the *Herald-Tribune* he'd been reading, just the phrase LANGUAGE BARRIER. His alarm buzzes two-thirty. He dresses, takes metro.

The agency is a replay of this morning's *Vogue* studios. A mob scene. In Beatrice's chair sits a gray-haired middle-aged client looking like a pope in a Francis Bacon painting. When Todd arrives Luigi grabs him, as if he's doing him a special favor, and leads him to a little room in the back.

Michelangelo jogs into the dressing room in a tan suit. Takes the suit off, arrogantly ignoring everyone, changes into his fatigues, leaving the suit in a muddle on the floor. Luigi gathers up the suit and hands it to Todd who's stripped down to the blue nylon skivvies he bought at a local department store. Pants way too big, Luigi folds the waist top over so they fit, and buttons the coat so the clowny waist won't show.

Luigi: (bragging as he leads Todd down the hall) My last job was a salesman in a men's clothes store on Monte Napoleone.

The client is not pleased with Todd's book or his forced pirouette in the tumbling suit. Todd walks, pent, back to the little room where the next, a blond, is waiting in underwear and socks for his turn.

When he finally steps out into the courtyard, though, after rushing to get out of there, Todd is suddenly thrown, blinded almost. Blinded not by the change from electrical to natural light, but by the return of an obliterating feeling of loneliness. A strain of nerves that had been temporarily eased during the earlier part of the day. He cannot bear to go back right now to his room at the Medici. So he decides instead to visit the refectory of the church next door to look at *The Last Supper*.

The mural itself, pastels, is hidden mostly by scaffolding. Along the walls are phones in every language. If you stick in a few *gettones* you can hear the history of a mural that can't be seen anyway because of the metal crisscrossing. It's being restored. Todd puts his *gettones* in the English phone. Not because he wants art-history facts. But because he wants to hear his own language undisturbed. Unfortunately he didn't anticipate the Oxford English accent of the speaker, and winds up feeling even more displaced.

So Todd walks back outside behind the church. There he finds a triangular park enclosed by a metal toothpick fence. He sits on a dark bench in the dark shade. The only other person in the park is a priest who is sitting half-asleep under his black sombrero. Pigeons and other birds are stalking about the pavement like restless travelers waiting for a train in a station. Todd concentrates on his tender painful spot. He could be anywhere in the world. Loneliness is a great leveler, an eraser of times and places.

Todd can almost taste his loneliness. It tastes to him like carob.

By now the afternoon is turning bronze. Todd rides back to Via Torino in an orange tram, a trolley connected by oblique tappers to overhead electrical power lines, its dark wood benches filled mostly with women. It's time for the *passeggiata*, between five and six-thirty, when the Milanese, especially men and teenage boys, walk the streets. Todd blankly watches these peacockish males through the windows as they eye one another, exchange gossip, show off new clothes.

At his *pensione*, he takes the small elevator up to the first floor lobby. His key is hanging like a man in a gallows from a hook on a board full of keys. Wrapped around it is a message. Todd unwraps the paper and bursts. It's from Frank.

Message: (in pencil scrawl) *My apartment's nearby. Sit in your room and wait for my call.*

Todd does wait as the pale white sun is replaced in one of the coin slots of the sky by a yellow moon, and as the atmosphere's red-green atomic tint (Milan is so industrial) turns purple-blue. He finally falls asleep grumpily, in a rumple like a beast.

Frank doesn't call the entire night.

MOTORCYCLE MOVIE

Just as Todd is beginning his long wait, Lucy is waking up to a hot, humid day. (Six-hour time difference.)

With both Frank and Todd now far away, Lucy feels like a lie detector without a liar. Useless, untapped. She takes a butt out of Todd's Florida-map ashtray she's keeping as a souvenir, schizzily smokes it down. Tries to flick on portable Sony color TV with her remote control. The ruby-red light lights up but no picture. So she walks over and pushes the power button manually. It's a story about terrorists hijacking a plane in the Mideast and forcing a landing in Syria. The Arab leaders look Old Testament in their striped towel hats. This confuses Lucy. She notices the detail in a hash way.

Lucy stuffs all her dirty laundry into her pillowcase laundry bag. The dirty whites, mostly underwear, go in a smaller pillowcase. She grabs a big orange-and-blue box of laundry crystals and drags on down the street. Over to Second Avenue. But when she gets there there's a sign on the door that she reads through the closed grate: CLOSED ALL DAY MEMORIAL DAY.

Lucy: Shit.

Lucy wants to go to a movie. The holiday special at the grungy theater on Second Avenue and St. Mark's Place is a motorcycle movie from the past. This youth epic is filmed in deep acid colors. When its motorcycle gang stalls by a lake to go skinny-dipping, the lake is a tincture of blues and oranges,

104

and the warriors rise out of the chilly ink pot themselves bluer and oranger than before. Much racier shades of blue and orange than those on the laundry box that Lucy is clutching as she sits in the chilled theater.

The Motorcycle Hero is a gawk with greasy black hair, dressed in a jasmine-green Korean War jacket with red decals, the only well-shaved cyclist. Lucy loves the scene where the young Motorcycle Hero's girl is moaning on the fire escape about how he tossed her off because she was on drugs. He didn't show her any mercy. But then later in the amusement park when she's high the Motorcycle Hero appears again and he dances her around, he twirls her slow, and then lets her kneel down on the ground in front of him and put her wet mouth on the cloth of his pants over his crotch. That scene makes Lucy's mouth water. She starts craning around a bit to see if there are any guys nearby that are Motorcycle Hero material. Right at the end of her row there is one, maybe. They glance at each other a few times as the bikers rough up a tender tumescent town school-teacher. Lucy wishes she didn't have that stupid laundry bag in her lap. She feels like a pregnant woman.

When the lights go on he is waiting for her by the doorway under the exit sign. He just starts right off talking, and she answers straight. He walks Lucy down Eighth Street, the busiest strip in the whole town; no one goes away for holiday weekends from this neighborhood, it seems.

Lucy: I just watched MTV for hours and hours last night. Then I put my sleep control on the TV. Where it turns off in one hour automatically. So it must have been around four.

Gabe: Did you see my jeans ad?

Lucy: (going through the roof) I did! I didn't say anything until I was sure.

Gabe: Can you believe that close-up at the end? And that girl all hot and bothered rubbing her pussy on the side?

Gabe looks Italian but he's not. He's a mix of many nations including Blackfoot. His father is an American Indian. He has an open shirt, black cloth pants with gold threads streaking through, and black wing-tip boots, antiques that he recently had fixed at a cobbler's on Sixth Street. His hair is black, his eyes are green, he's twenty-five.

Lucy: I have a friend, a guy, who's a model.

Gabe: Yeah? Who's he with? Oh never mind I don't care. I don't give a fuck. I went up to Elite with my contract for the print line of this ad and they started giving me this runaround about needing a few more pictures in my portfolio. But here I am with this national commercial and their faggot models aren't working. So they can kiss my ass. (his voice getting growlier) They can kiss my ass.

Lucy feels a mixture of repulsion, compulsion, fear, greed and desire. She invites him up, though just to be safe stipulating that he has to split in a half an hour.

So Gabe stops up, makes himself at home by taking off his wing-tip boots. The long boot part is made from the skin of some crocodile. Lucy offers him hash in a pipe that she is stoking. When they suck in, the ashes glow amber.

Lucy feels uneasy. Can't figure out why. Then sees Todd's Florida ashtray resting on a dictionary on a nearby table. She turns the ashtray over, ashes too, the way some Russian Orthodox people turn icons to the wall when they're having sex. Then she feels better.

Gabe: What kind of mood you in today? You relaxed? You have time to be with me?

Lucy: (cautious) I'm in an okay mood today.

Gabe: Can you go to the movies with me later?

Lucy: No.

Gabe: Then can I make a call?

Lucy: Go ahead.

Gabe pushes the buttons on the phone. Nothing. Brings his attentions back to bear on Lucy who is lying on the bed watching sports, tennis.

Gabe: You're so beautiful. Beautiful face. Beautiful body. You've got it all babe. I just wanna smooch with you.

Lucy is unusually quiet and passive during all this. She rolls over on Gabe and they start kissing each other out, feeling bodies.

Gabe: Is my breath bad?

Lucy licks around the unshaved stubble on Gabe's neck. That drives him nuts. They pause and he shows her pictures from his wallet, one of him in the Army looking pretty in his cap, like Elvis stationed in West Germany. Then he straddles her and squeezes her into the mattress.

Lucy puts her hand on Gabe's crotch. She slides down and opens the fly, unsnaps the snap. She is a bit spooked to discover that he has a curved cock, almost in an L. She licks on there for a while, so that moisture is already beginning to collect at the top of its Islam dome.

Gabe: I just want to eat you. I want to eat your whole body. I want to eat your pussy. And I want to eat your whole ass.

Gabe strips, except for his T-shirt that has a drawing of a banana (colored yellow) on it. Then he lets Lucy wriggle out of all of her clothes. He bends down and licks with his muscular tongue at her jelly and through her soft hairs.

Lucy: I have fantasies of being a woman with a harem full of men. You'd be great as a concubine. Your tongue feels so good. Good boy. Lick my. Lick my.

Then Gabe lurches on top of Lucy. She feels a little closed in, and his breath does have a medicinal taste. But his curved cock feels straight now that it is inside her. He makes her come and she feels during it that her heart is a whirlpool Jacuzzi. She feels more in her chest and heart than in her groin. Maybe she has anesthetized her erogenous zone. Gabe finally rolls back off.

Gabe: (after a few minutes) Do you feel good?

Lucy: Wonderful. I love your tongue. Did you come?

Gabe: A little. But I was holding back.

Gabe bends around and makes a phone call to a girl. He arranges to go with her a little later to the movies.

Gabe: (hanging up) Since you won't go to the movies with me, I have to get with someone.

Lucy: Do you have a girlfriend?

Gabe: Yeah. There's a girl I hang around with. Do you have a boyfriend?

Lucy: Yes. Sort of. He's the model I told you about.

Gabe: When can I call so I don't get in trouble?

Lucy: (protecting herself) During the day.

Gabe lies down on the bed again.

Gabe: I should start working out. I'm so thin.

Lucy: (smoking heavily now on a cigarette) You have a beautiful body. You said I have a beautiful body. But you have a beautiful body.

Gabe: (curling over on his side) Don't you think I look like a woman, this part? (pointing to his upper thigh) The name on the casting for this jeans thing was "Curves." I thought they were going to feature my ass. But they didn't. They didn't show much of the jeans though. Just to here. (makes line under waist)

Lucy: They're too smart. They know nobody cares about those old jeans. They just care about you.

Gabe: Looking street.

Lucy: (surprised) Yes!

Lucy walks Gabe to the door.

Gabe: Let's smooch one more time.

Lucy is a bit vague in her kissing right now. She misses one. But then decides to end this serendipitous meeting right. So they kiss full on target for a full twenty seconds.

Alone once again in the apartment Lucy feels a dip. Not a guilty dip. Just a lonely one. A mood she had been dodging by first going down the street to that movie. She picks up the heavy yellow telephone directory. Makes a call.

Lucy: Yes I'd like to know the price of a one-way ticket to Milan. In three weeks. Thank you.

Lucy makes her reservation.

AMERICAN GIGOLO

Beep. Beep. Beep. Soft digital-clock wake-up. Frank in bed goes into sit position. Moves lever in wall that raises the ceiling lights and plant lights to a soft white power.

His room is modern Italian Olivetti style. Low bed. Gray rugs. Push-button slat blinds that he now opens electrically from his bed, lowering the inside lights to get the light mix just right. Bookcases and mirrors made out of curving black and yellow plastics. Rubber plants under Grow-Lites. Frank plays around with his yellow Brionvega fold-out radio, looking for a good song. Then gives up.

Flips quickly out of bed. Takes a pair of soft yellow gym shorts off chair. Exercises with a set of barbells, then performs a military regimen of sit-ups and push-ups. In the adjoining wooden shower room he turns the sauna dial to release dry steam. Washes hair with herbal shampoo; soaps with a fancy soap on a rope; brushes teeth with Pasta del Capitano.

Then clears a porthole circle in the steam-covered mirror with a pink cotton towel so he can gaze carefully at his own face. Separates his blond hairs looking for brunette shadings. Flares nostrils to examine better the perforations of pores. Notices the way his light-blue eyes look at, yet also passively reflect mysterious cloudless distances. Fathoms how those bones, as solid as quartz, can affect others.

A knocking at the door. Frank wraps up in a plush red cotton robe before answering.

On the other side is Carlo, an Italian middle-aged man, short, balding, a sagging baby's face, with a big sincere smile, dying to be loved. Carlo is dressed in a blue linen suit, white handkerchief in pocket, striped tie, pale blue shirt, Italian soft yellow tie shoes with little heels. He slaps Frank on the back of the neck.

Carlo: It's ten o'clock. You said to wake you up at ten o'clock. Your agent is on the phone.

Frank: I pulled the plug.

Carlo: I wish I could get off the plane and five hours later look like you.

Frank: Fifteen. Thanks.

Frank goes back in room; shuts door; sits tensed in robe on edge of bed; plugs in gray phone. Then he lights into Jean. Frank's philosophy for stirring up business in a fresh market is to be a hard-ass, make trouble. Like certain celebrities who pick fights in restaurants to insure a mention in print gossip.

Jean: Just wanted to remind you Frank that you're working tomorrow morning at ten for Linea Italia. They're giving you a second chance. So be prompt.

Frank: (prepping the trigger) What second chance?

Jean: You remember when you walked off because they wanted you to stand behind Udo and splash him?

Frank: (blowing him away) I'm giving them a second chance. And you're working for me, I'm not working for you. Is there anything else we have to get right?

Jean, though, is always taken by Frank's reverse charm. He even agrees to set up an appointment for Frank to escort Todd over to meet Ferrati. Frank was last year's Ferrati man.

Jean: I'll try for three tomorrow afternoon. If there's any change I'll call you. And Todd I talk to every morning like all the small fish.

Frank: You shark's ass.

Frank clicks off. He lolls in the unmade silken sheets of the bed for a while, expressing a body language as luxuriant as Marc Antony in Cleopatra's barge. Then he calls Todd who grabs the wall receiver in his room.

Padrone: *Telefono per Signor Todd.*

Todd has been in and out this morning, but still has mostly waited for this call—his agitated stomach as riffled as the pages of a magazine in a barber shop. He is dressed kind of punk, black chinos, black velour zip-neck shirt, black Mao Tse-tung slippers. Bombs into the hall, picks up dirty pink phone resting on gray lace doily on wooden side table.

Todd: (crackling) Frank?

Frank: (smooth) How'd you guess? Are you Jeane Dixon?

Todd: (a complaint) You kept me hangin on.

Frank: (right back) It ain't me babe.

Todd: (inexplicably mollified by this establishing of same wavelength) Okay. . . . You know I was thinking a lot about you yesterday. Remember that time I talked to you on the phone in the middle of the night?

Frank: And then I called you back?

Todd: Yeah. . . . I was trying to think, was that before I went to see Soupy or after?

Frank: To tell you the truth I think that's one for the sports fans. . . . Listen. I'm at Twelve Via Nerino. Staying with my friends Carlo and Tania. His wife. Ask for directions at the desk and get over here. Okay?

Todd: Delivered.

Frank clicks down. Comes out of the bedroom dressed in yellow cashmere V-neck pullover, white chinos, sneaks. Strides onto the balcony where Carlo and Tania are having morning coffee. Tania is around thirty, Afrikaaner, with red hair, thin bony face and body. She is dressed in a white silk blouse with blue flowers, pink silky pants, white casual high heels.

Their balcony, a wide strip of strengthening sun along its edge, gives a great view of Milan from above. Is next to the Church San Giorgio: pigeons flying around its dome. View mostly consists of red tile roofs of the tops of houses. Part of the gray Duomo in the near distance. Pigeons on railing. Lots of TV antennas recede into a mess on a farther-away scrim.

Tania first found Frank backstage at a fashion show. She's an art director for a big designer. Carlo owns a French-furniture shop on Via Manzoni. She invited Frank over for dinner once and Carlo was crazy about him too. So now whenever he comes to Milan he stays with them. Both Carlo and Tania cater to him, feel relieved to bend to his moods. With each other, without Frank, they are more nervous and anxious.

Frank: You two look beat.

Tania: (patting a chair) Come here and sit down. I haven't even seen you.

Frank sits down on one of the metal chairs. Slips off sneaks and puts his feet in Tania's lap. She holds them there.

Tania: (to Carlo) See how at home he is with me. He treats me like a dog. (she laughs)

Carlo: I'm so jealous he doesn't put his feet in my lap.

Tania: (to Frank) Can you believe what he said?

Frank: Carlo you know that Tania saw me first.

Carlo: But I have all the money.

They go on playing at fighting over Frank. Then the front door buzzes. Frank answers. Todd is standing there fumbling in his black clothes. Frank pulls him in as if rescuing him from an orbit of weightlessness. They look their signs today: Todd, mid-winter Aquarius; Frank, high-August Leo.

Frank: You look older already.

Todd: (through his teeth) You didn't tell me this would be a pain in the butt. (then) But the carhops at the Fountain of Youth always get older faster I guess.

Frank: Do me a favor. Talk down to me.

Frank takes Todd out on the balcony to introduce him to Carlo and Tania. The four chat with no special expertise about sunspots. Then Tania puts a Frank Sinatra tape on the player. She and Frank do a slow dance. Carlo makes everyone Pimm's Cup on ice.

Tania wraps her arms around Carlo's waist and starts dancing with him to the tune of "Try to Remember." She coaxes him to stumble with her past the flouncy sofa in the sitting room and on into their bedroom. Sweaty foreheads.

Frank: (clicking off tape) Tania likes to get laid this time of day.

Todd: (not missing a beat) So I called Lucy. She sounded down.

Frank: Here we go again.

Todd: What's that supposed to mean?

Frank: Come to my big glamorous high-tech bedroom and I'll give you the present she sent. Get that over with.

Todd follows Frank into his bedroom. Frank immediately flops down on the bed, leaving Todd standing at the bottom corner, facing expectantly over him, like a statue in a port facing out to sea.

Todd: So where is it?

Frank: (baiting) Where is what?

Frank eventually reaches in a drawer by his bed. Pulls pulls pulls on a very long golden chain, with fine tiny links, dangling a golden heart locket. Reaches back in for a silver-and-blue envelope that goes with it. Tosses the locket to Todd, then sails the envelope to him across the room as if it were a silver-and-blue Frisbee.

Todd opens the locket. Inside there's a Kodacolor cutout of Lucy, in a white blouse, wearing black lipstick, her hair sprayed wet, with a bluish-purple flower stuck in.

Todd: Who took the old-fashioned picture?

Frank: Her friend Josef. He's an art photographer.

Todd: (suspicious) What kind of art photographer?

Frank: Not that kind. The other kind.

Todd opens the envelope. It's some lines from Lucy's favorite poem, "The Waste Land" by T. S. Eliot, written out by her hand in magenta ink.

—Yet when we came back, late, from the hyacinth garden,
Your arms full, and your hair wet, I could not
Speak, and my eyes failed, I was neither
Living nor dead, and I knew nothing,
Looking into the heart of light, the silence.
Oed' und leer das Meer.

Todd: (gooey) She's so clever. I bet those flowers in her hair are hyacinths. That's just something she'd do. Go to all that trouble. Some people are on Johnny Carson for writing poems or making paintings. And then she just does it all so naturally and spontaneously. Changes the dark into the light. I love her.

Frank: (ready to bolt) Okaaaaay. . . . Why don't you lie down for a while? You look tired. Maybe all the excitement of seeing me etcetera has been too much for you. And please don't wear the locket around your neck. For me.

Todd: (deep-voiced) I'm so tired. I didn't sleep last night. I need a rest.

Frank cups his two hands behind his head, arms making two triangles. He nods with his head to the bottom of the bed. Todd lies down with his head down there. The two are pointing in opposite directions, head to feet, feet to head. The white stripes of outside visible through the blinds' slats. Frank stands up and closes the door, resumes his position. Both nap.

Later on they hear a knuckle knock at the door. Carlo opens up. It is already shady afternoon now in the rooms beyond.

Frank: (groggy) Kaory? (his version of "Che ora è?")

Carlo: (quiet, looking down at Todd asleep in the bed) One. Tania is making pasta for all of us. Your friend too.

Carlo has a benign look on his face. He is unusually calm and kind, not tugging for attention.

Carlo: This is my favorite time sometimes. Just at the beginning of the siesta. With lunch cooking in the kitchen. Tania likes this time too. She is less the tiger.

Frank: (apologizing) My friend was so lonely. He just needed to lie down with me.

Carlo: I admire your display. It reminds me of feelings I haven't had since in the Army.

Tania walks into the doorway now with a big wooden mixing spoon in her fist and hits Carlo with it so that he will help her set the table.

Frank kicks at Todd's arm with his foot. Finally he comes around.

Todd: (soft) I was just dreaming. And I was wondering. Frank. Did you go to bed with Lucy when I was away?

Frank: (loud) Why does everyone always want to know that one thing? Like nothing else in the world matters?

Todd: (warning) Frank. . . .

Frank: No, sucker, I did not.

FRANK AND TODD'S SECRET

After lunch.

The light in the room now is rose. Todd is standing nude by the window. He is a statue.

Frank is kicking around in the clothes closet, throwing out pants, shirts, sweaters, in a chute of passing energy, onto the bed.

Frank: If you go to Ferrati looking like a down-in-the-face punk he won't let you near him. Dress like me. Healthy. All-American. Calvin Klein. That's what they want.

Todd: (protesting) But all those designers are fags.

Frank: That's what they want. They want straight boys to fill in the mold for them.

Todd: (thinking he's making some kind of joke) Then I'll put on Lucy's heart necklace.

Frank: (thinking he gets it) Then you'll be as sweet as a cup of cappuccino. You'll be a sweet pea.

Todd: I'll be a fag.

They both laugh as loud as a laugh track. But Todd then does walk over to the bed and puts the necklace gracefully over his head and lets the chilly metal heart bounce against his medium-hairy chest. He puts one leg on the bed, so that his phallus dangles down like a long purple fruit. Frank walks over and lays his hands on him. One on his ass. One on his stomach. And he looks into him with those strangely resonant flat light-blue saucers of eyes and Todd looks back at him with his weird cat-colored ones. What next?

Todd: You make me laugh.

Frank: I want you to make me laugh. (undressing out of his chinos and yellow sweater, standing only in orange nylon socks) I want you to make me laugh.

Todd: I'm not gonna do anything degrading to myself if that's what you mean.

Frank: How much do you want this job with Ferrati? The job I had last year? With your ugly mug in *GQ* and all those magazines all over America so your mom and dad will see you and be proud of you and know you're hot shit. Not just have to take your word for it?

Todd: (almost a whisper) Your parents are alive?

Frank: Yeah. My father owns gyms. And when my brother used to bring his friends home my father used to grope them and make passes at them and he used to like to smell their armpits.

Todd: Did he do that with your friends?

Frank: He didn't do that with my friends.

Todd: Is he still doing it?

Frank: He left my mom. And he's living with his eighteen-year-old platinum boyfriend and I don't talk to him. My mom is a holy saint and he's a garbage dump.

Todd: My mom is . . .

Frank: Shut up. . . . Think back for a minute. . . . Do you want the job or don't you?

Todd: (his phallus now pointing out at Frank like a thumb, or a stump) Sure I want the job. Can you guarantee it?

Frank: I can ninety-eight-percent guarantee it. I've got some hold on Ferrati. (gripping Todd's cock) I could squeeze harder.

Todd: I want to have my picture there where all my friends can see it. That would be a blast. Right?

Frank: Right.

Todd: I don't just want . . . I want not just . . .

Frank now is sticking his index finger up Todd's rear, pushing the red button of his prostate gland.

Todd: I just don't want to get fucked to do it. Can I fuck you?

Frank takes his other index finger and sticks it down Todd's gagging throat and bends him over the bed mattress. They are two tan bags of swirling trouble, their bodies more electrical or molecular than fleshy or bony or bloody. They are modern, and they are having a no-mind time.

Frank pushes Todd up on the bed using his finger-in-rectum as a prod. When he gets him splayed there he sticks his tongue in instead. Makes the inside of Todd's hole wet. Manufactures a frothy sweat.

Todd is lying there feeling bad and good at once, like a bad sandwich on good bread.

Todd: (head muffled in pillow) This is just a porn movie.

Frank: (sarcastically) Just?

Frank lowers his tan plumb bob at the end of plumb line down into Todd's unknown waters.

With the pain and the scraping, though, it's more like trying to hammer, rather than screw, a screw into a wall of scratchy Sheetrock. The linings are stripped. But then a steady settling position is finally reached. The cave of Todd's insides is illuminated in its rough-hewnness by the gas lantern of Frank's heated metal flesh. Todd feels lit up from the inside. Then the lights go out. Like the three-minute lights in Milan's apartment buildings. Frank pulls out his cock. And sprays the white paint over the tan wood of Todd's stiff back. Todd, humping into the mattress, lets out a splat of an ooze, like a water balloon bursting on the ground.

Todd: (in a moan while coming apart) I . . . wanna . . . go . . . home.

Frank (already rolled off) You wanna go home my ass.

When Todd has settled down he turns over on his back to unstick from the damp stain on the coverlet. Frank is already up at the closet again sorting through pants. Even though the room is almost dark with all the blinds zipped closed Frank's blond hair is a hazy landmark, a density of amber gases hovering over dark woods right after sunfall.

Todd shimmies his hands over his head, and opens his mouth wide in a noiseless hallelujah, like a spiritualist feeling the spirit. Then he rolls to the side and hugs one of Frank's pillows to his chest and stomach.

Todd: (pleased with himself) The world is one big Rorschach test isn't it?

Frank: Settle down over there. We have to get going.

Todd: One question.

Frank: No, I'm not gonna let you blow me. If that's what you're asking.

Todd: No. . . . What I meant was you're not gonna tell Lucy.

Frank: Beauty, sometimes you talk too much.

DO YOU EVER THINK ABOUT GUYS?

They are walking down Monte Napoleone in the spotlight of the sun. Todd has changed into some of Frank's white sporty clothes. Leaving behind him the shadow of black clothes out of which he emerged earlier. He was dressed like an etching and now he's dressed like a painting. Or for a Kodacolor photograph. Frank is the same yellow-and-white traffic sign.

Todd: What do you think about when you jerk off?

Frank: Girls. Why?

Monte Napoleone extends down on an angle from Via Manzoni to Piazza San Babila. On the stretch are the glossiest stores in town. The boutiques of the fashion designers. Loud glass walls cut by the angles-of-vision of mannequins. Those zombies, those sveltes.

Todd: Which girls?

Frank: Well last night I thought about this girl on the plane who had on a New York City Ballet jacket. I think she was a dancer. I jerked off thinking about her fucking with me in a dressing room. Why? What do you think about?

Todd: I think about Lucy a lot. One out of three times.

They walk past one after another fancy window on a downward path. Bald-headed men dolls in purple zoot suits. Twisted Sister men dolls in leather trous. Thin-as-a-pencil women dolls bent back as if ready to be plowed but in thick colorful woolen dresses. Not your average Macy's mannequin, staid in a comfy space. Lots of the women dolls are contorted or put into grotesque impossible postures. They are victimized more than the men.

Todd: Do you ever think about guys?

Frank: Yeah. But usually with a woman. Like fucking a guy's wife while he's watching. Or screwing his eyes out while his girlfriend is playing with herself. But not just guys solo.

Todd: That's bisexual. Pure and simple. So you think there are bisexuals, right?

Frank: I don't think. How about you? You ever think about guys?

Todd: Just to get fucked. That's the one thing a woman can't do for a guy.

Frank: (broadly) You mean I wasn't the first?

Todd: Yes you were.

Frank: Why should I believe you?

Todd: Why should I believe anything you said about what you think in the privacy of your head? Your perverted head.

Frank: You sick fucker.

Music is piping from each boutique. The same but different. Machine music. Nonmusic for nonpeople at a nonevent. Walkers on this street tend to have silk scarves tied around their necks. If this were the French Revolution they'd be hanging by those scarves. But it's not. It's the Rodeo Drive of Milan.

Frank: (pointing a finger) I don't want anything that happened before to come up again. Got it?

Todd: Nobody talks. Everybody walks. (getting excited as

they crest toward the Duomo) But what if they did? What if we knew what all these dicks and cunts were doing with their private parts at night? We wouldn't feel so funny right now.

Frank: I have my own problems.

Frank holds the door for Todd at the top of the curving marble staircase of the Renaissance palazzo where Gianmarco Ferrati has his offices. The two pass through one gilt-crusted eighteenth-century drawing room after another, each filled with uncrowded gray futuristic space lab furniture. As they lope they are reflected dimly in a series of smoky Venetian mirrors graced at their edges by candleless baroque sconces.

The two arrive at a young Italian woman, her dark face soulful and gorgeous, like the face of an animal when it appears to be deep in thought. She is sitting at a wide black marble table answering phones. All sounds are muted. Frank leans over and kisses the receptionist on her neck. She fusses over him.

Frank: (to Todd) I tell her all the time to go to Rome and make a mint in spaghetti westerns. (to her) The land outside Rome looks just like the Badlands.

A copy of Frank's Ferrati ad, him brooding in a brown suit on a bridge over the brown Arno in Florence, is framed on a wall behind her, where a picture of a head of state would normally hang in an embassy.

A short tan robust man in a stylish white cotton trench coat wearing very scientific glasses appears. It's Gianmarco Ferrati. He hugs Frank like a bear. He's balding with silver wavy hair, distinguished, has a kind of pig's nose and an absorbed glow. Legend has it that he drinks only water.

Frank: (rubbing his own ass, to Ferrati) I've been missing our Italian-food dinners.

Ferrati turns to Todd. Looks at him with his clear light yellow eyes. Smiles a tender smile. Holds out hand for book. Todd mistakes this move for a handshake. He scrambles his hands and arms in midair for a few seconds. Ferrati resolutely takes the book. Fixes it on the table. Studies the pictures using a little magnifier that resembles a diamond.

He settles on the photo that Soupy had first picked out: the one with Todd's legs stretched out, boxer shorts, in tile bathroom, wet.

Ferrati: I like you with your hair back, like this. If we use you, we will probably wet the hair.

Ferrati taps one finger many times in succession on top of the photograph.

FAST FORWARD

Time begins to go faster. Activity is the fast forward of Time.

Lucy gets her tickets in the mail in a big long envelope that stands out from the bills and club invitations. She calls up Todd to let him know. Wakes him up at seven-thirty in the morning his time. He stands there, sweaty, in light-blue bikini-style briefs that he bought at a nearby department store.

Lucy: I'm on my way.

Todd: (dimly) Thatsa girl.

Lucy: (disappointed) I thought you'd at least yodel. I think I deserve more feedback.

Todd: (waking up) I'll feed you all right.

Lucy: Better. . . . Now I'm coming sometime in the second week of July. I get to London on Virgin the next week. And then I'm renting a car and heading down from London by way of Paris.

Todd: (suspiciously) Who put these ideas in your head?

Lucy: (after a pause) What's your problem?

Todd: (thinking better of it) No nothing. The only thing is this Ferrati campaign I told you about looks zipped up. My face is really gonna travel. But it's supposed to be in July too. At Lake Major Something.

Lucy: Maggiore. I thought you were a map nut. Have you changed?

Todd: Beyond recognition.

Lucy: Then give me Frank's number.

Todd: (suspicious again) What for?

Lucy: (shouting) Todd! I'm asking because he might be able to help out a lot if you don't happen to be in town. Give me his number or something.

Todd does.

NECRONOMICON

Lucy sublets her apartment to Steve. Steve is a filmmaker. He makes horror movies that are rip-offs of *Night of the Living Dead.* He is also into voodoo religions of the Caribbean that use marijuana as the sacrament. Steve is tall and thin with red hair and reddish bug eyes. He always wears a gray pajama-top shirt. Before Lucy has even moved out—he moved in from New Mexico a few days early—he puts up his voodoo dolls around the apartment. Some of them are harmless, colorful and cute. But one or two emit the creeps. Over the doorway to the bedroom a demon stands with a metal spear and human teeth and human hair plastered on his horrific skull. Steve must keep certain stinky candles burning night and day. If they burn out, he's in trouble. His skin is pasty, too, from too much weed. He went to NYU Film School on East Seventh Street. That's when he met his dealer, Lucy. One of the books from his crowded library is *The Necronomicon,* an encyclopedia of evil spells.

MINOR ABOMINATIONS

Frank is not all that seamless and happy. He is trapped in what the poet Hart Crane called "a tower that is not stone."

Like now. It's night. And Frank is in Carlo and Tania's bedroom. The light is purple. A few tall black candles are burning in silver holders on different tables and stools and shelves. Smoky mirrors in gold frames reflect the tautness of muscles that is Frank riveting up and down like a pneumatic drill on top of Tania who is a slick of peach flesh beneath him. Her arm holding a leftover-seeming cat-o'-nine-tails, a prop long forgotten, that stretches out beyond the bed. It's pointed in the direction of Carlo who's wrapped in a diaper, his flesh abounding in rolls, kneeling in a corner at the base of a pedestal bearing an ebony bust of a sharp-looking man's head with a goatee and pointed ears. Maybe Mephistopheles.

Carlo: (while jerking his dick) Make her moan, Frank. Make her tell the truth.

Frank: (riding high now, riding for the fall) Shut up you piece of garbage.

At those words Carlo pops his cork, releasing the champagne of his own cum. It is a sauce running over his world. With him satisfied, Tania and Frank erupt, gradually lose momentum, slow down, easily disengage.

Soon Tania is lying in her bed drinking straight from a bottle of imported tequila in which a glowing green worm is preserved as if in formaldehyde. Carlo is snoring, rolled over on himself in that same corner.

Frank is standing in the buff at open pinewood shutters that reveal an unexceptional cinder-block city, like formations of dirty snuff powder, in the purple-lined pillbox of the spotted night. He looks as unsympathetically sad as Alexander with no more lands to conquer.

Tania: (croakily) You were great honey. I wouldn't care if you were twenty years older and thirty pounds heavier.

Frank: (has to reveal something, anything, to lighten his moodiness) To tell you the truth. I don't know if I'm coming or going.

I relish the idea that in the night, all around me in my sleep, sorcery is burrowing its invisible tunnels in every direction, from thousands of senders to thousands of unsuspecting recipients. Spells are being cast, poison is running its course; souls are being dispossessed of parasitic pseudo-conscious-nesses that lurk in the unguarded recesses of the mind.

—Paul Bowles, *Without Stopping*

THE MOST POISED PICTURE IS NEVER TAKEN

It's a gold afternoon on the Lago Maggiore. The models follow Bett down the steps into a village. She's in a red dress, no sleeves, with beige sneaks, no stockings or socks. Her hair is as red as a rusty wheelbarrow, brownish red. She moves in a slightly hunched-over way.

Bett is an American photographer known for her luscious off-beat pictures, often shot through gauze. There are lots of stories about her. Once she was shooting models in winter furs in Venice during the sultry summer. She walked them around all day looking for a good picture. By late afternoon the models were wilted. They collapsed, mad, onto some chairs of a wharf café on the Giudecca Canal. Bett exclaimed, "That's it," then shot them wrecked and sweating on those chipped chairs.

The village is pretty deserted, except for an occasional car trying to get through the too-narrow streets. They stop in a square that is bordered entirely on one side by the choppy blue lake.

Bett walks alone for a while, steps into a tiny cool dark church, filled with lots of gold statues, especially of the Madonna, and a second-rate painted rococo ceiling. She sits in the back row, occupying herself with her camera, changing film. Pretty soon Todd follows and slides into the same row.

Bett: (her face sort of beautiful-ugly, like a red donkey in a cartoon, her hands exquisitely ivory as they make unintentional mudras while changing the film) I love the cool and the musk in here. It reminds me of my basement when I was a kid in the South. It takes me back. (Loving to indulge in lyricisms, she seems to emulate plantation heroines.) Back, back back, to canned chili, and the acacias on the albizzia trees.

Todd: The what on the what?

Bett: I saw you reading a book on the van.

Todd: A *fotoromanzo.* You know? They have these corny photographs. Each one could be a B-movie poster. And then they put them together with words. To tell a story. I'm starting to do that in my scrapbooks. So it gave me ideas.

Bett: (picking up instantly) What scrapbooks are these?

Todd: (surprised) Well on my own time I've been making scrapbooks. With cutouts, drawings, words, photos, pressed flowers. You know.

Bett: I want to see them. It's a great magazine feature. The model who makes scrapbooks.

Todd, flattered, first smirks it off. Then puts his right foot up against the back of the pew in front.

Todd: I'll give you all the information.

The two walk out to find the rest. Bett leads the entire group on to look for a picture that doesn't yet exist. Past three old sailors sitting on a public bench in a piazza. Past racks of post-cards, all tinted blue. Past a tourist restaurant filling up mostly with Germans. The sun is dropping behind a midlake island crammed with the brown cubes and black slants of an old monastery.

She finally finds a luxuriant backyard of an English-looking country house at the edge of the village. A matron inside the house is peeking out through long velvet drapes.

Todd fidgets around in one of the white metal lawn chairs as if it were electric. Knows that he is in the gold, that the gold light is angled across his face. Reaches into his bag for the tube of hair grease, fingers it through his hair the way Ferrati likes it. Mari, Bett's ravenish assistant who used to work (rich girl) at MOMA, puts tan makeup under his eyes to erase the black half-moons, the opposite of football players and Nam guerrillas with their painted-on black dashes under the eyes, their terrorist makeup. Todd stretches out his leg straight. He's dressed in a fine linen suit, white, with light-yellow shirt, and blue polka-dot tie. His shoes are cane.

Bett tries to take a Polaroid but her camera keeps jamming. Mari comes over and takes it easily. Even though Bett's idiosyncratic photographs are hanging in museums, she still acts incompetent, pretending to know nothing about cameras, lights, meters. Maybe that's why she gets along so well with Todd. Their power in circuit lies.

Actually Todd turns in a solid and straightforward performance in front of her camera this afternoon. He has added many many faces to his one successful angry-in-the-shower look. And he plays them all for her, flipping through all the expressions like peek-at cards as he slowly turns his head from left to right. The extreme Rushmore profile. The tilted thinker head. The straight-on Bronzino portrait. The stud. The slightly-off Bryan Ferry. The one cheek that's just been slapped. Then back from right to left. The slack-jawed athlete. The straight-on Botticelli woman portrait. The tease, knowingly exposing his neck to the vampire in everyone.

But the most poised picture is never taken. It is life. It is the two other models, Maureen, auburn-redheaded, and Udo, American son of a West German policeman, sitting on a bluff, in the yellow grass, waiting their turn, able to see out over the entire lake as it darkens like a soup to which a tincture of teriyaki sauce has just been added. They appear attuned, as classical figures in a classical landscape. Though actually their talk gives them away as all too contemporary and mortal, as more scraps of enchanted human confetti.

Udo: Don't worry. Look at Marilyn Monroe. When she finished filming *Some Like It Hot,* you know what she said? She said, "I looked like a pig."

Maureen: (not at all relieved by these kind words) But she was. She was the heaviest she ever was during the filming of *Some Like It Hot.*

LUCY CALLS FRANK

Lucy is frazzled. She is somewhere in the middle of Milan, driving under medieval stone archways carved with figures, lit-up vanilla-gray. But she's not sure where, keeps going off on tangents. Stops at some corner to squint at a complicated pink city map by the light of the emerald-green radio dial. Finally she shuts off her noisy engine. Goes into a café and manages to buy a *gettone* and call the *pensione.* But the Medici *padrone* says that Todd isn't there. She can't understand the rest of what he says. Lucy scurries back outside and stands nervously on the street, the moon shining down on her as powerfully as the spotlights of a football stadium. Then she returns to put another *gettone* in the phone to call Frank. No answer.

What to do? She should have called ahead. But forgot in all the changing scenery. Now is alarmed. Gets back in the square car and shifts gears and moves ahead. Drives around and every half hour or so stops to call Frank. Finally rumbles up to the Giardini Pubblici. Parks next to its cast-iron fence, outlined in the full moon, gets out, sits on a fancy park bench in the would-be-shade-if-it-were-day of a fir tree. She is too upset to play at distinguishing the cats from the squirrels. Her mind is a blackboard on which she keeps scribbling the same worry words in chalk over and over again.

TODD BREAKS OPEN LUCY'S LOCKS

The Ferrati van steers down Via Vigevano past the canal worked on by Leonardo da Vinci back into Milan. They're all beat. Coming off the road can be more lonesome than staying on the road. Milan is muggy, familiar. As Todd exits the van, he swipes a pair of yellow linen pants he wore in the shoot off the rack and stuffs them into his knapsack.

Todd stops to get his key. It has a note wrapped around. From Frank.

Message: *Lucy's here.*

At first Todd feels distant from the news. He drops off his bag. Lies for a minute on his single bed and whistles the theme from *The Bridge on the River Kwai.* Then rolls off, pulls on the stolen yellow pants, with his smudged T-shirt, and sockless laceless boating sneakers.

Makes his way downstairs and out onto the baked streets of middle-of-July Milan. Stops at store windows on the way to check who the models are in the little cardboard placard ads. Looks longest at Frank in the Ferrati ad, at sea, leaning against the white railing of a white boat. Then stops in at an ice cream store on Via Torino. Its long glaring refrigerated display is all colors of *gelati.* Todd orders, by pointing, a mixed cup of lemon, chocolate and chestnut. The squat pumpernickel-skinned probably southern-Italian *ragazzo* behind the counter carelessly hands him a yellow plastic spoon. Outside, Todd leans against a police paddy wagon licking the mound slowly. It's as if he's savoring, lingering over his independence.

But when Todd pushes the doorbell (a copper button set in a large copper concave) a change begins. He becomes excited. His heart contracts faster. From inside the apartment he can hear some hushed moving around, as if boxes are being rearranged, or doors opened and closed. Then he hears footsteps coming closer on the other side of the plane of oak.

It's Lucy. She is looking demure, dressed in a long white shirt-dress, her eyes cast down at Todd's sneaks. Then she looks up. She is obviously in a virgin mood. Uncharacteristically so.

Todd: (as if not recognizing her) Lucy?

Lucy: Yeah. Come on in. I didn't know when you would get here.

Todd steps in, pushing Lucy in with his whole body and then he wraps himself around her. He licks at her earlobes. He can hear his own heart in his own ears. Her hair tastes like wet grass. He is trembling slightly throughout.

Todd: (choked up) I'm so happy to see you here. I can't believe what I've been holding back.

Lucy: I came all the way here to see you. (pointing to a decaled suitcase on the floor) With my suitcase. (starting to cry) And a car. (crying changing into sobbing)

Todd: (reassuringly) I'm a quiet guy. I'm not going anywhere.

Todd walks Lucy over to the modern couch covered with rough canvas material. He turns off the lamp. They sit in the dark.

Lucy: I feel like I'm in the Bible. Like I'm Ruth or something traveling a long way.

Todd: (tenor) I know what you mean. . . . (bass) Let's get out of here.

Lucy leans over and turns the lamp on again.

Lucy: It's not our house.

Todd: Since when did we ever have a house?

Lucy goes over to her suitcase. Takes out a flannel shirt that she bought for Todd in an Army-Navy store: a magenta-red field filled in with threads of light caterpillar-green and dark glow-worm-orange and deep indigo-blue. Looks as rich as any of Carlo's Persian rugs on the floors.

The door from Frank's room finally opens. He emerges wearing red jogging sweatpants, nothing else. Sits down in an auburn leather lounge chair, kicks back, and rubs his own moist chest and stomach.

Frank: (exaggeratedly cocky tonight) So me and your girlfriend haven't seen each other in a few weeks. Today I remedied that situation. I took her as my personal date to the local museum.

Todd: (through his recently whitened teeth) What museum?

Frank: (to Lucy) It was called the Berra or something? Like Yogi Berra?

Lucy: (to Todd, warmly) They had a foreshortened Christ there. I'll take you to it. If you take me to *The Last Supper*.

Frank doesn't like the bend in this conversation.

Frank: (callously, while ambling out to the terrace) Ciao.

Frank practices his calisthenics in the moonlit breezes, stretching his arms down along his calves, alternating, to tighten the sides of his waist.

Todd drags Lucy's suitcase out of the apartment for her. She has plenty of other sacks and bags to carry. They make their way like immigrants. By the time they arrive at the *pensione* they're bushed. Cram into the rectangle and ride up. Pile bags inside the room.

Todd: (exhausted, but worked up) I keep picturing the canals. Maybe we should go for a walk down there. I'll show them to you. (reining himself in) Or did Frank show them to you already?

Lucy: Don't you want to sit down alone together?

Todd: Not yet. I have to get used to you again.

Lucy: (brusque) Fine. Let's walk.

They walk back out into the vaporium of a summer's night.

Traveling down down down as if on a tilt toward the canal. Then look over the sides of a brick wall to the river water moving thickly but steadily along. A macadam highway traveled over by reflected stars.

Lucy puts her arms around Todd from behind and he lifts her up on his back and runs her piggyback down the sidewalk by the canal toward the outer walls of the town. She shouts different Italian words at random that she's heard—LATTE, SIGNORA, ASPETTA, SENTA, ASCENSORE—until they collapse laughing next to a wall where kids have scribbled their names.

Then they hurry back sweating to the *pensione*. The walk takes about twenty minutes. On the way they pass through some Roman ruins that now serve as a tram stop. The pillars look yellow in the light of the yellow flares surrounding them.

Lucy: We could've taken the car.

Todd: Shove the car.

They are back inside the *pensione* room. Lucy is lying with no clothes on under a white sheet, her eyes fastening rapidly on different slivers of the room. Todd is sitting hunched on a low bench by the sink, in toilet-sitting position. He's eating strawberries out of a plastic container from the deli across the street. Then he kills the two lights. Sets the alarm for nine so he can call the agency. Messes up Lucy's arrangement getting in.

Todd starts licking at Lucy's neck with his full tongue. She tenses up. Her neck is an ultrasensitive zone. In New York they had an implicit agreement that Todd wouldn't lick too long or too strenuously at her neck. It was dynamite. She would scream and struggle. But here Todd breaks that limit. He bears down on her neck, full mouth, as if devouring the fleshy isthmus. Lucy giggles uncontrollably and then screams and screams. Todd doesn't care who hears. Lucy can't help herself.

Lucy: (barely able to get the words to cohere) Please. Please stop. You're breaking open my locks.

The next morning is idyllic. Lucy wakes up first, lying there trying to remember where she is. The sun is total because Todd has forgotten to close the shutter doors. She shakes him awake as the annoying buzz begins. He presses the snooze bar. Todd has sticky pus keeping his eyelids closed. He begins to finger open the perforations to see Lucy.

Todd: (slowly) I dreamed I was riding on a big horse named Jailbait. The kind of horses they raise in Vienna. And you were in it as a performer who stands on horses wearing like a Playboy bunny's costume.

Lucy: (flattered) It's so much more fun when we're together than when we're apart. Fuller.

Todd: The worst thing about being empty is that you don't know you're empty when you are. Only after.

Lucy strains her neck so that the cartilage makes rib lines that stick out.

Lucy: What did you think of first when you woke up?

Todd: Today I thought of you first.

Lucy: All riiiight. . . . I'd much rather be one of those people who thinks about someone else when they wake up in the morning.

A pigeon with big orange legs and webs, and a green chest, grabs its way along the railing, squawking.

MUSSOLINI

Frank arrives home from a *Uomo Linea Italiana* shoot the next afternoon and can't relax. Carlo and Tania are both out working. He picks up the phone to call Todd and Lucy, but then smacks it back down.

Frank: (out loud) Let them call.

He changes into a smelly black T-shirt, green fatigues and brown hiking boots. Goes for a long walk. Keeps seeing fresh models along the way. Can spot them. Girls dressed for a night-club in the daytime—constructivist earrings and blue jeans, but fresh as milk—traveling in pairs. Guys—solo—Paul Bunyans in seven-league Tony Lama boots plugged into a Sony Walkman.

He ends up at the Milan train station, that monument to Fascist architecture with its belittling dimensions, stone textures, Samson pillars and flexed doorways. Rides escalator up through a gray excavated boulder of a foyer, like the inside of a tombstone, that communicates the thrill of grand emptiness and substance unexplored.

Frank bangs around the second floor for a while. Trains, whistling and screaming, arrive and depart. A brown de Chirico waiting room, haunted by a huge white clockface, fills up with benched travelers, then empties out, then fills up again, like an egg timer with sand. Hawkers at carnival stands strung with Christmas-tree lights try to shout out syllables among the speakered din of the pervasively broadcasting omniscient narrator's voice announcing times and tracks.

Frank then leans impatiently near a tall poster that shows him drinking some twerpy fruit drink from a tiny shaped bottle. An ad.

Exiting from a nearby men's room is a young man in his late twenties, about 6'3", his brown hair cropped close to his head, wearing a gray workshirt, green work trousers and white bucks. Has on pretty thick glasses with transparent frames. Catches the juxtaposition of Frank and his ad, stalks around there for a while, trying to make eye contact. No luck. Finally, in a somewhat skulky fashion, walks over.

Richard: (a voice as clear as a middle-range organ pipe) If I'm not mistaken, aren't you the model in the picture over there?

Frank: (startled, not realizing the poster was nearby) Yeah. You American passing through?

Richard: I'm Richard Hayworth. I live in Milan.

Frank really looks at him now, not shy about his moving stare that rolls over the stranger's face and strange clothes as coolly as a buyer appraising a suit of clothes on a rack.

Frank: (lazily) Studying? Working?

Richard: (vague) No.

Frank: (his peeve at this mysterious answer making him involuntarily more interested) What'll it be then?

Richard: (Tony Perkins's voice, or maybe Roddy McDowall's) I just thought we might talk, as two Americans.

Frank: (suspicious) Do you always walk up to strangers in this train station?

Richard: I never did before. I am just coming off a train now from Rome. And I always try to follow my impulses. I hope that you do too.

Frank: No. Wish I did. Could kick myself for some real doozies I missed. (testing him) Especially pussy.

Richard: (a closed book) I live nearby. If you'd like, you may stop up for a soft drink, or a negroni, and I'll show you my collection of eight-millimeter films.

Frank: What kind of films?

Richard: Old ones. *Dracula, Frankenstein.* Mostly monster movies.

Frank: (hooked) I'll go for that.

They ride down the escalator with the walls and ceilings expanding farther and farther outward from them as they descend. They are finally on ground level. Walk past rows of stolid stone eagles carved at attention, wearing badges, staring ahead all in the same direction, beaks like pointed weapons.

Richard's apartment is in an outlying neighborhood of Milan with room for its own circles and squares of classical parks. The apartment building is one of many toast-brown fortresses lined up without a break like brownstones in Manhattan, but wider, and with more detailed bumps and grinds. These have the color and feel of falling leaves, bringing a melancholy mood of autumn to all four seasons, even now in sultriest summer.

Richard takes Frank up the old-fashioned copper elevator cage that rises through the middle of the building. Down the hallway lit, or rather just sketched out, by pale green overhead light bulbs. Through his cool, dank, many-roomed apartment that seems mostly unused waste.

He leads Frank finally into a bedroom that looks like a teen-ager's room. There are plenty of models of monsters around. The shades are pulled down over the windows, and the movie screen is down too. A projector is set up behind the bedboard. One Visible Man model shows all the veins, arteries and organs in the human body. Most curious is the Nazi paraphernalia dis-played: flags, picture of Hitler, books, a uniform on a hanger, tall SS boots, badges and metals.

Richard: Have a seat.

There is no seat. So Frank sits gingerly on the side of the bed with its red-black flaglike bedspread. He feels slightly revolted.

Frank: How the fuck did I get myself into this?

Richard: Into what? You can leave. But I have an old movie of Lady Godiva you might like.

Frank: Who's she?

Richard: She's the one who was forced to ride naked on a horse through Coventry in the Middle Ages.

Frank: Oh yeah? Sounds hot.

Richard: It is. It is.

Richard turns off the lights. The projector streams its light like an oversized flashlight onto the blank screen. Then the black-and-white images begin to appear jerkily, filled with sepia tints and shadows that attest to the age of the stained print. Frank gets turned on watching this rather thin young woman riding on a horse through the gabled town, the townspeople hidden behind their shutters, her waist-length hair draped over her breast, her crotch pressed into the neck of the obliging stallion. He rubs the nail of his curved thumb up and down the outline of his camouflaged cock while Richard watches him, his head resting on the back of his desk chair. The whole film only lasts about fifteen minutes. Then Richard turns on the lights again.

Richard: (sputtering) I have *Playboy* magazines from the States.

Frank: You can get those at any tobacco store here. What is this anyway? A stag party? Do you have any other porn?

Richard: (relieved) I have one full-length feature called *Pink*.

Frank: I'll watch that.

Richard: It's one thing to have my loneliness relieved. But to have it relieved by a celebrity.

Frank: (flattered) Please.

The movie is long, in color, with high production values. In one scene a woman boss wearing a suit and tie tells her secretary to hold her calls while she confers with a squat Mediterranean-looking salesman. The salesman turns her out of her swivel chair, and plays boss for a while. He swats her with a riding crop that he pulls out of her drawer. In another scene two female roomies live together in a homey, humble apartment. A fella in a team jacket comes by to date one of the girls but ends up, to his delight, in a threeway.

Frank enjoys looking at these tales. Although they do nothing to calm him down.

Frank: (spastically) You trying to buy me or what?

No answer. During the whole show Richard is sitting at his desk with a pen flashlight paging through old yellowed papers, studying them closely at times with a round hand magnifier. By the time the movie ends Frank feels like crawling out of his skin. But he also isn't comfortable just walking out. This complex of urges causes trouble.

Frank: Turn on the lights willya? I can't see a thing.

Richard moves slowly, like Uriah Heep, over to a lamp that he turns on, grinning.

Frank: What's so funny?

Richard: (fussing with its plastic-covered red shade) You seem nervous today Frank.

Frank: What do you mean today? How many days have you seen me on?

Richard: Is modeling getting to you? Too much limelight?

Frank: Don't start fantasizing about modeling to me please. But would you tell me what you're doing over there at that desk of yours?

Richard: (moving back to desk) I'm trying . . . it's confidential, but I can tell you. . . . I'm trying to compile a history of Fascism in Italy.

Frank: (catching on) Sympathetic or no?

Richard: Good question. Rather sympathetic actually. That's its special claim to fame I hope. No one has taken that position in the last thirty years. It's a radical step.

Frank: I'll give you a radical step. And what about that uniform hanging on that door over there? Is that an Italian Fascist's uniform?

Richard: You said it.

Frank: (goading) Why don't you put it on for me? Is it your size? Do you wear it around the house?

Richard: As a matter of fact I belong to a group. It's my size, though authentically 1940s, from the 1940s.

Frank winces. All his anger and frustration is now being focused, the way kids in a playground focus the heat of the sun through a cheap magnifying glass onto a piece of paper that catches flame eventually without a match.

Frank: (lockjawed) Put it on Richard.

Richard goes into the hallway and makes noise getting into his uniform and boots. Then he returns looking like an extra. He is a piece of the shrapnel of the past—black and orange and red—lodged in the bony tissue of the present. His uniform is so starched, and boots so shiny, he hardly seems to belong in them at all with his unsettled expressions and hopeless eyes.

Frank: (standing up and walking threateningly over toward Richard) I have a friend named Todd. Now his uncle got hurt flying bombers over the people who used to wear these uniforms. (grabbing Richard around the neck in a choke gesture) Now he wouldn't get a kick out of this American traitor stomping around in this uniform would he? (screaming) Would he?

Richard is suddenly scared. Frank has him in a trap.

Richard: I was just kidding. I just wanted to impress you. So you would be my friend.

But Frank isn't mollified. He is already raw, his nerves over-exposed. A bomb of many megatons goes off inside him larger and more powerful than any he has ever felt.

Frank starts to pound Richard. He smacks him hard across the cheek with the flat of his hand. Then punches him in the stomach so that he doubles over. Then knees him in the balls. And when Richard is bent over double on the floor Frank squats over him and starts beating on him with his fists while Richard is shaking and screaming and even crying but can't pull his muscles together, or mind together, to yell any words. Frank then stands up, straddling his victim, looses his penis from his pants and lets out a yellow shower of perfumy-smelling piss all over. A discouraging rain. When he finally pauses, he looks over, hardly recognizing himself in the full-length mirror hanging on the closet door. He has been transmogrified into one of the shelf monsters.

Richard: (eyes burning) You got me all wrong. You're too dumb to understand.

Frank: Who's calling who dumb?

Frank knocks over a side table with an ashtray and some pens and pills that clatter onto the wooden floor.

Richard: (still lying down there) I'm calling the police and your agency and having you deported from Milan. I have powerful friends in Milan.

Frank takes a walking stick with a metal top and smashes the light bulb in the ceiling.

Frank: What are you going to do Mussolini? Little Mussolini?

Richard is now smart enough not to say anything else. He just lies there, playing dead. Frank opens the door to leave. Stands heaving in the doorway, his silhouette outlined by the chartreuse hall light. He is a Shadow Man with an alien aura.

Frank: (a word that sounds like a gunshot) *Duce!*

MORAL DISORDER

Frank turns around tipsily on his heel, tears down the stairs, and sprints through Milan trying to find the Pensione Medici. Is harder than finding the way through a forest. He races down streets only to find himself back where he started. No one can tell him where he's headed. His Italian isn't so good. All the life in Milan is hidden away behind big fortress doors. It's not on display. Like Rome. So the streets are nowhere.

When he finally gets to Todd's door his clothes are sopping wet from sweat. His face doesn't look at all familiar. He is heaving up putrid breath from deep in his lungs.

Todd, immediately concerned, puts his arm around him and leads him in. Sits him on the edge of the bed. Lucy returns from the terrace and registers the dramatic change that has come over. Frank tells the whole story with his face hidden in his cupped hands. He never looks up once. Todd and Lucy look at each other many times during the telling, trying to get some clues from each other how to act. When Frank is finished they stay quiet.

The inside phone rings. Todd lifts the device from the wall.

Padrone: *Telefono per Signor Todd.* (he always pronounces Todd's name like "Tod," the German word for death)

Todd irrationally feels that the police have tracked down Frank. But they haven't. It's Jean.

Jean: (rushes the words together at double speed) If you see your friend Frank tell him he has to leave Milano pronto.

Todd: For getting in a boys-will-be-boys fight?

Jean: I'm so angry at him I don't want to say anything else. (changes to a sweeter tone) Now you, *caro.* Two agents are here from Paris. They are taking some models out to dinner who they are interested in tonight. Be at Rigolo at eight. Also you have a booking. You leave tomorrow for Sicily. Be at the agency at nine in the morning and they have a car for you. Aaaaaaand, I received a telex from Anna in Munich. She wants you in August. That could be good. You know Milan and Paris are dead for three weeks in August.

When he returns to the room, Todd relays the news. But Frank doesn't react much.

Frank: (unusually timid) Is it all right with you guys if I go with you to Munich or Paris? Or wait for you there?

Then he just sits on the edge of the bed, his spunk sunk, toying with stray strands of his blond hair that he is examining by pulling them down in front of his eyes.

MAIOCCHI

Maiocchi is a typical upper-middle Milanese restaurant. Dark wood tables. Carts with creamy desserts. Waiters in black smoking jackets. It was disrupted a month ago by one of the new-style restaurant robberies. Proletarian burglars barged in with machine guns and held up all the customers, taking jewelry, cash. This tetchy terrorism had been irritating Milan recently in its most sensitive organ, its esophagus.

Five models, including Todd and Paul, are sitting at a long white-tablecloth-covered table. But Todd is the only one wearing a blue baseball cap turned around backward on his head. He and Paul are talking baseball statistics, as if to justify the hat. Todd doesn't like going to games, or playing, but has always collected the player cards. Many are pasted in his high school scrapbooks. He learned the stats from the cards. Knows how to flip them, too, to trade up for betters. Favorite player: Clete Boyer, a third baseman for the New York Yankees in the mid-sixties.

Bertrand and Simone, the agents from Premier in Paris, are

there, too. Throwing the dinner to snatch the best bets first. Simone is a man about fifty with well-coiffed gray-white hair combed back, wearing a cream-colored silk shirt open at the neck, necklace with gold dog's-head charm hanging down, black dress bells, brown boots, very garish-looking. Bertrand, Simone's partner, is about twenty-five, messy brown curly hair, wearing a matching outfit with Simone, shirt, pants, boots, without a necklace, with a diamond pinned in his left ear.

Bertrand: (to Todd) Baby, you know Soupy send me the pictures of you coming out of the shower, in the shorts, and I send right back a telex saying you should come to Paris, we take care of you. You know I just get a feeling from this picture. That's how I work. Just by . . . (he flutters his fingers to represent some kind of special intuition he gets apparently from the air) Isn't that right, Simone?

Simone, who always seems a bit on Quaalude, looks up with an abstract smile from a conversation with another model.

Bertrand: This is Todd Eamon. You know he is about to be Ferrati.

Todd bites hard into his breadstick, and chews it as if he were chewing on tobacco.

Simone: (not ready to acknowledge Bertrand's find just yet) This is Alan Blaire. (pointing to a tall blond innocent with a bony face.) Ooooh. You know Blaire speaks a perfect French. These Americans. They are very serious. (to Alan) Talk to Bertrand in French.

Alan: (in Alliance Française French) *Oui, je peux parler, je l'étudiais dans l'école.*

Bertrand: But that's very good baby. I mean first thing is we want you to be happy in Paris. You know, to have your girlfriend, your whole life there, because if you're not happy, it's hard to work well.

Todd: (to Alan, testily) Tell him how much you like that doggy necklace of his in French.

The other models, except Alan, and Paul, laugh. But Simone doesn't get the sarcasm.

Simone: (holding the lump in his palm) It's gold. Pure gold. And pretty soon you see I get an even bigger piece.

Todd and Paul leave together. They stand for a few minutes in the perfect circle of a park in the middle of the square under a mulberry tree packed with multiple false fruits that resemble raspberries.

Paul: Whatever happened to that Yankee-boy gentleman I rode over on the plane with? One major campaign and you're a shit?

Todd: (sorry) No. It's not that. It's not that simple.

Paul: I heard about your buddy Frank Yastremski.

Todd: It could be. It could be that.

When Todd arrives home, Frank and Lucy are both asleep. Frank out on a lounge chair on the terrace with a few itchy blankets over him. Todd watches him breathe up and down for a while. Lucy is under the sheets. Todd feels the dampness as he sidles in and sets the alarm for seven.

HAIRCUT

When Todd wakes he knows right away that something is wrong. He doesn't feel right. Has a thrush throat. Is warm when he crosses his forehead with his palm. Lies in bed in a shadow of his own sweat. But he gets up anyway. No one else does. It's too early.

Todd turns on the bulb over the mirror. His face doesn't look right either. Skin is sallow. Pores are big. Some pimples. He notices a general puffiness. His hair is dull, dry, flat. By now Todd knows his face so well that he can tell from his first look in the mirror in the morning how well it will glow that day. Like farmers who can predict a day's weather from their first crack at the sky through a bedroom window at dawn.

Todd is working today on Panarea, an island off Sicily. To

142

get there the client has rented a private prop that flies from the Milan airport. There are seven on the shoot and they plan to stay a few days. One of the male models is an Australian, built big, who tries to come on to all the women. One woman is Sophia. She is seventeen, and lives with her mother in Verona.

Todd, fevered, takes risks in his plane chat.

Todd: Lookalikes do well in this business. (to Australian) You could be Mel Gibson's stuntman. (to Sophia) And you look like your name. Sophia Loren. Why is that?

Sophia: Is true. Is true. Alessandro, the Bolognese model, is looking just like Mick Jagger.

Australian: Twins are big, too. Brother acts. Sister acts.

Todd: There's this thing with replacing one human with another. Xeroxing. Cloning. Erasing personality in the meantime. We have no personalities.

Following that last comment the Australian gives him a bugger-off look.

Their plane flies close down to the sleek highways that cut through midair above the dark, vampirish region of Calabria in the South. The seven finally land in the port and wait to take a little boat to Panarea. In the distance, a volcano is puffing away like a cigar left on an ashtray.

The art director and her photographer husband tell the crew they have one hour until the boat to Panarea embarks. The island, one of the Lipari Islands, formed from black volcanic ash, is only reachable by boat, has no electricity, just generators. At night the people on the island carry flashlights to light their way along the narrow snake paths on the inhabited side. One disco blares away on generator power until midnight or so. The other side is left to rocks, ruins of ships, and skeletons of giant fish. No one goes there.

Todd decides to use the hour to recoup. He's so dizzy that he can't even talk anymore to the other models. He lies down next to a crate of fruit on the wooden deck. The sun is hot and getting hotter. He lies in the sun, not in the shade. Sailors come by and step over him. A few birds cackle every so often. Then

Todd stands up and heads for a line of stores along the harbor's main drag. He finds a barber shop and decides to step in to get a buzz cut. He feels so hot that he intends to cool off by cutting off his hair. Plus he wants a change. A change from the fever and the broiling state he's in, period.

Todd shows the young apprentice barber with gestures that he wants all his hair cut off. The long-haired kid, probably fifteen, his transistor blaring tinny rock, is surprised, slow to start cutting. But Todd prods him on. Every five minutes the boy barber stops and gives Todd a chance to call a halt to the session. He gets his round mirror to have Todd approve the snipped back. Todd stares in the globe at his shorn neck and then further in, gleefully, at the reflected messy newspapers and *fotoromanzi* on a little side table and the reflected color photos of soccer teams taped on the walls. Then he motions the boy to go on, go on. Todd looks through the windows onto the wooden walk where people in colorful outfits pass carrying cases and bales as they must have in the nineteenth century whaling towns of New England. Finally Todd has the same crewcut he had when he was nine and he's satisfied. Feels momentarily cooler. Cool and rebellious. He pays his 5,000 lire and leaves smiling, walking a bit like a drunk up the street, up the wharf to the waiting boat.

When Elga, the art director, a sophisticated but hard-lined woman from the North, near the border of Austria, the daughter of some money, sees Todd, she tightens her fist. Then she starts screaming at him in Italian. Todd just stands there. The rest gather around him. They all look shocked.

Todd: (jokey) I just got a buzz cut. What's the beef?

None of the models answer. Not even the Australian guy who understands that slang phrase. They feel threatened and repulsed by his act. He may ruin their job.

The screaming Elga marches off to the boat office. She is missing for forty-five minutes. During this time the others on the shoot stay away from Todd. He sits on a post looking down at the water. Feeling only half there. The turquoise water is shimmering as if electrified. Todd listens to the music of the boats revving up, splattering water, tossing like soccer balls on the restless shoulders of the moving waves. Finally Elga returns from the wooden shack. She talks as much with her stiff arms and hands as with her tongue. Her husband, slow and heavy, approaches Todd.

Husband: (spokesmanlike) You must go back to Milan. You are not wanted on this shoot with your hairdo. My wife is very angry to kill you. So go over to that house and you will wait there until someone comes. (then, obviously finding his own words) I hate children like you.

The husband walks away. Then the rest of the crew, including the models, slowly join in the departing procession, not looking back. By now Todd is a bit delirious, or thinks he is. He sits patiently on a dark-blue bench, waiting. About three hours later a lackadaisical middle-aged Sicilian man in a white uniform, looking like a cafeteria attendant, arrives to pick Todd up. The two don't try to talk. Todd feels as if he's being led to a prison.

It's almost dark now. No other passengers on the six-seater, the last plane allowed to fly back through the orchid sky. Todd sits way back in the seat and imagines representational shapes for the voluminous, and variously shaded, cumulonimbus clouds. At Milan he is met by another car and is driven straight to the agency.

When he arrives only Jean and Luigi are still working. They look at him seriously, so seriously that Todd can't help a nervous laugh sound. They are sitting on the same side of the table, facing him.

Jean: So you and Frank decide to go insane now on me in the same week. And to lose me, both of you, much money, and more important, much respect. I have no use for you now. Your hair is too short.

Luigi: And Milan doesn't have any use for you either. You can't work this way.

Todd: (a plea) It's just a new look.

Jean: If you want to sell yourself with this GI look, then you have to begin a whole new book, with new pictures. But I warn you this look is not very commercial here in Europe. And I do not believe in the States either.

Luigi: Europeans like the long hair. In America too. Look. (He throws Todd the latest copy of an American men's fashion magazine. Todd doesn't bother to check.)

Luigi grips his hand on Todd's shoulder for the last time this summer. He walks him toward the door. Todd feels choked up. He didn't intend to mess up more than this one job. All of a sudden, just when he was hitting, he is going to be without work and money. He feels his insides go woozy.

Luigi: *Senti.* The hair will grow again in time for the season in Paris in one month. The shows are even in six weeks, for men. So I would take a vacation and go to Simone and Bertrand then.

Todd: But I didn't know I was doing this.

Luigi: You have to grow up. But then if you grow up, who knows, maybe you won't look good, or right.

There might as well be drums hit one by one in military-disgrace fashion as Todd walks back down the tunnel he had first entered three months ago.

Todd is almost packed. Lucy is over at Frank's. The quiet is positively violet, so light, so crystalline. He walks out on the terrace and sees the same housewife making the same spaghetti bolognese, but her boy isn't around tonight.

Slinks back inside, takes his scrapbook from under the mattress. He will have to buy a new one when he gets to Paris. This one is completely full. Three months is record time for Todd. But then cutting and pasting had been his only activity during all the flat hours between go-sees.

Todd sits on his bed and flips through. At first these pages resemble the New York pages. He has mementos juxtaposed.

Here a matchbox cover from Primadonna with its seventies silver-on-black written script logo. There a painstakingly scissored-out advertisement for an ambulance service, with nurse and doctor drawn next to a jaguar of an ambulance.

The middle pages, though, turn into a kind of homemade *fotoromanzo*. The characters are all cutouts of models, guys and girls he knows, mostly from his agency. Under their ad or card photos are captions, written out on white pasted-in labels. Because the characters are so posed, and often romantic, his story line tends toward melodrama, about love or murder or both, along the lines of the cartoon strip *Rex Morgan*.

The last ten pages or so are expressively abstract, a flamboyant breakaway. Recently, after Lucy's arrival, Todd started working purely with colors, at first greens, to make patterns on the page. For days he traveled around collecting any scraps that were, say, lime-green: movie tickets, candy wrappers, blades of grass. Then he moved on to rose, then robin's-egg blue, then black-white television gray. He meshed these flecks and blotches and sinuous rivers of paper into whole swirling pages that look like those marble-papered notebooks that are sold in one tiny shop in Venice a bridge-hop away from Piazza San Marco.

Finished looking, Todd now closes the book with a satisfied sigh, as if he had just read a fat nineteenth-century novel. He wraps the book fastidiously in lemon tissue paper and packs it in his L.L. Bean bag. Then stretches out on the mattress. Waits for Lucy to fetch him, while languorously listening to a tape he bought of pop love songs, "I' sto bene con te," "Car' amico ti scrivo," "Solo noi."

Feels funky.

The train is pulling out of the Milan station where Frank met Richard Hayworth a week before. Click click click of train windows passing by. Todd, Lucy and Frank have two interconnecting cabins with the door now open between them. Both sides have two bunk beds, a sink with mirror, small refrigerator. Standard train photographs, black-and-white, of parts of Italian cities, decorate the walls. First class.

The three are crowded into Frank's side, with Lucy as odd-man-out leaning against the sink. She is swaying along with the motions of the train. An Italian official interrupts to check their tickets, a maid to fluff their beds, a waiter to deliver the three bottles of *bianco* wine Frank ordered before. Each now has a bottle.

Frank: (vengefully) I'd rather be a Burger King salesman than ever go back to that armpit of a city.

Todd: (supportively) Burger King's food is better anyway. Not so much sugar and starch.

Lucy: (dreamily) Imagine *The Last Supper* set in a Burger King.

Through the square windows, the land of northern Italy is flickering. Or the three passengers see it as flickering. They see orange rooftops give way to brown patches give way to green patches give way to a thicket of fruit trees give way to a factory smoking up ashen clouds into a pink sky. But of course the land is not moving. Is not scenery. Is saturated, is sunk in itself.

PARIS

JAZZ

Jackie (pronounced jaw-kée) is dancing on the low-slung ramp of a chichi cellar club on a backstreet of Pigalle. Renaults and Peugeots are pulled up out front. The club is filled with a cloud of gray smoke that never disperses. The crowd—in costumes, and black tie, and rhinestone drag—moves in and out of visibility according to the hovering rumba of the smoke that moves through over and about the red velvet couches, chairs, banquettes, drapes, rug, the black plastic tables, round, rectangular, triangular, like molecules of exhaled smoke refusing to float away from a pair of gaudily lipsticked lips.

Jackie moves down the ramp in a purple G-string, tassels on his tits like a belly dancer, clanging bracelets, thick black North African hair dyed blue. He is part Algerian, part Egyptian, part French. His body is no attraction. Is thin, is a canvas of dark oily skin. Like an Abyssinian cat he pushes up from the ramp with his feet. Dancing an evocative-of-everything-and-nothing tease dance to the tune of mild jazz from the twenties. His black eyes fluttered with gold sprinkle flashing at many tables of hookah friends.

Jackie: (almost inaudible while twirling his tit tassels and delivering his lines) *Tu veux l'entendre de ma bouche. Eh bien, oui, j'ai aimé. J'ai souffert. Mais je n'ai pas été aimé.*

Jackie moons the audience with his dusky ass.

Paris by day. Joggers running along the ups downs and arounds of the brush paths of the Bois de Boulogne beneath a sky so clean and light-blue it seems it must be scoured by the white Brillo pads of clouds. Honk honk. Drinking a red wine as nourishing as blood to a vampire in the café said to be Hemingway's second favorite in Montparnasse. Catholic uniformed schoolgirls lifting their scarlet skirts (the fronts) to each other in front of the gray tablets of tombstones in Père Lachaise on their way to the most popular grave, Jim Morrison's. Metal café chairs kicked over by a gang of beefy truck drivers from the *banlieux* gone over the top across from the gold emulsion of a palace of Louis XIII. Flying kites in the alleys of the Jewish ghetto, the water-stained Marais. Roissy Airport looking like a construction from H. G. Wells: lots of bubbles and tubes, big gray metal space helmets of buildings, anonymous travelers passing on black moving sidewalks. Spokes shooting out from the vertical sepul-

chral obelisk of Place de la Concorde as dizzyingly as those of
the wheels of a Le Coq Sportif bicyclist on a span of Napoleonic
bridge over the smelt Seine.

LOST GENERATION

Soon the drizzle is intense enough to feel like rain. So Frank
ducks Todd and Lucy into a café on Châtelet Square. He has
been touring them around.

They sit by the streaked windows. Plenty of noise from glass
clinks, French talk and pinball bleeps. Damned-looking people
pass by in a yellow glare. The artificial light at this time of early
evening in the rain resembles gaslight. Lucy has a medicinal-
tasting *infusion* Verveine, Todd a glass of red Beaujolais and Frank
a draft beer. Lucy sticks in her black leather skirt to the red
vinyl seats.

Frank: (wrapped in a green Army trenchcoat) Let me try Jackie
again.

Todd: (extra-light black cashmere sweater, jeans) Yeah. Do
that.

Frank drops *jetons* in the wall phone, lets it beep, sounds like
Morse code, no answer, returns.

Lucy: (her body compressing from frustration of wanting to
get to the next stop) So how did you meet Jackie?

Frank: One night walking home from a club. It was dawn.
The birds were singing. And there he was in a park behind a
church on St. Germain smoking hash next to a statue. He offered me some.

Frank tries again. No answer. So he invites Todd and Lucy
to spend the night at his place. Tomorrow he's sure he can
secure them a room at Jackie's. They walk in the direction of
Odéon. Todd pretends to look at used books at the stalls along

the river but doesn't know what he's looking at. They descend to the cobble path by the river. The smell isn't too much today. The rats aren't showing their hoodlum heads.

Todd: So if this Jackie likes to dress up like a woman he must be a fag.

Frank: No way. If he were to fuck, he'd fuck women.

Todd: What do you mean, if?

Frank: He likes to watch. He's a whatever, a voyeur. That's his scene. Watching someone else make it. He gets me whores and pays me to fuck them in front of him.

Lucy: I have no problem with that. Like there are straight men who are turned on to transvestites. What they like best is the dick.

Todd: (interrupting) That's what women are most interested in anyway. Big dicks. No so much face or body. I read that in *Playboy*.

Frank: I thought it was ass I read they were most interested in.

Lucy: Let me finish. They like these pseudo women because they have tits and they can get fucked by them.

Todd: If they have tits then they're not transvestites.

Lucy: I get them mixed up. I'm dyslexic as far as that goes. Which is it?

Frank: I think pre-op transsexuals shooting up hormones have both tits and cocks.

Lucy: The best of both worlds.

Frank: Then real transsexuals have it cut off. But they don't feel anything when they get fucked. That's the price they pay to have real men.

Lucy: Spare me.

Todd: If Jackie just likes to watch it either way then that's primal scene. Watching Mommy and Daddy fuck.

Lucy: The ultimate TV show.

Frank's agency apartment is a studio down the street from the Odéon metro stop. When he's away, he lets the agency rent it to other models. Because of the steady circulation of single men the place has a call-boy-apartment ambience. The clutter of personal dibs and dabs only adds to rather than softens the anonymity of the blank white walls: piles of dirty clothes, socks lined on the radiator, pastel-colored cassette boxes scattered, musty musky smell, venetian blinds, comfortable bathroom with large mirrors and recherché men's cosmetic products randomly stashed.

Frank: (arms tucked across chest) Who wants to sleep where?

Lucy: But our bags are still at the train station.

Frank: Can't you sleep without them?

Lucy: Okay. I'll sleep in the bed with you two.

Frank: Todd?

Todd: (barely suppressed anger) I'll sleep here on the floor if you have a sleeping bag, or blankets.

Frank: I have a sleeping bag. (incredulous) So you want to sleep on the floor here at the foot of our bed?

Todd: (sneeringly said) Yes.

Frank: (shrugging innocently) Do it your way.

Frank unrolls a sleeping bag that has sponged up the musky smell filtering through the humid apartment. The outside of the bag is dark green. Inside in bright oranges and reds and blues are stitched scenes of hunters hunting and campers camping in primeval forests. The outside of the bag is functional, the inside fantastical and luxuriant.

Todd is asleep quickly. His hypothalamus shot its load as soon as he got in the bag. Lucy and Frank have a harder time. They are careful to stick to the edges of their sides of the mattress. But the distance is not natural. Their muscles and ligaments are aching to touch other muscles and ligaments, and be touched. Sometime in the middle of the night Lucy gets up and squeezes into the single sleeping bag with Todd. When he wakes up in the morning she is pressed flat up against him like a pickle wrapped by a deli man with a rye sandwich.

THE WHITENESS OF THE GHOST

It's noon. Jackie shuffles in a sarong of a bedsheet onto the cool blue linoleum of his slick modern bathroom in a geometric, plain, flat apartment building on Place Blanche near Place de Clichy. The kind of apartment building in Truffaut's *The Bride Wore Black.*

He pulls down the pouches of his eyes exposing the yellow tint of his whites in the mirror. Then breaks open tubes of medicinal gooey liquid that he takes for, as he says, *"la force."* Drinks down the gelatinous pee. Then slides into a bluish bathtub and hoses himself down. Dries off. Returns to the main room where he sleeps every morning on a blanket on the floor, like a bat in a phosphorescent cave, metal shutters shut tight, only the yellow light from his halogen pyramid producing a gloaming glow. He spins a Pink Floyd record, followed soon by Leo Sayer.

By the time the three get there, Jackie is dressed and has finished the shopping. He is wearing his striped blue-white sailor's jersey, tight-fitting dark blue-jean bell-bottoms, brown Italian boots, gold-chain necklace and gold-chain bracelet. When he sees Frank he presses him in a spontaneous strong hug and drags him in.

Jackie: (to a slightly creeped Frank) Now I remember you. You are the Chariot Driver from the tarot. *Bien sûr.*

The four sit at a long modern table in the main room. The sun in the window casts everyone in a cleanly outlined group shot, graphic. Jackie has fixed a giant salad in a Japanese bowl. The endive is broken up in oval leaves and covered in a pasty vinaigrette. They drink red wine out of Mickey Mouse glasses.

Jackie: (showing his manners) I am sorry that the room is so little. I wish I had a television for you. But feel free to come and use this room as your room too. I travel often. To South America. To New York. To Maroc. So you will be alone too.

Lucy: I can't believe how sweet you are. Your heart is as sweet as a heart of palm, *un coeur de palmier*. (her eyes flicker blackly for an instant) But then people who have *coeur de palmier* hearts often can be mean I've noticed. Not acting from self-interest they can confuse, or fool, themselves. That's dangerous, no?

All three look at Lucy, surprised. Her change in tone causes a change in mood, a drastic temperature drop, but then Jackie acts as a thermostat.

Jackie: (laughing) I like you. I like you the best of anyone here. You have . . . flavor.

Lucy is now pleased with herself.

Lucy: (returning the favor) But you know I was only talking in generalities. I don't know you, and don't have any intuitions about you either.

Frank: (to Todd) See I told you these two would get along. They're already talking Deadhead talk.

Todd: (leaning back, balancing on just one chair leg) They're bogarting the joint.

Jackie: (to Todd) Do you like modeling?

Todd: (coming down unpleasantly on all four chair legs) I did. But now I'm not so sure.

Jackie: I think the not sure part of you is the best part.

Frank: Now you're talking as bad as Lucy. But at least you've got an excuse. You don't speak English.

Jackie: Models who love modeling are usually monsters. But they confuse you because they're beautiful monsters, not the ugly monsters we can identify so easily.

Frank: (bored) I gotta go.

Todd and Lucy spend the rest of the afternoon in their blank new room. It's a rectangle with metal shutters, shiny wood floors, a double bed, chair, table, little else. A Paris motel room.

As the sky begins to turn Hiroshima-pink they walk out to Rue Lepic to buy food for supper. Rue Lepic is very small-town.

A food street with a few of each kind of store built on a hill that leads up in the direction of Sacré Coeur and Montmartre. Tonight there are lines for everything. Working their way down the center of the street is a small marching band of school students. Their teachers are walking along the side collecting money and handing out pamphlets. The band is divided in two. The first half are the girls in red. They are twirling batons and swirling around in little skirts. They are not professional enough to take the gum out of their mouths. Behind them is a larger group of boys dressed in blue uniforms. They play woodwinds and trumpets and drums. Shoppers watch from the side, not really smiling wildly, just watching. The loudspeaker from the *boulangerie* is interfering by playing Edith Piaf crooning.

Lucy: (squeezing a lettuce ball) Were you in the band in high school?

Todd: No I was too busy with my own club, the Texas Chainsaw Massacre Club. We watched horror movies, snuff.

Lucy: (very Long Island) Gross.

By the time Todd and Lucy return to the apartment, it's dark violet outside. Jackie now has a very theatrical group of friends over, sitting with candles around the dining table. They stare over distantly when Todd and Lucy walk in. The two feel like pups who've trotted into a snake pit: warm-blooded up against cold-blooded. But when Jackie makes introductions, the curios at the table turn instantly animated and friendly. One is a South American woman with long earrings who chatters. A French guy and French girl, both teenagers, around thirteen, in black beatnik dickeys, sit very close making out, forming a single four-eyed octopus. A Bulgarian deposed duchess in a bronze lamé dress posed on the edge of her chair, crossed-over arms resting on crossed-over legs, black sunglasses never removed. When Todd and Lucy excuse themselves, the table chatter subsides again into low serious murmuring.

The two eat their chicken in their own room, swigging the red wine straight from a green bottle. They balance the plates on their laps while sitting on the narrow bed pushed up against the wall. The green beans are from a can, warmed-up. Lucy made dressing for some endive left over from lunch. She mixed oil, vinegar, mustard on a wide spoon, scrambled them with a fork, then let the liquid glue splatter from above onto the salad below. When either of them walks into the kitchen the cabal outside hushes.

By eleven they are under the covers, nude, lights on. Todd is reading a filler story to Lucy from the *Herald-Tribune*, the print rubbing off on his fingers like charcoal.

Todd: It was in Florida. The kid yelled out, "Help! Mike! Shark!" And listen to what his seventeen-year-old fishing buddy said. "The sun was in my eyes and I thought I saw a shark's fin." The kid had just dived in for a swim. Then his friend says, "He was gone when I got there. There was just some blood on the water."

Lucy: I don't believe it. It sounds like a misfired drug deal to me. Who goes swimming when they're fishing?

Todd: Hmmmm.

Soon Jackie walks in without even knocking. He has on gray trousers and a slightly-different-shade gray shirt over that.

Jackie: I am going out. Please don't answer the phone now that it is late.

They look at each other after he leaves. Neither wants to say that something is funny.

Lucy: I feel chilled.

Todd: (nudging into her, comfortingly) Sugar.

They turn off the lights. A couple hours later both wake up. Todd muffles a shout. Lucy breathes in a whistle. She sits up quickly and turns on the lamp. They look at each other startled.

A startled face resembles its opposite, a poker face.

Lucy: Who's there?

Todd feels a cold sweat begin to break all over his body, most intensely on his forehead. His lips feel wrong, neither hot nor cold.

Todd: Did you feel something too?

Lucy: (her voice not calmed down to normal yet) It all happened at once in a scrambled order. I'm not sure if I was sleeping. But I saw this man and sat up and turned on the light and shouted all at once. I don't know which came first. I could have dreamed it but what about you?

Todd: It just felt chilly. You know it's been hot all night. And then I was in this cold spot.

Lucy: You think there's a ghost here? I've never seen a ghost in my life.

Todd: And you didn't see one now. You just felt it. But it's funny it happened at all. That we both felt it.

Lucy: There's something weird about that guy.

Todd: Maybe not.

Lucy: What were they doing out there? Having a séance?

Todd: I doubt it. Let me ask Frank.

Lucy: Can we sleep with the light on?

Todd: Absolute.

So the two of them put their arms around each other in a protecting cuddle. And they lie there trying to sleep inside the circumference of the annoying lamplight.

About an hour or so later Todd gets up to go into the bathroom. He stalks around the apartment in no clothes then circles back. Stands in the middle of the room.

Todd: It's gone. Whatever it was.

Lucy rolls over bleary and moans. But now Todd feels lusty, almost bloodlusty, like a cat preparing to eat a warm, freshly killed bird. He lies on top of Lucy with his full weight. The unexpected pressure rouses her. She understands immediately.

Lucy turns over on her back and they stick their tongues in each other's mouths. Barely inside the lips at first. Then Lucy rolls out her tongue full in Todd's mouth, and makes suction sounds with it. But when Todd tries to put his tongue full in her mouth, she resists, moving her jaw up to block the insertion. So Todd just goes down on her neck for a while to jiggle her sense of time and place. Then sticks his thick muscular tongue back inside her mouth. This time she relishes the big fish of a tongue swimming bumptiously about in her little mouth.

Todd grabs Lucy's hand and pushes it down there by his stick. Then with his own hand he starts fingering around inside her front hole. He rises up on the mattress on his haunches then bends his head down and starts to lick where her legs meet, as two limbs of a tree meet in a crotch. He is preparing her. Lucy's heart is going fast now. Todd lies on her again but this time with his stick in her hole. He begins to go up and down, up and down, like a lever on a jack that raises a car so that the driver can change a flat. They are both breathing in through their noses strongly.

Lucy: (yelping) I'm coming alive.

Todd: (even louder) It's the only time.

In a few hours, when light cracks are showing in the shutters, Jackie arrives home. He opens the bedroom door and Todd watches him silhouetted there but pretends to be sleeping. Then Jackie clicks the door closed once more.

THE CUT

The showroom is streamlined Versailles. It's long with curving interlocking sofa-chairs on one side. Big mirrors loom from the golden frames on both sides of the room, offset by folding mirror screens. A green velvet imitation Louis XVI armchair is positioned near the door.

Todd, dressed in loose brown cords, black shirt, pale-blue smoking jacket, tan pale deck shoes, his portfolio in a navy-blue shoulder bag, pushes back into one of the purple-tan couches and pretends to read European *Time*. Next to him is a Spanish model, Matteo. They try to stumble through some talk.

Todd: *Tu travails pour Oller?*

Matteo: (grainy Basque face, speaks French slowly with a Spanish accent) *Non. J'étais en Espagne pour juillet. Et après en Allemagne. C'est très bien pour l'argent, Allemagne.*

Todd is still trying to catch up to the end of Matteo's sentence, but lags behind like a UN translator.

At the end of the room, Alessandro, the dark Italian model Sophia, on the plane to Sicily, said resembled Mick Jagger, is smoking Marlboros, talking to a group of guys, mostly Americans.

Soon a short woman in fancy clothes with gray hair pulled back walks in. She never lets up.

Woman: (claps hands) Monsieur Oller is arriving any minute. Now we all go back in this room. When Monsieur Oller is ready, you will come out one at a time and walk for Monsieur Oller. (claps hands again)

A Blonde: (rebelling) I'm gonna go grab lunch. (walks out)

The rest of the models saunter loosely back into the cloakroom, too small for them, filled with coatracks. A few hang around outside the door with Todd.

Patrick: (French with red curly hair, thin, to Todd) Are you taking your card with you?

Alessandro: I take mine. I don't care. (he bends his composite and sticks it up inside his jeans leg) You see? (stands up and pretends to bow before Monsieur Oller and swipe the card out of his leg to hand to him)

Woman: No. No. No. You don't need anything. No cards. Monsieur Oller has the perfect eye and a total memory. He just has to see you to know if you are right.

Todd: So where is Monsieur (executing a flamenco finger click) Olé?

Patrick: (warning) Swallow your spit.

Woman: Oh. He has a rendezvous. He is seeing the girls for the show. But the boys are much better this year. (looking out into the filled coatroom) It's nice to see so many good-looking *têtes* this year. I see a lot of new *têtes*. And young. The clothes are very young this year.

Frank barges in in a hurry, slapping five along the way, and pushes his way over to Todd. Is dressed all in different blue denims. Gives Todd a shove.

Todd: (unbudging) You want to step into the back?

Frank: You say that like you mean step outside.

Todd, much more confident with Frank these days, jerks with his head, and the two push to hide among the long coats.

Todd: (slowly beginning an interrogation) Now tell me about your relationship with this Jackie character. And what he does with his life.

Frank: I told you. It's pretty much a zero. He has this kind of hero-worship thing to me. Kinky though.

Todd: So Lucy and I are there to test his devotion to you?

Frank: (irritated) No. It was just the logical place to put you up. If you don't appreciate it, then go to a hotel.

Todd: (modulating) No, it's not that. But last night he had these strange people over.

Frank: Could be art smuggling. Or drugs. What do you care? Look at Lucy's purple past.

Todd: And then in the middle of the night a ghost came. We both felt it. And when he came home he just opened the door and looked in, no knocking.

Frank: There's no free lunch. Anything good happen in there?

Todd: (high school buddy tone) Yeah. I fucked Lucy.

Frank: (tenses then twinges) Is that any way to talk about Lucy?

Todd: (his interrogation beginning to produce leads in yet another case, he squeezes eyes narrower) Do you have a better way Frank?

Frank: Yeah. Just watch.

Shouting across the room, to no one in particular, Frank cuts away without a backward look. Todd is left standing alone with all the hanging coats, feeling a fountain of acid spraying in the Tuileries of his stomach.

Woman: (confiding haphazardly) The women are ugly this year. Strictly prêt-à-porter. And we're only haute couture here. . . . (announcing) Monsieur Oller is here. He is arrived.

Oller, a man around fifty-five, medium height, thirty-four waist, with thick glasses, talks to his assistants who have been looking, peekingly, at the crop of models from the hallway. Oller moves like an experienced stage actor, a Laurence Olivier. No hand gesture, or facial expression, or command, seems entirely casual. He is a Madame Tussaud wax statue of himself.

Woman: (starts fluttering her hands) All right. One at a time.

The ceremony that follows looks nice and simple, but is actually brutal. The models must walk out one by one, turn at the end of the room, walk the length toward Oller sitting in his chair, turn again, and walk out a side door. Sometimes he makes them do it twice. By the time they exit he has said yes or no. If this were Kabuki theater the losers would be beheaded stage right, or fall into a choppy ocean and drown.

When Todd does his walk for Oller, he feels like a basic mammal. A locomotion of muscles and bones. Is only aware of his own heavy breathing, his lungs a butterfly opening and closing tan-blue wings. He unwittingly holds his composite in one hand like a fan. When he does finally get to the end of the rug, Todd starts to limber up relievedly. Heads for the door.

Oller: (calling after him) *Comment vous appelez-vous?*

Todd: (startled, forgetting his high school French) What?

In the tenor of the old Three Stooges skit "Slowly I Turn, Step by Step," Todd walks back into the off-limits zone where Oller sits.

Oller: *Comment vous appelez-vous?*

One of his assistants swipes the card from Todd's hand and announces his name.

Todd: (catching on) Todd.

Oller: *Vous êtes de quelle taille?*

Assistant: What size are you?

Todd: A hundred eighty-one. (very very slowly) *Cent quatre-vingt-et-un.*

Oller: Wait there.

Assistant pushes Todd over to the side, where he joins a bunch of other models separated out.

When Frank walks down the middle of the room he is not easy. Does not seem to have been affected by the royal scent

164

that Oller has been spraying. Looks lunky, unhappy. His heart is not all there. Like the woman tennis player who replied, when asked why she did so poorly at the U.S. Open, "I'm not a machine."

Frank: (arriving at the dais) We already know each other. Right Peter?

The other models off to the side sputter, impressed.

Pierre: (amused) Right, right, *très bien.*

But Pierre doesn't call for his card, or point him toward the set-aside group. When Frank realizes what's happened he looks back to Todd sharp and straight. He is blaming him.

Right now as Frank walks down the circular stairs to get to the street, the unheard music changes. It's close to the tinkling dissonant piano music that plays in the next to the last section of Fassbinder's *Berlin Alexanderplatz,* when a vulnerable villain charms his best friend's girlfriend, then starts to rape her in a tilted forest that grows darker and darker as the scene wears on, as the rapist coils around the trunk of a thick tree like a snake in the Garden of Eden. The music is hollow, kindergarteny, chilling. Could be played on a toy piano.

Todd feels the shift strongly. He feels bad for Frank, guilty almost. And is afraid of what Frank will do, how he'll be the next time they meet. But his down is interrupted.

Oller: (making an arc with his hand) Now stand in line. Make a line.

The remaining models, twenty-two of them, make a semicircle. Oller tells who he wants where. He puts Todd between Alessandro and a Japanese. Then Oller starts eliminating from even this tiny circle.

Oller: I am sorry but I only need sixteen. You. (pointing) You in the white pull. Let me see you walk again. (the model walks stockily toward him) No. I'm sorry. *Je suis désolé.* You, in the red jacket. Take off your jacket. I want to see the body, *le corps.* (model steps out from the arc, takes off his red windbreaker) *Non. Je suis désolé.* (Oller counts them with his finger) *Un, deux, trois.* No. I'm sorry. No. But I only need sixteen. *Je suis désolé.*

(the assistants are whispering to him, pointing) *Un, deux, trois, quatre.* . . .

Todd is in the last sixteen. The ones left clap, the way athletes clap at the end of a sports training session.

Todd almost forgets to come home that night. He goes on appointments until seven or eight at night. Drinks with a few of the other Oller models at an imitation English pub across from the Beaubourg Museum, the glass-and-plastic museum with vacuum-cleaner-tube passageways stuck on its sides.

When Todd does get back to the apartment Lucy is already stiff asleep. At first he is relieved. He has been trekking on another planet all day. Feels funny seeing this face from the past. But once in the warm bed, filled with Lucy's musty smell, he wants to tell her how he was picked. He kisses her back to try to wake her up. But she hugs flat against the wall, angry even in her sleep that Todd never called.

He's working hard. And the harder he works the harder he gets inside. Like the Vietnam War soldiers who became so hypnotized in their work that they became less than human yet larger than life, actually killing and pillaging and raping as if they were characters in a B-movie or a B-novel. Real life is mostly B. But there, drugs were part of the cause. Drugs and money can make the bad look good.

'TIS PITY HE'S A WHORE

Todd gets up five hours later, not rested. It's seven-thirty and he has to be at work at Studio Alésia at nine-thirty. When he looks in the mirror he sees that morning face: red eyes, yellow skin, black under eyes, hair angular and wild. In a groggy panic he starts making one-by-one cosmetic adjustments. A do-it-yourself airbrushing. His morning routine has many more steps than it used to.

First Todd splashes cold water on his face, especially rinsing out his eyes. Then brushes teeth. Then squats down in tub-shower, runs hose over head, shampoos with Roger & Gallet shampoo, letting vanilla suds sink in while scrubbing body with stinging green soap, hoses off both cleansers together. Towel dries body except for hair and face. Puts special antibiotic shaving cream on face. Shaves with dulled throwaway Gillette blade so as not to make bloody cuts. After shave, puts on special astringent to close the skin pores. Rubs a dab of Tenax in hair Vitalis-style to give some greasy definition to hair without going too far into slickness. Applies orange skin cream on face to keep skin moist and a little tan. Drops Murine in eyes. Under eyes spreads white Nivea cream to camouflage black circles.

Next he takes his medicines. Improved multivitamins and minerals supplement in a natural base. Natural chewable Vitamin C with acerola. Surgam Acide Tiaprofénique for middle ear infection plus antibiotic nose spray. Boric acid for right armpit fungal infection plus antifungal cream. Butterscotch-flavored cough medicine with codeine.

Gets dressed. Tight fitting blue T-shirt. Old blue jeans. Black Adidas sneakers with heavy raspberry socks. Not necessary to wear Tony Lama cowboy boots today for added height because booking is already confirmed. Tan twill sweater over T-shirt. Green Army jacket with padded shoulders and an orange marksman's patch on the sleeve.

Todd leaves at eight-thirty and takes the metro, breaking the usual rule of metros to go-sees, taxis to jobs. He is the replacement in the middle of a three-day shooting of ski clothes for a catalog. Three other guys and two girls are already sitting around in the dressing room when he arrives. Todd sits on one of the folding wood chairs and starts to wait. Didn't bring anything to read. Is trying to ride out the fear of boredom, the mounting panic of it.

Jay, who wears a diamond stud in his right ear when dancing at night at the nightclub Elysée Matignon, removes it by day, is reading a spy thriller about double agents in Nazi Germany.

Jay: (complaining) I can't get shit from this book, or any book but Stephen King. He rules.

A Swedish girl with yellow hair sits on Ron's lap. Ron is a twenty-two-year-old tennis champ, over 6'2", with Mount Rushmore good looks. The Swedish girl puts her tongue in his ear.

Todd: (sarcastic) Is it nine in the morning or nine at night?

Jay: Ron likes to fool around with women a lot. But when it gets down to some serious fucking, that's when I arrive on the scene. Flash! Like a bat out of hell. She's from Sweden. They don't care about fucking either. Everything's a blue movie, or a yellow movie. I've been there. Bo-ring.

Swedish Girl: Where are you from then? Fuck heaven?

Jay: Portland, Oregon. Did you ever see *The Shining*? I used to go skiing at that lodge.

The Swedish girl leaves Ron's lap, sits down on her own chair. Jay then sits on her lap, facing in, making mouth-watering sounds. Ron returns to reading *The Real War* by Richard Nixon.

Todd: (to Ron, trying to shift the base of operations) What is the real war?

Ron: This guy's theory is that the real war is with Communism, and that it started in 1945, even earlier than 1945. I'm amazed at how many facts he's got in the first sixteen pages.

Matt is reading a novel about a computer miscalculation that almost plunged the world into a nuclear holocaust. He's a Jew from South Dakota who was in the Marines four years. He's dressed today in fatigues.

Matt: (not concentrating on his book) Hey break it up. Break it up. (to Swedish girl) Teach me some more of those dirty words you were teaching me yesterday. I wrote them down in my matchbook.

Matt recovers his matchbook and shows the Swedish words to Jay who pushes him away.

Cindy, twenty-four, blond hair, dressed like a baseball player, props herself up on the long dressing counter in a haze of pop-bulb lighting. She looks over Todd's shoulder while he tears through *Être beau*, a French translation of the American picture book of male models, *Looking Good*, photos by Bruce Weber.

Cindy: I hear you're from P.A. Me, too. I'm from Hershey.

Todd: I used to go there on the tour of the Hershey Kisses factory.

Cindy: (a contrived slinkiness) I haven't really been working so much in Paris. Neither has my roommate. (motioning with her head to the Swede) We got this job because we met the photographer, Patrick, at Matignon. I just don't have that many photographs yet. I think I'm going to Milan next week. I hear it's easy for someone like me to get work there and get photos. (stage voice) But I'm not going to sleep with anyone to get a job. (intimate again) Do you have a girlfriend?

Todd: Yup. Here in Paris.

Cindy: Then I want you as a friend. Do you go out?

Todd: Well I've been to a couple bars.

Cindy: Can I come with you sometimes?

Todd: (starting to pull back a little now) Yeah. Sometime. But I'm going home tonight.

Cindy: Me too.

Todd: Where do you live?

Cindy: We live in a dirty hotel room near Odéon. It's a disgusting mouse house.

The makeup man has arrived with his big red metal kit that looks like a box of tools. He is already smoothing his black hands over the face of Cindy's roommate. The three guys are looking for baseball scores in a copy of the *Herald-Tribune*.

Cindy: (going on inconsistently) I'm so poor in Paris and I love it. I love living like a tramp.

Todd: How old are you?

Cindy: Twenty-four. But I pretend I'm twenty. I act like a little girl, especially around middle-agers. My boyfriend in New York is forty. He's in the music business. I don't like men my own age. I think they're silly and immature. (then) Do you love your girlfriend?

Todd: I haven't thought about that in a while. I've been working so hard. It's like I can't do both at once.

Cindy: Hmmmm. I hope you don't end up alone.

Todd: Would that be the worst thing in the world?

Cindy: Yes. Didn't you know?

Around ten Patrick Martory shows. He's wearing a blue-silver jumpsuit and giant goggle glasses. His frizzy sizzling blond hair makes him look like Fearless Fly. He is as speedy and funny as a comedian in a French comedy, the kind screened on Air France flights. If he doesn't have anything funny to say, he says whatever he needs to say faster so that it sounds funny.

The six now have to tramp out onto a demarcated white snowy zone, tissue paper, with the catalog logo behind them, a big K. In one shot Todd stands off to the side, on skis, bending and swaying, pretending to ski with his poles twisted up behind his neck. In another he flirts with the Swede who gets carried away and kisses him on the cheek, leaving a rouge smudge, which a woman assistant wipes away with a Kleenex, making her kiss Todd then on his other cheek, then wiping that, to make both sides the same tint. Todd is standing off to the side smiling mellifluously at the camera.

Ron: (nudging him rough) Who are you relating to?

Todd can't answer that question. Feels the cogs of his own stomach stripping themselves of their gears. He just can't hack it today. The out-of-body feeling he first felt on Louis's balcony that first day keeps coming back. Each time differently but the same. Not just the camera, but now the other models, the backdrop, all are magnifying mirrors, funhouse style, of the condition his condition is in.

Lunch is more than lunch, it's a birthday party for Patrick. The client's assistant brings in a cake with candles and lots of champagne. He made salaam bows earlier to Todd when he was buckling his ski boots. Todd dubbed him on both shoulders with his ski pole.

Todd: (to Cindy) I gotta get outta here.

Cindy: There's one more shot. But you do look crazed.

Todd: I'm just waking up.

Cindy: (handing him a cup) Smell the coffee.

Ron and Jay are making jokes to each other.

Ron: Do you have a match?

Jay: Yeah. Your face and a buffalo fart. (makes sound effects)

By now Todd has swallowed three glasses of champagne, three cups of coffee, smoked five or six cigarettes. The studio secretary, a Phyllis Diller, peeks in, giggles at the mad mad mad mad whirl, disappears, shows up again, suggests in broken language that Cindy take Todd to a vacant room upstairs.

Studio Secretary: (proud of the phrase) Try him on for size.

Todd takes Cindy by the hand and leads her upstairs, finds an empty storage room, they rustle in and sit among the abandoned boxes. He feels as if he's going to puke.

Cindy: I'm glad to see these shoots make you crazy. They make me the same way, the same crazy. I thought I was the only one.

Todd and Cindy fade out together for a half hour.

TALKING TREE

Todd is standing on a hill in the Bois de Boulogne. Far away, the sound of motos driven up and around rotted tree trunks. He's barefoot in Lee jeans, five o'clock, in a wind, eating tomatoes out of a picnic basket with two girls and another guy. The photographer is set up behind a tripod down the slope a few steps, wearing a red beret.

Todd wanders off. Comes to a thick gray tree trunk, its slices of bark as hard as house shingles. He touches his one hand on the bark. A bird clatters the branches above, branches where a few leaves are growing, stuck on by rubbery stems, arranged like notes on a scale. Todd hears the tree talk to him. Well not exactly. The voice is inside. As thoughts. But the thoughts are audible, the way they are in a dream, dubbed over a scene where no lips are moving at all.

Tree: Don't worry Todd. You have to give up worrying. You have to be free. Free to be brutal. Free to be tender. A man is as alone as a tree. Stuck in his aloneness. Don't worry.

Todd walks away from the tree, and back to the shoot. He doesn't know anybody, really, there.

Todd: I could have sworn that tree just talked to me about how everybody is as alone as a tree.

Ha-ha-ha. The photographer's assistant translates to the photographer and everyone has a good time.

Alex: (young angel-headed American model, on his prep school rugby team until he ran away to do this) He's crazy. He's crazy. Take his picture.

EMOTIONAL PILLOWS

Todd is home by nine. But no one is around. Jackie's room is dark. A light is on in the bedroom, but Lucy obviously just made a mess getting dressed then left in a hurry. No note.

Todd walks around without stopping. He can't sit down, or lie down. He even looks in the closets the way you look for a pet cat that might be stuck under some clothes, or that might have climbed inadvertently into a refrigerator before the door shut it in a temporary Siberia. No Lucy.

Todd sits up for an hour watching French TV on Jackie's set. It's a show on the government arts channel—three men in suits are heatedly discussing some latinate concept word. Todd understands next to nothing, and finally brushes his teeth. His heart itself is a rumpled bed.

In the middle of the night Lucy sneaks in. This time Todd is turned to the wall. At first he is too stubborn to ask where she was. She lies next to him perspiring through her cotton T-shirt pretending to sleep, but her heart is going pit-pat from too many cigarettes.

Todd: (finally barging through to her) Where were you? It's the middle of the night. And I'm here alone, not knowing where you were.

Lucy: I was with Frank. He was upset because Sharon's found another guy. (almost shouting) *Because Frank was not the emotional pillow he should have been.*

Todd: (snapping shut) Fine.

More minutes go by.

Todd: (pushing again for a truth he can feel hidden) Is that fine?

Lucy: (putting her hand soothingly on the side of his skull) Don't make me start talking. There's no time.

Todd: That's right. And tomorrow I have to work all day.

Lucy: (sitting up) Then where were you before at dinnertime?

Todd: I don't want to tell you.

All of a sudden Lucy starts crying and crying. It just comes out.

Lucy: This won't work. This won't work. We're not compatible.

She is crying these words. Todd doesn't know where to begin.

Lucy: It's miserable here.

Todd: (mean) Stop it please.

Lucy: I will stop it. I'll stop this.

Todd: No. Stop that, not this.

Lucy: You don't know what you're talking about.

Neither of them can really get to sleep. The birds start up outside in the morning like annoying newscasters on a clock radio. The daylight keeps getting turned up, turned up, turned up. As if voltage rather than wattage.

Todd stands up again and washes up again and can't take it. Lucy's head is under her pillow. She is an uncovered sleeping body with a big pillow for a head. Like a Halloween kid with a gruesome bag over its head. Like the victim of a crime of passion.

Todd: (ready to leave, standing over her body, in jeans, sneaks and a raincoat, speaking softly) Lucy. Home is a jungle more savage than any of Nature's. It has its own diamond-headed snakes and red ants. Living together is a mortal expedition.

No response.

MONSIEUR SAINT-LAURENT

Todd walks into M. Ricard's office at Saint-Laurent. He sits down on a sofa. Then M. Ricard and the other fitting model for the morning, David, walk in.

David is a young guy from somewhere on Long Island. He is no taller than Todd, has dark skin eyes and hair, and a curved nose that juts out. He's dressed like an American suburban high school student in gray cords, white shirt, white socks, black penny Loafers.

M. Ricard has white hair, is dressed in a deep-blue distinguished suit made of the kind of fine corduroy that blurs into velvet. He is a haughty coyote. His two assistants follow right behind, both of them in new tan Saint-Laurent sportscoats made to look like safari jackets.

M. Ricard: Well today Todd you are lucky. It is an all-American morning. You two are American. And the man here, the manufacturer, is an American too. So you will be able to follow along. (claps both hands together, almost like Oller's woman) So you two will dress in here. They (nodding to two assistants) will dress you (nodding head back to Todd and David).

M. Ricard sweeps on out of the room, unsteadily, like the fidgeting hysterical broom of the sorcerer's apprentice in *Fantasia*. Todd and David sit on the couch in the shadowy office, no lights turned on yet, as the businessmen begin to arrive and sit around a big rectangular table in the next room.

Todd: (yawn-talking) How do you like Europe?

David: Not so much to do. Not enough girls I can get my hands on yet.

Todd: Why did Soupy send you here?

David: My picture came out in *Puritan*. It's a skin magazine. I did them before I got into modeling, a year ago. So he wanted me out of the country for a while.

Todd looks away. He's tired of talking to other models. David doesn't seem that interested in Todd either.

Then the assistants enter, flourishing lots of clothes on hangers that they lay over the desk and office chairs. They get the two young men dressed. Todd has a yellow stain on his BVDs that he tries to keep in shadow. His T-shirt collar is also stained, maybe with soup.

The models are sent out, one at a time. Todd walks back and

forth across the room, watching the eyes of the men in suits, the regular men, watching him. He feels like the woman in the Maidenform bra ad walking nude across a conference room table. M. Ricard obviously doesn't get on with the manufacturer, a man with a Southern accent, short brown silky hair, jowls, dressed in a brown suit that is not Saint-Laurent. All the manufacturer's factories are in France, so he spends about seven months a year here. He doesn't budge much, while M. Ricard is always moving, either twitching or getting out of his chair or gesturing nervous finger taps on air.

M. Ricard: Todd. Tell me the truth now. Would you buy this sweater you are wearing?

Todd: (looking down at the white heavy sweater he has on over yellow silk corduroys, his feet lost in the oversized pink bucks beneath) No.

M. Ricard: Good. Go away.

Todd rolls his eyes at David who is coming out of the office in a tweed overcoat, his hair all wet. David must have run into the bathroom while Todd was out wearing the ugly sweater with his hair dry. The assistants give Todd a pink starched shirt, they tie on a tie with a bugle design, and he wears black pants. Same pink bucks. David is executing a dance-strut out there, bounces back charged. Todd's not. He walks out and M. Ricard does it again.

M. Ricard: Todd. Tell me the truth. Would you ever buy these pants in America? Or in France for that matter?

Todd: (hasn't bought dress trousers in five years) No.

M. Ricard: I can see you share my taste. Perhaps you too should be an executive at Saint-Laurent.

But now the manufacturer, who has been breathing in harder and harder, decides to strike out. These little exchanges between M. Ricard and Todd are costing him his Alfa Romeo, his airline tickets to Alabama at Christmas, his daughter's medical insurance, his nights in Pigalle buying dark women who stir up some dull enchantment in his mind.

Manufacturer: (sloppily rising) I think our problem here is not my clothes, it's your model. Look at him. He's too small. What's the point of bothering to have a model who doesn't fit the clothes? And look. (he squeezes Todd in the shoulders, actually pressing in severely) He's all bunched up in his shoulders. I can feel the knots, like knots in a rope. (sits down again) That comes from weightlifting. (Todd stews) Plus all our clients are not pretty boys, they're men, on the street.

M. Ricard gasps, hyperbolically.

M. Ricard: (to manufacturer) I do not condone your opinion, your image, of the Saint-Laurent customer. It is so so-so. Here. You want to see men-on-the-street in your clothes. These with you, they are men-on-the-street. They are overweight, plain, serious, tired, soft, brutal men. Let's see them in your ordinary men-of-the-street fashions. (shouts out like a drill officer) Go ahead! (claps hands again)

The manufacturer's three colleagues stand up uncomfortably, pushed between the two heavies at the conference, as Todd has just been pushed. They lumber over to the coatrack, and M. Ricard dresses them in sportscoats and motions them to walk toward the manufacturer who glares, most of his skin burning under his clothes. The enlisted models stand sheepishly around in big lumpy jackets, showing embarrassment by their fluctuating Adam's apples. Todd just hangs there, one hand fluttering on a tabletop corner.

Manufacturer: (ruffled) Saint-Laurent's pants did not sell very well last year. They were nothing.

M. Ricard: (pouting theatrically) Nothing. (walks over to the three *mal à l'aise* recruits) This gentleman says that the Saint-Laurent pants are nothing. (louder) Nothing. (barking the command) Sit down.

So the three find their chairs, noisily. And M. Ricard starts pacing. He will not stop pacing for the rest of the hour.

M. Ricard: (his chalky complexion turning pink) You have such a gift for language. That you can with the simple word "nothing" sum up everything that is to be said about the pants of Saint-Laurent. I see this gift. I see it in the name of your own line. "New Classical Line." But, excuse me, could you explain how you arrived at this nice name?

Manufacturer: (trying to control his mouth) No. I forget.

M. Ricard: Because to me the two words seem to be opposites, to erase one another. I mean new is new. And classical to me is the fables of La Fontaine, perhaps, or the essays of the *philosophes,* of Voltaire, the author as well of *Candide.* Are you familiar with these?

Manufacturer: No. Let's get on with the show.

The show lasts for three more hours. Todd and David alternate, with plenty of interruptions from M. Ricard.

M. Ricard: (during one of his lectures) Last year you made some very successful designs. You and your company. So successful, unfortunately, that this year you have just made the same designs in different materials. Taking last year's cotton (his hand now on Todd's sleeved arm) and redoing it this year in wool. But what you fail to recognize is that when you have changed the material you have changed everything. Suddenly a belt that meant something in cotton looks like a donkey's tail in wool.

Manufacturer: I don't see the difference at all. I think you're different. Nervous because your pants did so bad this year.

M. Ricard dismisses the models, signing their manila *affiches.* While they are dressing, he puts on his own fashion show for the manufacturer, taking on a character he names "Monsieur Saint-Laurent," a kind of rich man's man-on-the-street. He models in succession three or four old Saint-Laurent coats that have worked in the past and that he considers epitome. He accompanies the show with a running commentary.

M. Ricard: Here is Monsieur Saint-Laurent taking a stroll in the Bois de Boulogne in his new training jacket.

He makes complete pirouettes and dramatic turnarounds, as if turning his heel vengefully in the manufacturer's gut.

Todd: (to David, as they lean in the doorway) You think he's suffering from lead poisoning?

David: (more impressed) No way. We could learn our shit from this man.

BETRAYAL AND/OR BALANCE

Frank's looking good today. Fresh. His hair is pushed back from his shiny waxy forehead. Is wearing a blue short jacket with the Yankees NY symbol on the back, blue jeans, springy white Nike sneaks, cut low, a light-blue stripe, a chevron, on the canvas sides. He's coming home after posing as a groom for the cover of a brides' magazine.

Frank's apartment is on one of the streets that veers up to the right at a juncture where a V-shaped café fits just beyond the Odéon hotel. Most of the buildings along the street are five stories, pigeon-gray, busily shuttered, as finely textured as corrugated cardboard, topped with maids' rooms' gables.

Lucy is standing outside his building waiting for him. Her hair today is a floozy black chaos, an exploded puff bomb, and her eyes are switch-hitting so you can't quite tell where she's looking. She has on a Leatherette jacket (tannish orange, the color and texture of the banquettes in Le Drugstore, the Woolworth's of Paris), a short black corduroy dress, black imitation-lace stockings, and low white pumps.

Frank puts his arm around her at her shoulders, and pulls her toward him. She goes along. He can smell the smell of plastic (the smell that permeates American shampoo) in her hair, and something within him moves. Something that feels like love yet is not love. As homonyms are words that sound alike yet have different meanings.

They walk down the cool long dank narrow confining protecting hall. Release themselves into Frank's smelly apartment. The only furniture is still the mattress, so Lucy sits down on it and inhales the stank. She likes that male mammal smell today. Is in one of her mouth-watering moods again.

Frank: (standing over her, taking off sneaks, laces already untied, by rubbing one foot against the other for leverage) So what's up?

Lucy: Todd's show is up. Are we going?

Frank: (squatting down in front of her) You had to mention that didn't you? (stretches back out on the floor) You want to get me going? Is that what you're into today? (he's only kidding at belligerence)

Lucy: (basic Marlene Dietrich accent) Yes. I want you to march over me like the German army over the plains of Europe.

Frank: You turn me on. . . . But I don't like your boyfriend anymore.

Lucy: Just because he got the part and you didn't?

Frank: No. Just because he's not the same. Not to me and not to you.

Lucy: (stretching seductively back on bed) It's true. He didn't even come home until late one night.

Frank pushes her down farther, and for about ten seconds lies on top of her, then rolls off.

Frank: Come and get me.

Lucy: (wriggling toes) You playing or what?

Frank: Come . . . and . . . get . . . me . . .

Lucy: You've sure got animal magnetism today.

Frank: Show me your little tongue.

Lucy rolls over sideways, unzips Frank's zipper, separates the oval of his cloth underwear fly, lets his round balls pop out, with hairs sprouting, black thorny hairs. Then she puts her tongue on the balls and starts licking around and around. While Lucy is wetting and softening Frank's balls, she keeps looking up at him with a delirious little-girl look that gets to him, is powerful in its powerlessness.

Frank lies back and unsnaps his jeans and pulls them down more, and the shorts along with them. Then he pushes Lucy's head down on his up cock. She loves the strong rhubarb taste.

180

Todd usually goes down on her, while she draws him in, like a *Dionaea muscipula,* the swamp flower commonly known as the Venus flytrap. This new position has her all heated up. She comes up to gulp air.

Lucy: (aha) This is what it's all about.

Frank: (playing, pushes her back down) Down bitch, swallow bitch.

Lucy swallows and swallows, as if she is swallowing a rope that won't stop uncoiling in her insides.

Frank: (hands back behind head) Take off your clothes.

Lucy, disoriented, stumbles out of her clothes. Frank stands up and presses her against a wall. As so often in train stations, after rush hour, at ten or eleven at night, when a guy in his hooded pullover and jeans and big sneakers is pushing a girl with tiny red heels into a giant stiff pillar, the railway cavern filling up with a roaring of trains from a nearby gate.

But Lucy and Frank are not in a train station, so they can finally orgasm that way. Frank still has his T-shirt on, his jeans down around his ankles. Lucy's nude. She feels the heat of the electric heater warming up one side of her calf, and the rest is just numb. The more she gives in to this supposedly physical sensation, the less she actually feels of most of her body, could be lying on a bed of nails. Slowly, though, feeling, and its little pains, returns.

Frank and Lucy sit or lounge down around and on the mattress. He places her hand on his bare foot and she squeezes mindlessly into its bottom muscles so that all the other muscles in the body which are tied into a knot there will relax.

Lucy: (first to speak) You know what song I'd like to hear now?

Frank: (no need to be clever) No.

Lucy: I'd like to hear "Alfie." I think that's my favorite song of all time. (she sings) "What's it all about, Alfie? Is it just for the moment we live? What's it all about? When we sort it out, Alfie? La dee da da dee da da dee da." That's all I remember.

Frank: That's beautiful honey.

Quiet, for five, ten minutes. Then Lucy stands up and swipes Frank's black cashmere coat from his closet. She spreads it on the bed and lies down, her cheek grazing the wool. Every so often she wraps herself inside.

Frank: (emotional) I love feeling that I own you.

THE VOW IN THE COUSCOUS RESTAURANT

Later that evening Todd and Lucy walk down into Pigalle to have some couscous supper in one of the greasy-spoon Arab restaurants along the Boulevard de Clichy. They sit at a wooden table in a hepatitic light against a wall covered in dirty red silk alongside a bleary window that takes up most of the entire front wall of the haunt.

Todd knows that something is up.

Todd: What did you do today?

Lucy: (her mouth filled with teeny grains) Saw Socrates.

Todd: (through the fingerprinted window catches sight of a vinyl red ass disappearing around a corner) Wha?

Lucy: An old man in the Gare de Lyon with white hair and shaggy clothes yelling at everyone for making too much money.

Todd: (irritated) Don't change the subject.

Lucy: How can I change it? There wasn't any subject to start with.

Todd: (prosecuting attorney) But you saw Frank, too. And you haven't told me one word about that.

Lucy: If you saw Frank and Socrates on the same day who would you talk about first?

Todd: You smelled like Right Guard when you got back.

Lucy: (pretending to give in) Oh okay. I know what you want to say. And then I'll say blah-blah back. And you'll say blah-blah-blah. And there'll be some slap. Is that what you want?

Todd: Do you know any way around it?

182

Lucy: Yeah. Look at Socrates. Or Mahatma Gandhi. Or Queen Victoria. They had fantasies of themselves like no one ever had before. And they lived them out. Every lunch, or dinner, or phone call they handled differently than anyone ever had before.

Todd: (only hearing an anachronism) Lucy! The phone wasn't even invented then.

Lucy: (coming down heavily on the word) Meaning . . . meaning we can handle this whole Frank thing differently. We don't have to be soap-opera actors about it.

They finish their plates filled with steaming pale yellow crushed grains of couscous covered in chips of brown lamb. Todd is digesting both the food and Lucy's curious maxims. She lights up a Gitane and passes it to Todd. He tokes.

Lucy: Let's take a vow. Just so we feel securer.

Todd: A wedding vow? Now?

Lucy: No just a vow vow.

Todd: (amazed) In the middle of this crisis you want to take a vow? You blow me away. Don't you have any feelings?

Lucy: (as if to a dummy) Todd. I'm trying to get us into our higher feelings. Trust me.

Todd: (with a weakness for the surprising) Okay.

So Lucy slips a safety pin from the inside of her belt that she's kept stuck there for emergencies. Holding Todd's thumb over his halvah cake, she pricks it so that a jewel of crimson blood dots up. Then she pricks her own. Then they mix the blood, like two teenage boys. The Arab waiters smile hysterically.

The couple just sits there for a while in the new calm.

Todd: I do feel better. Can't say why. Maybe because we can each interpret this vow any way we want. Or maybe I just needed a bloodletting.

Lucy: (knowingly) Or maybe it works.

The mood outside is pretty strong. The people in crowds are developing excited looks in their eyes as the night thickens. Arab teenagers, transvestites, an old Scottish couple with gray skin, tourist buses mainly for Germans and Japanese, fat people with hanging cheeks, scrawny vendors for the bottomless shows, pickpockets, everybody just burning. Some of them turn unexpectedly from what they are pursuing to burn laser looks at Todd and Lucy right through the muffled window, its visibility not much better than Lucy's plastic-covered window on Bleecker Street.

POWERFUL UNCHECKED NARCISSISM OF THE YOUNG

At noon the next day Frank and Todd are walking down the Boulevard de Clichy. The mellow Paris sun gives a muted tender quiet feeling to this otherwise Times Square *quartier.*

Frank is dressed all in shades of yellow, Todd in black and red. They are keeping their weekly swim date even though both feel like unflung grenades.

Todd: (pointing at the other side of the street) That's where Lucy and I took our vow last night. Couscous and blood.

Frank: (spitting) I don't want to hear about it.

Boulevard de Clichy turns into Boulevard Rochechouart. Clichy's free municipal pool is housed in an old armory. The two shuffle silently down into the cold wet locker room. Dank. Gray. The floor sloshed with a thin layer of mildewy smelly water. All the mirrors steamed up from the showers. It's not too crowded now. Lunchtime. The two change into their Speedos, Frank's orange, Todd's white, and head to the swimming pool.

Todd lowers himself into the pool at the shallow end and starts a rhythm of stroke swimming, arms over head, hands cupped, legs kicking. The more laps he does, the more his eyes burn, and the louder the hum in his sinews. Frank is a diver. He climbs over and over up the high tower, diving down frontward, with one or two spins, and one one-and-a-halfer, piercing the surface of the water dangerously close to Todd swimming in the next lane. The green bottom of the pool is striped with straight lines that appear to undulate.

Frank stretches out on a bench. He's leaning back with his legs out on either side. Todd walks over, dripping, and sits facing him on the same bench, pulling his legs up in an A frame (arms used as the crossbar) in front of him.

Todd: (gloating) So the vow was that Lucy pricked her thumb and my thumb and we mixed the blood. In that Turkish atmosphere.

Frank: (burning) I don't believe it.

Todd: What's not to believe? Unless Lucy has been feeding you other information. Has she? Is she a double agent?

The swimming hall, huge, is filled with echoing shouting splashing sounds, like the ones on a stereo demo album, *Sounds in Space,* given away free with the first stereos in the 1950s: you could hear the sounds of footsteps walking closer out of one speaker then walking away into the other speaker; the record cover pictured a transmitter sending waves—parallel parentheses—out into a purple solar system with red planets and yellowish-white moons.

Todd: (starting up again, more directly this time) I have reason to believe you're screwing my Lucy.

Frank: (purposely bad-acting) That's wacko. I think we have to put you on a pill. How could you say that to me? Your big brother?

Todd: Lucy even admitted it.

Frank squeezes his palm on the back of Todd's softened neck and rubs up and down at the even bottom of his haircut.

Frank: (sycophantic) You're my idol. I would never screw your girlfriend. If I did, I swear you could cut off my donkey dick and I'd eat it. Let's go see her right now and ask.

Back in the locker room a dozen high school kids are indulging in the powerful unchecked narcissism of the young. One swimmer stands in front of a shower-room mirror, smoking a cigarette that's almost too big for him, wearing a jungle-print bathing suit. He watches himself from many angles, shaking his head to rearrange his hair, then puffing again, examining, posing. He seems most satisfied with his hair when it falls down in shocks like Elvis Presley's, and when he holds his cigarette between his thumb and first finger. Next to him his friend does chin-ups in the frame of the doorway to the john.

Todd paces around the long bench, walking around in rectangles, while Frank is fastidiously changing out of his trunks and into his street clothes. The more that Frank denies the truth, the more Todd's insides whirl in a storm, like Cremora dropped in a cup of coffee. He finally stops pacing only when he bangs his knee against a corner of the bench.

Todd: (shouting, simultaneous with the knee bang) You hit me where it hurts. I felt it. You can't deny it.

Frank: (starting to lose it now too, embarrassed at this public cat fight in front of the young toughs) I'll hit you in the fucking face then. I'll punch you in the fucking face and you know I can do that when the ropes are cut. You don't want a giant machine exploding in your face, a big fart exploding in your face, do you punk wimp?

Todd shows his teeth, his lips curling back like a rubber band stretched to its limits.

He is sick from self-expression. Has to get out of there. So he opens his locker and methodically puts on his clothes, no shower, no nothing. Walks out without saying a word to Frank.

Frank: (shouting after him, maybe worried) Hey bozo!

Todd doesn't see a thing. Walks as if he is marching. Thud thud thud thud. Back down Boulevard Rouchechouart. Past the Anvers pissoir, the sun making its fluted roof gold, its green rusty metal walls speckled. Past the movie theater crowded all over, inside lobby, outside door, at the posters, with locals, mostly Arabs. The movie is *Master Bruce Lee: Conqueror of the Manchurians.*

Frank is on Todd's trail. Runs out of the swimming hall, his bag strap slipping off his shoulder. Stops at a phone stall to quickly call Lucy.

Frank: Lucy. He knows.

Lucy: (noncommittal) Yeah?

Frank: And I know.

Lucy: Know what? You're talking like Maxwell Smart, sweetie.

Frank: I know about the vow.

Lucy: (sighs a full sigh) Frank. We're in this over our heads. It's yucky. Please try a little tenderness. I feel yucked up. Totally.

Frank: Okay. I'll cut it out. . . . For now.

Todd keeps in the same direction, toward Place Blanche. Stops for a *demi* at La Nuit, a honky-tonk café. There is a soldier at the table. Two fat men seem to be introducing Gallic johns to Arab boys. The music from the violet jukebox is Italian love songs, crooning. One boy leans against a Barbarella pinball machine. He resembles, from the waist up, early Frank Sinatra, wearing a striped blue mafia coat with double buttons, but his crinkly burgundy pants give him away as not.

Todd glugs down a gold smooth thick ale, as unaware of drinking as he was of walking. Frank turns into the café and confronts him at the bar. He orders them two beers. They are both trembling, using emotional muscles that have long been slack.

Frank: (as if talking to a far wall) Okay. I did screw Lucy one time. Because she was lonely. Here in Paris. Under my roof. But it won't happen again. (voice drops a third of an octave) And I was lonely because of Sharon.

Todd: (voice box crackling) You were lonely cause you missed my ass.

SACRÉ COEUR

When Lucy intercepts Frank's phone call from the street, she has on only a black bra and beige-colored panties. Has already drawn a bath in the powder-blue porcelain tub. After their short talk, she climbs into the clear broth and settles. The heat rises through her as it does through a piece of bread in a toaster. The warmer she gets inside, the more she sweats, enjoying rubbing her hands over her oily skin.

Lucy stands up, dripping, in the compact tub. Steps out, letting hot water droplets drop on the pink mat with tan shag border on the tile floor. She wraps up in a gray, high-tech towel, and shimmies on her toes to the bedroom. Lets the towel fall off and walks about the room nude. Picks out white clothes from the closet—white blouse, white dress skirt, white shoes, white leather purse. Dressed, she sticks a veil and a pair of gloves into the purse.

Lucy walks up Rue Lepic. It's dusk and the steep incline is filled with shoppers. The electric light in the stores grows stronger and brighter as the sunlight dims. Lucy keeps walking toward Montmartre. She is soon at the bottom of many stone steps that lead up to Sacré Coeur, a nineteenth-century oriental fantasia tourist spot of a church that looks like it belongs in Constantinople. Lucy is on her way to Saturday-night mass. She ascends the steps while bells are ringing that cause steeple birds to fly up in a temporary holding pattern for a few minutes until the vibrating stops and they can roost again. A trolley, like a ski lift, transports passengers up the declivitous hill. But Lucy prefers to walk. She might as well be at Lourdes, fastening the veil on her head, and muffling her hands in little white gloves, with the piety of a Spanish village teenage girl.

Lucy enters, taps the cool holy water on her forehead, sits on one of the severe wooden-plank benches. The lighting is harsh, almost fluorescent, from above, like the lighting in a department store. The altar is covered in a polyester linen that's stitched with simple gold designs of eagles and crosses and chalices and lambs. Slowly the front twenty or so rows fill up with parishioners who prefer this early Saturday-night mass to the Sunday festal mass. They want to get it over with. Lots of beat women. Women with their children. A big gray-suited fat man leading his wife and three children. Some tall thin members of a Catholic school basketball team sitting all in a row up front, nonchalantly.

The priest enters abruptly, flicking his white skirt, with two altar boys assisting. A laywoman from the congregation with a turtleneck gray cashmere top and gray skirt leads the singing, into the microphone, of old Lutheran hymns adapted to Roman Catholic uses. The mass is in French, not Latin. Lucy doesn't know what's being said, but she doesn't care. She likes sitting in this damp cave. She likes the absence of fancy people. The crowd is like the traditional populace of her Lower East Side. At the climax, she steps forward in a patrolled line, sticks out her tongue, almost bratlike, and takes on the white wafer, letting it melt slowly in her mouth as she crosses herself and returns to her bench. Her heart is warm and gooey. An old-fashioned lamp has been lit in her chest cavity.

The mass ends fast, and everyone is up and out of there in a noisy racket. No coffee hour, no chatting among families. This is not a small-town or suburban parish. It's more like the Catholic churches near train stations in big cities that draw anonymous travelers. The sanctuary is a big waiting room.

Lucy walks back out into the blue-black air, a bit chilly. She clacks in her white pumps down the many stairs to the bottommost landing. Finds a corner café and calls home. Todd answers.

Todd: Where were you?

Lucy: Church.

Todd: (confused) Church? You've never done that the whole while I've known you.

189

Lucy: I feel fresh now. (only half-kidding) Washed in the blood of the lamb.

Todd: (reassured by that eccentric remark that it's the same old Lucy) I just want you to know that it's between me and Frank. Always was. Has nothing to do with you. He used you as a pawn. I don't blame you. You don't know all the facts, don't want to.

Lucy: (appreciating the easy out) I want to eat lamb.

Todd: (suddenly overly jovial) Get real.

Lucy: (back on track) I am. I want to eat at one of those shish kebab places in Pigalle.

Todd: No.

Lucy: Then at one of the big two-story red fish restaurants. Let's have a meal. I'm dressed.

Todd: Okay. I'll meet you in twenty minutes. At the one next to the movie theater at Place de Clichy. You know what? I bought a Henry Miller novel today called *Quiet Days in Clichy*.

Lucy: (expletively) Too much.

An hour later they are sitting at a white-clothed table on the second floor of a vast tinkling restaurant eating sea urchins, those round balls with black porcupine pins sticking out, sliced red cabbage with lemon, vinaigrette, *steak frites*, and *crème fraîche* with dainty poinsettias of strawberries sprinkled over. They drink two cold sweet bottles of white wine.

All the while, Lucy, her hair tonight as wildly curly as Robespierre's, expounds gustily on the validity of the "trans" doctrines, transubstantiation and transfiguration.

PENSÉES

Frank has been frying in a pan of lust for the last few hours. He is lying on his mattress in just a flannel bathrobe. Rubbing his balls. Licking his palm and pulling at that little hat of flesh, resembling a Saxon helmet, the head of his cut cock. The apartment windows are blackening.

Frank: (out loud, whining) What's wrong with me?

He walks over to his half-refrigerator and takes out a little bottle of Alsatian beer. Opens the top with an opener hanging on a nearby nail. Then shuts off the kitchenette light and stands in front of the blank window drinking the beer. Stalks around his bed as disconnectedly as Todd had paced rectangles around the gym bench earlier.

Frank phones Lucy. Jackie answers.

Jackie: *Allo? Oui?*

Frank: Jackie. Frank. Is Lucy there?

Jackie: No they went to dinner.

Frank: Together.

Jackie: *Tous les deux.*

Frank: (after a long nothing) Do you have any of the black pills?

Jackie: I can give you four or five black ones. If you meet me at the Tuileries at nine. The moon is full tonight.

Frank arrives at the park on time. The moon lights the lacy buildings so they glow elegantly. Only one light is on in the entire Louvre complex, up at maid's-room level. Perhaps a dowager empress lives there. Or a janitress. Frank paces up and down the gravel paths, past statues, past gold fences, past perverts cruising. It's too late for tourists. Sits down on what looks to be a pure shadow molded in the shape of a bench. Eventually

Jackie arrives, all wrapped in scarves, a draped statue in transit. He sits down next to Frank.

Jackie takes four black pills out of his billowing white quilt full-length coat and passes them to Frank. Just then a cop van roars up.

Jackie: (paranoid) *Viens vite.*

After their quick exit from the gardens, Jackie guides Frank on a tour of the different prostitute promenades in Paris. He wants Frank to find someone to take home to fuck so he can watch. Along the way they stop often at different *tabacs* for a glass of Vichy each for pill-popping.

First. Near Opéra. Regular women street prostitutes dressed like extras for *Irma la Douce*—red dresses, overt makeup, tight black tops, fishnet stockings, flirting musically with *les gendarmes, les flics.*

Second. Montmartre. Where transvestite whores solicit from doorways and stairwells. They are thinner, younger, darker than the Opéra ladies. Wear hipper clothes, beehive hairdo wigs or Diana Ross slit gowns. No cops are having fun with them.

Last. Behind Métro Barbès-Rochechouart. Here in locales that shift around as furtively as drug-shooting galleries on New York's Lower East Side, the three-minute whores ply their trade. A line of men will stand outside a metal door. When the door opens one man zipping up his fly leaves. Then the next pushes in, the cold metal door slams, and the line restlessly reconstitutes itself, the incontinent fidgeting with bottles of liquor in the linings of their long coats. A madam mans the door.

Frank: (to Jackie, after a fascinated spell) This is the armpit of the world.

So Frank returns home alone, covers himself, naked, with his sheets. He lights a low-burning strawberry-scent candle that smells generically sweet. Plays a Pretenders tape. "Stop Your Sobbing." Ingests the second of the black pills. And about ten minutes later the third.

The pills go to Frank's head. They turn out to be wake-up pills. They are head sugar. And heart sugar. Making his life box shake rattle and roll. Doesn't know what to do next. Reaches over for his tape-recorder Walkman that he uses only to record music to play for himself on trains or shoots or working out at the gym. But now he decides to push the RECORD button and talk into it.

Frank: (low into tape, its electric red light flickering to the sound of his voice) This is Frank Yastremski in the year of our Lord the late twentieth century. This is my diary that I'm starting tonight. Since I don't have a girlfriend to share my secrets with. And I don't know why I don't have a girlfriend, except that I'm an A-one shit. "Sometimes you just gotta say, 'What the fuck!'" That, folks, is a line from a movie that meant a lot to us back here. Somehow, by fluke, this tape has survived the atomic blasts that shook this planet in the 1990s. But that great movie starring Tom Cruise hasn't. I'd tell you the story if I could remember it. I have nothing to tell you. I never had anything to tell my girlfriend back in New York either. I'm one of these guys who talks all the time. But I have nothing really to say. Maybe I'm lonely because everyone is out partying tonight. My fellow models. I won't explain to you what a model is. Anyway. Those airheads are out partying. And my two best friends are probably shitfaced by now from wine. And my head is just spinning so fast I can't come down. So what do I do? I'm maybe the only guy on the whole planet who's taking the time out to talk to the future, a time when I don't even expect to be alive. But that's bullshit. And I'm what's called a "bullshit artist." So, later, citizens of the future. Thanks for keeping a lonely god company.

Click.

Frank is out, his head throbbing, his bed warm, and his body relaxed for the first time in hours.

DÉFILÉ

Todd doesn't have to be at the fashion show until seven at night, Sunday night. Oller believes in spontaneity so there have been no rehearsals. As the models arrive they are passed assembly-line-style to a barber for fifties haircuts: buzz cuts, mohawks, ducktails. Todd's hair is greased back to look like his Ferrati ads.

Todd: (mumbles, to an adjacent surfboard-style model) Now I know how a waxed car feels.

He and the other hepped-up guys are then led backstage for Oller's directions. Backstage is filled with racks of clothes, as well as stacks of shoes, belts, suspenders, hats, ties, socks, guns, canes, masks, boots, jackets, coats, pajamas, bathrobes, cigarette holders, lighters, watches, rings.

Oller, in a suit of yellow silk corduroy, speaks into a hand mike, trying to rally the bunch of overly casual models, trying to overcome the gap between his precious sense of the filigreed history of couture in France, and their blanks on that subject. Todd toys with a prop, a Bat Masterson gold-topped cane, while Oller orates.

Oller: (on a box) I want my show this year to be young, to be spontaneous, to be fifties, to be poetry. That is why I have chosen you. And why I will have no rehearsals. I detest to see these shows where the faces are dead because the heads are dead. I do not know who will go out in what costume or when. I will be reading, not reading, saying, poems into the microphone that I will invent spontaneously for the audience. I too am on the edge, as the Americans say. *Avant-garde,* as we French say. (raising his voice, liberation style) I am with you.

A middle-aged, probably Basque, dresser takes the cane from Todd's hand and smacks it down on a flat table. Then snottily starts to dress him in his first outfit, a paisley dinner jacket with black Lurex trousers and painted black tie shoes. Cartons of champagne arrive, the assistants pouring plastic cups for the models. Then cocaine is circulated, smuggled in.

Todd: (after a few hits, enunciating clearly, to his dresser) My hands feel like they're swelling up. Like a rubber monster's.

The show starts. Oller grabs Todd and pushes him out. Todd walks stiffly toward another model who's wearing a startling electric-blue sportscoat. The two meet and turn to walk down the aisle. Then Todd, feeling suddenly like a moving spectator, loosens up. He discovers the real fashion show is in the audience: red velvet pillbox hats, black canes with silver-eagle tops, rock-star suede vests, gray tuxes with purple velvet collars, feather necklaces, women with shaved heads wearing lurid green Martian makeup. Sees a living photomontage of faces he'd almost forgotten: Soupy, Dom, Bett, Louis, Sandy, Jean, Luigi, Ferrati. They are lined along the sides. When he nods at a familiar face it's as if two live wires are touched together. At the end of the ramp he and his partner smile in sync, smack each other like baseball players on television, and intercept the two teenage girls maneuvering awkwardly down the ramp wearing long silver Academy Award gowns. The four link arms to the tune of digital music and exit back up the ramp while cameras pop like exclamation points, and the clapping deepens.

Nine Ping-Pong games playing simultaneously. That's backstage. About a dozen dressers panic nonstop. They are throwing shoes or belts or ties to each other. Todd, feeling no pain, is dressed in tennis clothes, is then transferred to another dresser for white socks and sneakers, then to another dresser for a visor and tennis racket. He touches his toes ten times to try to regain possession of his own body. Finally Oller pushes him out onstage.

Oller: (invisible, his amplified voice filling the auditorium as Todd shiftlessly plays the ramp this time for its sex appeal) Spring for summer. Winter for fall. There are no seasons. Only moods. This year Oller is introducing mood dressing for the modern calendar. Just because it's winter, you can still play tennis. Play it in South Africa. Play it in the gymnasium.

Two shows tonight. Frank and Lucy are booked for the second. During intermission one of Oller's assistants, a Frenchman as pale and fragile as porcelain, dressed in a soothing tailored gray suit, takes Todd on a tour. He introduces him to Andy Warhol and Fred Hughes in the lobby.

Warhol behaves like the poet Henry Gibson in the sixties television comedy show *Laugh-In*. His hair is silver and combed straight to the side. His Cary Grant assistant, Fred Hughes, dark hair, dark skin, is wearing a blue pinstriper. Warhol is a walking oxymoron, high-strung poker-faced. Hughes is suave. Doesn't seem as happy as his boss.

Andy: (melodic) You were wonderful up there. You looked just great. We want to do a story on you with your photo for *Interview*. Don't we Fred? There's a boy in New York now named Todd, too, who's your size and look and who is making it. He looks beautiful in the McDonald's commercials saying, "I'm gonna make it big, Big Mac big."

Fred: Come to dinner with us after the show. Oller will be there.

Todd: (pixilated) Sure.

Andy: (to Fred) Don't you think Todd looks like the young Terence Stamp in *Billy Budd*?

The second show is looser than the first. One model develops a crimson nosebleed from the cocaine. For the finale they all must run out and run back, sprinting. Then they must carry Oller on their shoulders, and clap, and horse around. Todd, akimbo, looks down and sees Frank and Lucy at the end of an imaginary line drawn straight out from his feet. Lucy is staring up quizzically, an unsure pup. Frank, steely, is too busy appraising his emerald pinkie ring to look up.

Backstage Todd leans into one of the oval mirrors wiping his makeup off with a round cotton pad dipped in coconut cream. Frank and Lucy show up. Lucy hugs Todd and tells him how good he was. Frank just stands there. They then had planned to go to Les Trois Petits Cochons restaurant in Les Halles, the nineteenth-century farmer's market district nicknamed "the stomach of Paris" by Victor Hugo. But Todd discloses that he is going to dinner with Andy Warhol instead. The news hurts.

Frank: My picture was in *Interview* five years ago.

Lucy: (gloomy) Why wasn't I invited?

Frank: Because you're not a good butt-kisser.

ANDY WARHOL WAS AN ACCUMULATING MIRROR

The dinner table is crowded: Andy, Fred, Todd, Justine a model whose father owns a newspaper in England, Carol a French actress slated for a Chanel campaign, Gerald a young photographer secretary to Andy, Oller, Oller's assistant and David a young Midwesterner whose face and body appeared in *Playgirl* once.

Fred: (staring into the long wine list) Is it okay if we order a two-hundred-dollar bottle of wine?

Andy: Yes.

The waiter, all in white, with a white apron, brings over the wine already poured into a giant old chemistry flask and places the empty moss-covered original bottle down next to it. Todd picks up the bottle and looks at the label. 1966.

Andy: They probably added food coloring.

Gerald: (dressed in a black leather jacket with an American-flag pin in the collar) You said something like that before. (announcing to the table) This idea of fake color came up earlier, when we were driving past the Eiffel Tower with its spotlights on. (straining with his voice to evoke hilarity) Andy was sure the monument had been painted white. I said it was the way the lights made it look, that it's still gray. (plea to the jury) It is isn't it?

Andy: (case dismissed) So what did you do in Berlin after we left?

Gerald: I won't say.

Andy: (to Justine, after seconds of silence) What do you think Cecil Beaton's sex life was like?

Justine: I had a picture Beaton took of me when I was a little girl which I threw away because it wasn't any good.

Fred: (teasing) Andy. You're showing an excessive interest in sex these days.

Justine: Speaking not of sex, I went to Notre-Dame today, to mass, even though I can't speak French. It was wonderful. I love things like that. Church. Tarot cards. White magic.

David: (rumbling to Todd) The last time Justine and I had dinner she spent the whole time talking about how her Cardin watch fell on her wrist.

Justine appears in this month's issue of *Interview* looking just right, stark and sophisticated with pillows of white camera light behind her.

Todd: (not liking David) I'm satisfied.

Andy takes lots of pictures of a boy cooking a lamb in the fireplace. The boy wears a white cook's hat over his German haircut with hairs cut evenly all around in a reverse bowl.

Oller Assistant: (who spends all of his vacation in America) I saw young David's picture in that magazine and I think he has classic pecs.

Andy: Maybe that's true. But I'm sure that Gerald's are bigger.

Oller's Assistant: I think that David's pecs are bigger than Gerald's. I'd be willing to wager the price of this meal.

Todd starts jiggling his crossed leg, as if it were a propeller or lever that could transport him out of the acting-out of this wager.

Gerald unbuttons, not turning any less pale than usual. His chest is a plaster-of-paris cast of concaves and convexes with brown nipples like stains. David obliges too, though he blushes and gushes a lot, a tanned Roman marble copy, a study of tension (sinews, ropes) in high resolution. It turns out, though, that Gerald indeed does have the more developed chest, in size if not definition. Much roar. Oller comically world-wearily reaches for the check. And everyone else, except the spent Oller and his assistant, travel on.

The next stop is an enormous house where a starched wedding party is under way. The room is big and stone-walled, like a wing of the Metropolitan Museum of Art. The fireplace is twice as tall as Todd, who is standing in front with Justine.

Todd: (awkwardly) I feel something terrible. Maybe I should call my girlfriend.

Justine: (tony) Don't be such a terrier.

Andy starts snapping Todd and Justine's pictures, while asking a question of Justine at each snap.

Andy: What books are you reading these days Justine?

Justine: I like *The Glass Bead Game* and *Magic Mountain.*

Andy: Then you like thick books?

Justine: No. I don't like Tolkien's books and they're thick.

Andy: Who are your favorite poets?

Justine: I think Ted Hughes. And then T. S. Eliot. (having trouble with this question, giving schoolgirl answers) And Sylvia Plath.

Andy: (snap, snap, snap) Oh I like rock music lyrics. They're the real poetry. They're better than T. S. Eliot.

Andy is wearing a Sony Walkman, but the headphones are down around his neck now. The tape half-wound in the box is Puccini's *Turandot.* He was listening to the part about the three questions on the way over from the restaurant.

Fred and Andy leave for the evening, but Justine and Gerald and David want to continue. Todd is starting to feel a gnawing inside. He phones home from a pink phone on a pedestal. But no answer. The gnawing grows and grows into a gutting of insides, interrupted only when Justine taps him on the shoulder to leave too.

Justine and Gerald and David sit tight in the rear of a cab.

Todd sits up front next to the driver who has thin brown hair, middle thirties, looks a little like Bela Lugosi, a dog pushed down in his inky shadowed lap.

Cabdriver: (to Todd) *Vous êtes sado ou maso, monsieur?*

No one hears. Todd thinks he understands but isn't sure, and won't take a chance. So he just sits back and watches the rain streaking down the front windshield as the tiny wipers squeak back and forth. The only color that seems to glare though the wet is amber. All of Paris is amber, except for white buildings at corner turns. The streets cut this way and that making a cubist collage.

They are on their way to John Edmonton's party. He's a "tax deduction," one of the many young English lords living outside England as an income-tax loophole. Edmonton is a tender trap. He's twenty-one, just started studying philosophy at the Sorbonne. Always very sweet and very spacey. And very liable to be used.

When they arrive at Edmonton's nineteenth-century apartment, done in deep dark-blue plush, many rooms of the stuff, a butler takes their coats. First Todd uses a phone on a side table. No answer. Then Justine and Gerald walk him into the big room. The two are immediately fixed in a momentary bouquet of guests whose picture is snapped, leaving Todd free to check around.

He watches Roger Pale for a few minutes, another "tax deduction," the most animated, a devil, early thirties. Pale looks like a shark, or a rock star. Blond hair cut ragged. He spills a drink in a friend's lap on purpose, acts drunk. Pale's secretary is a tall gray-haired American wearing a red baby rose behind his ear, mid-forties, with a dummy laugh and a woman in his lap.

Justine: (to Gerald, about Pale's friend) I think he's a CIA agent. Do you think he's straight?

Gerald: His voice is too deep to be straight.

David slams up with a plate of food for Todd who's squatting on a purple ottoman. Five minutes later circles back with a mirror striped with lines of coke, the double image of the lines making a curious perspective. Todd sniffs in, one nostril open, the other blocked. Justine somehow squeezes onto the ottoman beside Todd, her chin in her palm.

Justine: How old are you?

Todd: Twenty-five.

Justine: It's wonderful to meet someone who's twenty-five and hasn't turned into a ghoul yet. It happens to so many people.

They pass into the next room where more people are standing up talking and drinking and smoking. One tall bald gent in a mauve quilt suit is doing hand puppets. Justine introduces Todd to new people who each say a few sentences. Todd keeps fingering the goo from the fashion show that gives his hair its New Wave flip.

Danielle: (young, wispish, with stiff collar, works at Sotheby's) Buying always lifts me out of a depression.

Alexander: (a fat man in a red tie and red Adidas and thick glasses who is supposed to have been an interrogator for the British army in Cairo during World War II, now teaches French to English speakers) The key to the French is that they are secretly individualists who want their culture to remain a mystery to everyone including themselves.

Anne: (an *ancienne* princess supposedly of French royal line, has cigarette voice) The Anglo-Saxons are the best storytellers. The French, like Proust, write memoirs.

Finally John Edmonton comes round. He is sensitive-looking with fine bones and thin red hair brushed back showing a full bulging shiny forehead. He is dressed in a brown corduroy suit, white shirt, thin orange tie, silk socks and embroidered Moroccan slippers. Has the honed spirit of a much older gentleman. But also an adolescent lostness. Though lostness is not a trait limited to the young. John's fingernails are lacquered. He's smoking a thin English cigarette from a plaid pack.

Todd: Hello.

Edmonton doesn't answer. Just smiles, then glides away. Todd is peeved. About twenty minutes later he walks into the cocaine toilet by mistake. He excuses himself and turns right around into Edmonton in the doorway.

201

Todd: Where's the real toilet?

Edmonton: (a new person, putting his arm around Todd) I've been wondering when I was going to see you again. We didn't get to talk enough yet.

Then John walks off without answering Todd's question. Todd is starting to feel extremely jangled. Everyone is talking in non sequiturs. Along comes David, the friendly gigolo.

Todd: (to David) Where's the real toilet?

David puts his arm around him to take him there. But on the way he stops to show Edmonton's bedroom.

David: It's just like John to get mixed up. He had them make wallpaper from the curtain design. And curtains from the wallpaper design.

The bathroom is a gleamy bleary white-tile submarine where Todd and David perch on the side of a tub to confer, their faces distorted in all the sizes and shapes of mirrors that subsume or explode the others' reflected territories. David unawaredly turns a tub faucet on and off, on and off, giving and taking away a waterfall in the middle of their talk.

Todd: (slurred, summarily) I don't need Frank and Lucy anyway. They're from the past. They're slow. It's best for all of us for me to end it by cutting loose. Don't you think?

David: (alarmed) You're sweating.

Near the end of the evening, or the beginning of the morning, John sits down to play the black grand piano in the main room where Todd had been suppering on the ottoman. His fine hands move over the keyboard like a secretary's at a typewriter. He is playing Scriabin. His guests each come up to him to say goodnight, but he just goes on playing obliviously. Eventually they move awkwardly away. John plays away all the politeness and all the guests with his renditions (full of parentheses of modulation) of the sonatas of the great mystic Russian composer. It's as if he is powerful enough to make all his guests disappear when he wants, only because he doesn't really notice them. Is he making the sun come up too? It's a Paris fairy tale.

Todd doesn't say good-night to anyone. Just breezes out the front door. The butler disappeared with the light. It is light. Todd walks out of this house near the Eiffel Tower and squints at the gold bright light in the empty streets. As gold as the inside of Welsh teacups. He walks and walks. There will be no cabs. The metro isn't running. He walks until he gets to a bread shop. Bread shops are the first to open. The metros will be next. He buys a loaf of bread that is shaped like a long nimbus cloud. He buys a short bottle of purple confiture as well. He doesn't recognize the fruit painted on the front label. Then he takes his bread, wrapped in a thin sheet of paper, to a triangular park. Sits down on a green wood bench that's curved to accommodate the body with the finesse of a recliner. Todd unwraps the bread. Opens the compression-sealed bottle. And dips the bread that he has torn off from the rest into the purple Dippity-Doo jelly. The birds in the park are awake. They are gray, noisy. Todd watches them paying so much attention to the A.M. He is up with the birds but for the wrong reasons. He eats half the bread until his belly begins to feel too full. The starch explodes fast in there. He walks to the metro, one of the stations with the replicas of art-nouveau signs. It's open. He escalators down. The tunnel is filled with workers, mostly dressed in blues and grays. They might as well be Maoist workers in China. He takes the train to the Clichy stop. He walks up the Boulevard de Clichy. Listens to the birds that are in the center-of-the-street parks, and lined along the eaves of houses that look like orange gingerbread houses.

Todd: (numbly) Hallelujah!

The phone rings around eleven. Lucy leaves bed. Todd is sleeping so hard he doesn't hear. She is wearing yellow cotton pajamas with feet and a repeating design of fuzzy white bunnies.

She answers the phone in Jackie's room. He's asleep too. A breathing pile of white sheets, snow-covered hills.

It's Frank, as unsettlingly wide awake as a host on *The Today Show*.

Frank: What time did he roll in last night?

Lucy: Around seven.

Frank: Where was he?

Lucy: I haven't had a chance to quiz him yet.

Frank: Listen. I have some big news. If it were New Year's, this would be my resolution.

Lucy: I'm quivering.

Frank: (lapsing) Yeah, quiver. (then back on track) This is it. I'm getting out of modeling and I'm moving back to New York to start living a straight life. I'm tired of being a gigolo.

Lucy: (screeching) I love it.

Todd walks by in white boxer shorts with a repeating blue pony design. He is carrying two GQs. Hands one, opened to a page, to Lucy. Then turns into the bathroom.

Lucy: (enough said) Him.

Frank: One more thing I've been thinking about.

Lucy: Frank! You've changed so much in Paris. You've gotten so, so introspective. It's not like you.

Frank: I want you to fly with me.

Lucy can't swallow that news so quickly. She has to detach. She travels for a few minutes through a no-visibility-sector of excitement and worry. Leaves the magazine, closed, on the table. Knocks on the closed bathroom door.

Lucy: (angry-housewife tone) Todd? That was Frank. He's flying the coop. And he wants me to fly back to New York with him. (walks away)

Todd is sitting on the toilet with the magazine open. He hears Lucy but doesn't respond. Then he shifts over to the bidet. Lets the water spray all over his ass while he sits and reads for five minutes, feeling the scintillation of the pinpricks. He is reading a tiny feature in *GQ* about his scrapbooks. Bett had mentioned it to them. They printed a tiny inset of his Ferrati ad. And a page they came by the apartment one morning to photograph: one of the *fotoromanzo* series. Todd is tickled.

But his lilt soon passes. When he hurries back in the bedroom Lucy has disappeared. He doesn't want her deciding with Frank on today of all days. He begins to feel the headache of his hangover. Takes out his scrapbook from the closet. On the first page is Paris spelled out with different styles of letters that he found—art-nouveau P, lipstick A, Panthéon column I. But all the rest of the pages are blanks. He hasn't completed one since he got here. He lies down on the bed, then spreads the open book, pages-side down, over his face, as an escapist siesta sombrero, while yawning a groan.

MORE J/O

Even though Matt and Todd are the only guests in the empty ski lodge—renovated, not yet open for business, at the top of a very steep mountain with winding narrow roads, lots of stars matched by twinkling of lights in lake valleys below—they are assigned two narrow beds in a single knotty-pine room.

(They are on a ski-clothes job in the Dolomites. The day after Lucy said that through the door.)

Matt immediately dresses down to his white boxer shorts and lies sideways on his bed, his magical-looking Hebrew-letter necklace dangling. Matt is the South Dakota marine who worked on the catalog shoot with Todd—tall, curly blond hair, an expressive masculine face, dark and lined and malleable, like a catcher's mitt. Todd, on his stomach reading a brochure, is warm in his black-orange Harley-Davidson muscle shirt from a sixties store in the East Village, and Calvin Klein briefs.

Matt: (after an obvious think) You ever read *The Story of O*?

Todd: (warily) Yeeeah. . . .

Matt: (perking) Cause when I was in Hamburg we went to all

205

these bars with these chicks with red boots and whips and stuff. And this buddy said it was like *The Story of O.* So what's the story?

Todd: Oh. Well I don't remember. But I do remember that this rich French girl . . .

Matt: Girl or lady?

Todd: Chick. This rich French chick becomes a slave to this ugly older French man. He makes her wear a short skirt and no underwear. Then when she gets in the back of a cab she feels the cold vinyl on her rear and upper legs.

Matt: Is that the worst of it? Isn't there more?

Todd: Read it. There's definitely chastity belts in it. And piercing rings. There must be whippings. My favorite though is *Venus in Furs.*

Matt: (his heart drumming) Tell me that.

Todd: (turning on his side now, facing Matt) A man lives as the slave to a woman, in her boudoir, with her suffocating furs and heavy drapes and perfumes. Drinks urine out of her slippers.

Matt: (disdainful) You like that stuff? And I'm sleeping in the same room with you?

Todd: (reprisal) Sleep it off.

As Matt leans over to turn off the light he gives Todd a look, curious, leery. Then, click, black. Todd can't fall asleep. Doesn't hear Matt sleep-breathing yet. Wets his hand and starts pulling on himself, trying to stay mostly still, to steady the mattress on the springs. Then he hears the sounds of Matt stirring. Matt stands at the foot of Todd's bed, his face silhouetted like a kindergartner's cutout George Washington or Abe Lincoln in the window. Moistening himself, Matt moans, makes grunting noises, finally sprays all over Todd's quilt. Then back to bed. Todd fakes heavy sleep-breathing.

The next morning when Todd wakes up, Matt is performing hundreds of push-ups, with his legs locked somehow in a chair. His talisman necklace is slapping against him as he moves up and down, the hair on his chest in clumps of varying densities, some places soft, others spiky, others barren.

Matt: (breathlessly) I couldn't fall asleep. I don't like new beds.

Todd: (irritated at the attempt at muffling, throwing his blankets off) Last night you stood up and you came all over me.

In ancient Greek "apocalypse" means with no veil or no blanket. An uncovering.

Matt glowers at this remark. He disentangles himself from the chair and pounds into the bathroom to floss in front of the bathroom mirror. Then walks back out to blow steam.

Matt: (belligerently) I went on a trip to the Canary Islands and the client wanted to get laid every night. I said no. So the client fired me. When I got back to Munich I found out, A, that my agency didn't demand full pay for the week from the client, and B, even accepted less for the work I did. They were more interested in keeping the client than me. I kicked ass. So they threw me out. When I went around to other Munich agencies I found out I had been blacklisted.

He returns to the bathroom mirror. Starts squeezing blackheads, his light green eyes squinting to discover more.

Todd, concerned at the overkill to his tease, makes his way over to lean in the bathroom door frame.

Todd: So what?

Matt: (turning around, second explosion) I went to dinner with Barberi, the Milan fruitcake designer. He said I could have his fall campaign if I went on vacation with him for a week in Greece. I said No. You know who went? Bobby Branlin, the blond guy, and I know for a fact he's married and has kids. Now when I go by Barberi's for go-sees, this Branlin is always hanging around back in the back with all the clothes and the seamstresses. Like a wife.

Todd: (piping down, sensing psycho) Uh boy.

For the rest of the trip, during the shoot, on the train on the way back, Todd and Matt don't communicate. The silence between them grows thicker and thicker, like smoke in a house on fire where all the oxygen has been used up, only carbon monoxide and sulfur remaining.

SOMETHING NEW

Lucy and Frank are riding on an Air France flight back to New York. They are sitting on the side in a two-seat section. Frank is next to the window, moving his legs around, not able to find a comfortable position, trying to sleep. Lucy is on the aisle, her fold-down down, writing in her journal. She doesn't ever write long entries, just a few lines, every few weeks. She's kept this black journal for a year now and only about fifteen pages are written on.

In a black felt-tip pen, an extremely upset script, all caps, she scrapes, "LIFE IS A TRAIN OF MOODS."

Eventually Frank falls asleep, his head on the pillow the attendant in the dark-blue uniform with the Air France wings insignia pin handed him earlier. The lights dim for the movie. Lucy leans over and pulls down the window shutter, a little square, like the squares that cover the clues on a TV-game-show board.

Ninety minutes later the lights resurge, Lucy is crying hot, quiet tears. Frank wakes up but doesn't notice. The attendant dispenses Evian mineral water in little cups. Cups of salt-free tears.

THE KING OF CUPS

Jackie: (wearing a red silk robe covered with gold-thread swords) Hold the cards in your hands and mix them like this. (simulates shuffling)

Todd, sitting at the dining-room table in white T-shirt and

blue jeans, shuffles the tarot cards in the weak lemon-whitish light of mid-afternoon.

Jackie has already eliminated one card from the deck. He wipes its face with the red silk rag that he usually wraps the deck in before placing them in a metal box with a Playboy bunny drawn on its cover.

Jackie: (holding up the card) This is you. The King of Cups. With light brown hair and hazel eyes.

Todd holds the flat card in his hands. Sees an old-fashioned king (crown, scepter) seated on a barge of a throne that floats upon silver-blue waves.

Todd: I look better than that.

Jackie: (authoritative) He is a man of business, law or divinity. (pointedly) He may be a bachelor. . . . Friendly, of creative intelligence in the arts and sciences.

Todd: (sarcastic) That's me.

Jackie then lays down the shuffled cards in what is sometimes called the Tree of Life method, four down the center, the trunk, and two branches of lines of three on either side.

Jackie: You may ask a question. You may tell me the question out loud or you may hide the question in yourself.

Todd: (beginning to cooperate) My question is . . . should I go back to New York even though it would be better for my career to work in Europe for another year? Should I pursue Lucy and try to get back together with her or take her as a thing of the past, a stepping stone? Am I doing the right thing with my life? Is modeling just a part of extended adolescence? Am I too juvenile? Too narcissistic? Is that why I lost Lucy? Or did I lose her because I outstripped her? Should I pursue my artwork? My diaries? Go back to the student travel center? What?

Jackie: (furious) The tarot only answers one question at a time. But I do it anyway. Even though it is not right.

Jackie muses poutily over the cards. He begins talking about horoscopic abstractions using all these fairy-tale characters, descending farther and farther into a dark forest where shadows are personality flaws that accidentally veer from little paths into wide swaths because of a misjolt in the chariot of the ego, and where light that filters through leaves or shines as directly as a flashlight from heaven is the be-all and end-all.

Jackie: (his finger resting on Eve's belly) This is the card of Love, as part of the way and the truth. This does show the danger of a breaking-up of lovers, and with it the chance of a wrong mistake.

Todd: See?

Jackie: (overturning a card picturing a tall gaunt man in a hood holding a lantern) Is sad. He is *tout seul* as he lights the way on the old mountain for the spiritual travelers on their way to the top. But your card is in reverse. This is very bad. It shows immaturity, foolish vices, the refusal to grow old.

Todd: See?

Jackie: What do you see?

Todd: We call it Peter Pan.

Finally Jackie turns over a Hanged Man, right side up. But he has trouble with the interpretation. Walks over to his cabinet where he stashes his candles and tits jewelry to find his book of tarot in English to choose the right words for Todd.

Jackie: (walking back) . . . suspended decisions, a pause in one's life.

Todd: (dashingly pushes back his chair, stands, stares out into the same old off-white) I'm taking the Concorde.

Jackie seems very happy with this decision. While Todd violently packs in the next room, Jackie nonviolently dances around his apartment, smoking his hash, bending backward and forward to the tired tunes of a French television version of *Soul Train*.

NEW YORK

Chelsea is mostly sienna red.

Lucy and Frank and Todd are all now living in this neighborhood filled with red brick buildings between Fourteenth Street
and Thirty-fourth Street on the lower West Side. (The Upper
West Side has brownstones, the Upper East Side limestones.)

It's six months later. Late winter early spring.

FRANK'S NEW LOOK

Frank is sitting at a table-desk in front of one of his living-room windows. The place is spiffed up with Milan-style furniture. Metal skeletal chairs with black leather wraparounds. A red-and-black sleek couch. Gray allover carpeting. A tall halogen lamp with its own custom-made fifty-dollar light bulb.

He looks different. The wire-rim spectacles make him a Russian revolutionary intellectual, say Trotsky in his Mexican periods, or Pasternak. The lighting from the lamp turns his blond hair whiter. His face is lit up from below by the reflecting pages of the book open before him, *What Color Is Your Parachute?*, a handbook on career switching.

FIFTIES HOUSEWIFE

Lucy is in Frank's bedroom. Her excuse is that she sublet her own apartment for a year. So she has been staying with Frank since they returned. It's like the love cave in the German medieval poem, *Tristan*. Though without the crystalline ecstasy that took away their need to eat. Tristan and Isolde dined out on each other. The worst that can be said is that Frank is the fulfillment of many of Lucy's fantasies.

Lucy is down on the floor putting together a new vacuum cleaner. Only wearing a pair of black silk panties with a hole rudely cut out with scissors so her black pussy hairs show. Her big breasts are hanging down. The empty box and Styrofoam filler pieces are scattered around. She has the cleaner stem attached but can't get the plastic screws in. No instructions. She takes an hour, and has a rush of pleasure at each move: the attaching of the refuse bag, the insertion of the metal fastener, the plugging-in of the three-socket plug. She stands up and presses her foot on the starter. A headlight goes on at the front of the blue-and-white Eureka vacuum cleaner. If she wasn't as undressed as a native woman in a *National Geographic* she could be a fifties housewife.

Frank walks in from his desk in his tan pants and white T-shirt carrying a red-black-cover magazine called *Hellfire*, with shots of suburban swinging couples from Long Island and Queens and New Jersey tying each other to couches and chaining each other to stoves. Frank spreads it open on the floor like an instruction manual to a page showing a fat woman with black lipstick (cf. Cat Woman in late 1970s Roxy London), her breasts and arms and legs and crotch strapped in black snap-leather straps. Frank unsnaps his own straps from the closet and starts binding Lucy to look like the bonded woman in the picture.

Lucy stares out with a garish look at the bedroom and the living room beyond—where Todd first unbuckled his pent-up back on the wooden floor, where she first visited Frank and rocked in his lovely rocker. But that was then. And now is now. Now is a world whose only sense (fun) seems to be sensation.

EMPTY APPLIANCE CARTON

Todd rents a new two-bedroom apartment, found by the agency, on Twenty-ninth Street and Eighth Avenue. It resembles a motel room, barely lived in, with wall-to-wall brown carpeting, model-home cabinets and dishwasher, and a flashing sign outside the window advertising an Italian salumeria below, the Italian map neoned in black and red on the jazzy sign. His apartment is at the level on the map of Lake Como.

Todd hasn't concentrated yet on turning his empty appliance

carton of an apartment into a home. Like Perry Street, it's a mess. Unpacked boxes are the only furniture. But he does have a drafting table with clip-on bright lights set up between two front windows. That's where he works on the scrapbooks. Since the *GQ* article he's been receiving queries. One gallery wants to give him a show. Now he is sitting there making a melancholy grotesque collage. On dark violet paper, glued over the black page, he sticks on somber symbols: skull, black rose, nuclear explosion. His new scrapbook is an anatomy of moods.

The front bedroom is furnished with a mattress on the floor, but the back bedroom is still completely empty.

S & M

Frank's bedroom has no windows. No time of day. When he shuts the door it's night in the middle of the afternoon. The overhead track spot is its moon. The mirror on the back of the closet door reflects a tiny string of lit bulbs along the wallboard, like stars. Frank inserts a cassette of vaguely menacing electrical music. He strips down out of his clothes, Lucy tied now thoroughly in all the straps.

Lucy: I have somewhere to go at five-thirty.

Frank: You want me to gag you with the mouth dildo?

Lucy: (warming) No. Not yet.

Lucy is a shiny-and-dull, leather-and-flesh mound, like a dark mountain in the chaos (black emptiness) of the floor. Frank has slipped into a pair of black leather underpants, still wearing his double-rim glasses that catch light and make him look as ominously impersonal as a political speaker.

He takes a pair of tiny scissors. Slices them together musically to prepare them, in the way barbers used to flick their razors up and down on a strap to sharpen them. Then he kneels down and carefully starts to snip all of Lucy's little black hairs between her rigid legs. He drops some of the hairs in his mouth, some in hers.

Lucy: I'll be a hairless beast.

Frank: Are you excited?

Lucy: (leveling) I'm still a little bored. Sorry.

Frank stands up and smokes a joint, walking around and around in the palpitant blackness, in what could be prehistory, feeling empty of his names and his screens of behaving.

Frank: (angry) Everyone has it in them. It's not just me. I went to the store next door to buy that dirty magazine and the guy behind the counter punished me by not giving me a bag, making me ask for a paper bag. But he has it in him. You know he does.

Lucy: I'm getting into it now Frank. Talk to me.

Frank: (bending over her, swatting her every so often with a gigantic rigid feather attached on a knob) I'm the New York vice squad. And I know that you've got it in you. And I'm here to plug it out of you. To tickle it out of you. To make you beg and confess. (is tickling the tips of her tits) Tell it to me. Blurt it out to me.

Lucy: (sirening) I wanna live under your thumb. I want you to have a low opinion of women like Mick Jagger does. And I want to deal with it.

Frank: Good girl. Good girl Cindy.

Lucy: Cindy?

Frank: I just changed your name for now. What's your name?

Lucy: What's your name?

Frank: My name is BladeMaster.

Lucy: (whining) Why does everyone have these same limited four or five fantasies? Why do ten million people like to get spanked?

Frank: You're getting out of it again.

Lucy: (closing eyes, trying harder) I see myself in a harem, I want you to have other girlfriends, and I want to have to watch you fuck them. Pick them up on the street. You can do it. (opening eyes again) Look at you.

Frank: Yeah. Spanish girls. Black girls. Every kind of submissive. Every kind of girl cake.

Frank undoes the belt around Lucy's thighs, and around her calves, and around her ankles. Then he spreads her legs open wide, like a wishbone.

Lucy: (excited) That drives me crazy. Now I'm an open book.

Frank: What does the open book say when it's getting fucked?

Frank sticks his dick in Lucy's shaved hole. He rams into the soft wall in there that gives way like a sidewall on a car-racing circuit when hit head-on by a turbo sporty. Like a low bush into which a horse falls sideways during a jump.

Lucy: (shrieking) I love you. I love you.

Frank: (coming) You do not. You do not.

The worst, or best, is over. They lay in the dark of the solar system of a bedroom. The tape is shut off. The quiet feels like emptiness to both of them. Now they have to change into something less, or more, comfortable. The mood is Elgar.

Lucy: (lying there as Frank is undoing the last of the straps) I have to be somewhere at five-thirty.

Frank: You said that already. I thought I was making all the decisions from now on.

Lucy: Ugh.

Frank: (crossed) Mmmmmm.

Frank leaves Lucy to lie on the black floor. He dresses and returns to his lit desk. Lucy lies there with her head snapping from left to right. No. Then from right to left. No. It's not guilt. No. It's not the tired recesses of spent excesses. No. It's simply the forces of No spilling up like the guts of a volcano. The No music that is what they used to call "the music of the spheres" that is all the empty winds blowing through the saloon doors at either end of where we live, the Sun end and the Pluto end. No.

ST. PATRICK'S

At five-thirty Lucy pulls on her brown wool overcoat. It's already dim outside. She draws a thick brush through her thick hair. Stops at Frank's table on her way out.

Lucy: (confronting) It's Ash Wednesday. I'm going out.

Frank: You complain about my bondage and domination.

Lucy: I don't go to church for that. I go to get out of the house.

Frank: (staring at a page of personal ads) I'm gonna answer one of these ads.

Lucy: (impatient) Frank. You're not thinking big enough. Throw that paper in the trash. (leaning over and opening the window, papers blowing around from the cold gust) Just look through the window of the world for a few days. Take walks.

Frank leans over, annoyed, and closes the window. Then he touches his palms against Lucy's breasts and makes swirling motions. Lucy's feet stamp as she draws back.

Frank: (seducing, from habit) Baaaby. Come to Daddy.

Lucy, heart-fallen, walks toward the door.

Frank: (calling after her) Lucy!

She wheels around. Frank winks at her, his right eye wrinkling shut. Lucy is glad to see that wink, a universal sign of innocence.

Lucy: (with understanding) I guess it's not your fault if there's trouble in Tahiti.

Her stomach now does not feel so turned as she sticks her hands in her big coat pockets and walks through the door. First time out in days.

Lucy takes the Seventh Avenue IRT to Fiftieth Street and walks across town, past office-building slabs, to St. Patrick's Cathedral. Fifth Avenue is whistling with traffic, few honks. The streetlamps are on early. Lucy walks up the finely graduated cathedral steps, enters through a side portal, taps her forehead with blessed water from a wall well, lines up for her ashes. The color scheme is similar to Sacré Coeur's—white and light gray. The line of communicants is similarly beat. Mostly workers just let out. Lucy catches a young brunette priest eyeing her when she is still three penitents away. Then he quickly fixes back on his pot of black ash. Lucy finally stands before him.

Young priest: (not reciting the traditional "From dust thou art/ Unto dust shalt thou return") Read the Scriptures daily, and pray.

Lucy, disappointed at the whitewashing of the gloomier saying, stops off at a side chapel to light a votive candle. Actually she lights four.

Lucy: (warbling between whispering and deep gutturals) Lord here are four candles, one for me, one for Frank, one for Todd, and one for the souls in Purgatory. I know that love can neither be created nor destroyed. So this mess will work itself out. But I'm starting to think I made a big mistake. Please send a sign.

Lucy shuffles along the side aisle by metal and stone statues of saints and "space travelers" (her phrase for angels). She walks down Fifth Avenue past windows full of oriental rugs on her way back to Chelsea. Past a Protestant church that has a catchy slogan in its announcement box. She pulls a crumpled bank receipt from her inside coat pocket. Copies the quotation down, planning to transfer it later to her journal.

Quotation: **The greatness of a man can nearly always be measured by his willingness to be kind. G. Young.**

Lucy makes a right, walks west. Even though the sky overhead is black, she can see orange squibs over New Jersey, the last pullulations of sun. The only one on the block, she feels free to begin singing a song made up only of la-la-la's. Rubs her own tummy soothingly through the pocket of the coat. Knows she needs that.

TODD AND FRANK LOOK THE FUTURE
IN THE MOUTH

While Lucy is at church, probably at the moment she is lighting those candles, Todd calls. It's the first time since he returned to New York. Frank invites him over.

Arrived, Todd sits tensely on the stark couch, his one black chinos leg crossed over the other at a right angle, black construction boots jiggling, not taking off his knee-length black cashmere coat. His hands are as cold as wet dishrags. This is not the tenseness he felt almost two years ago, sitting in the since-sold rocker. That was tenseness at trekking in new territory, its traps not known, its signifiers not signified. This is tenseness at knowing the territory too well, of tiptoeing by land mines located in pinpointable spots of psychic patches.

Frank, plushly dressed in brown French dress corduroys, a gray wool V-neck sweater over a white T-shirt, and brown cordovans, sits with his desk chair turned around so he can grab its back while facing Todd, his rubber soles pressing in on the sides of the chair's legs. His pipe, a recent toy, balancing on a glass ashtray, looks like a brown walrus beached on a slag of ice. Frank is swigging from a tall bottle of St. Pauli Girl beer.

Frank: (absorbed) I could open a downtown club with live bands from Hoboken and performance artists on trapezes overhead.

Todd: (hip) But nightclubs are always sleazy, man. You get visited by the Shadow of Death. If you know what I mean. You'll get involved in sting operations.

Frank is taking in this advice, putting on his new deliberating face, overdoing it.

Todd: (suddenly electrified, plugged into some socket) Let's get out of here. . . . I've got just the future for you. . . . I passed it on my way over here. . . . It's a property.

Frank: (standing up) Relax. Then tell me about it.

Todd, feeling strongly that he doesn't want to be there when Lucy returns, doesn't want to be in the same room with those two, stands up and paces, his hand every so often rubbing on the bronze doorknob.

Frank doesn't notice. Instead he slowly walks out to the kitchen then reappears with a thick wedge of Jarlsberg cheese on a plate and a box of round orange sugary crackers. He sees no knife, returns to the kitchen, emerges with a steak knife to cut the cheese. Sees no mustard, returns to find a bottle of peppery Dijon to spread. In transit around the main room, finally makes himself an hors d'oeuvre. Points to the hunk to indicate that Todd may serve himself.

Todd: (extremely) There's this building on Eighth Avenue in the twenties. It's been a funeral home, and there was just a fire, and the building is on the market. Please let me show it to you. Now.

Frank finally has his fill of those sweet cheesy crackers. He gives in to Todd's urgent prods. Zips up his blue quilt jacket and tries to remember where the keys are. Then, on the way down in the upright coffin of an elevator—same red velvet draping over metal as an inexpensive coffin—he repays Todd for coming over and helping him with his future.

Frank: (out of nowhere) I mean this thing with Lucy. I don't know if it'll last. I think we're like halfway houses for each other.

Todd: (acting nonplussed) Well that could be.

Todd is now determined to help Frank with his future. His own future is implicated. It's only once every so often that someone says a sentence that changes a life course, or at least indicates the change before it's under way.

So Todd guides Frank enthusiastically down one of the side streets in the twenties between Seventh and Eighth avenues. Most of the apartment buildings on the block are subdivided colonial brick houses, many with lights on in the windows, people inside dressing and undressing, watching television, shadow-dancing to unheard music, talking on cordless phones. These domestic boxes look warm, filled with a soft yellow light, like the oven where chickens are heated in delicatessens for workers to pick up on their way home, and eat, with a side order of slaw, or a buttered corn on the cob.

Todd's red brick building is on a corner, gutted from fire. Lots of charred crossbeams lie at Xs to one another. The windows are just empty black sockets, like the eyes in skulls. Notices have been pasted up by public departments to warn trespassers away.

Frank and Todd stand across the street and stare.

Frank: (his old robustness coming back, the arms circling) This is the kind of building that could really get me up in the morning. I see an empire. A real-estate empire started from scratch. I could be like that.

Todd: (philosophical) If you can love a person I guess you can love a building. Even if you can't love a person you can probably love a building.

Frank: (ebulliently trying to express his pleasure) I want to . . . fuck . . . a . . . duck.

Todd grabs Frank from behind and buries his face in his back, in the padded blue nylon of his jacket.

Frank: (taking it) You still love me don't you?

Todd: (propelling both of them into a walk) I can't help it.

They cross at the next corner, over toward a gay bar on the opposite corner called Jarhead. Its vent blows a sirocco wind of beer and cigarette smells out onto the street. Right now local teen guys are throwing sleetballs at its gray steel door. The attackers hoot and holler.

Frank and Todd continue down the side street to fetch Lucy. But Todd still can't bear to go up. So Frank calls her from a pay phone on the corner of Seventh and invites her down to see the building. The sidewalk where her two lovers wait for her is covered with dark gray ice snow, the compressed accretions of a month of snowstorms and rainstorms.

Lucy is more excited to see Todd after six months than to see Frank's building. "Whatever that is," she says out loud as she pours the rest of the can of beer she's drinking into a glass and drinks the foamy brew. Then she looks in the mirror on the inside of the closet door. Predate behavior. Slips into the same brown sackcloth-and-ashes overcoat, turns off the lights, and hurries downstairs.

When the three finally get together after so long they are awkward. No kissing. No touching. Only conventional hellos. They stand in a triangle, then converge into a horizontal line and walk up the street with no more exhibited feeling than characters in an algebra problem. They come to a full stop directly across the street from the vacant building.

Lucy: (standing between Frank and Todd, wailing) It's so hollow. It's so forlorn-looking. It's such a big empty black zero. Are you sure you want it Frank?

Frank: (dismissive) That's because you don't have the right kind of eyes like I have. Money eyes.

Lucy: (fervent) Let those with ears to hear, hear, and those with eyes to see, see.

Todd: I can tell where you've been. (makes a middle finger to no one in particular)

Lucy finds that gesture the funniest thing. She kisses Todd on his cheek, after having inhibited herself for fifteen minutes. Lets it out.

Todd: (feeling bad) You always did laugh at my jokes.

Frank: (pointing to the building, trying to butt in with a vengeance) You two could never handle a building like that.

Todd then walks them back to their avenue. Pats Frank on the shoulder with forced diplomacy, less fond of him now that Lucy is there. Kisses her on both eyelids the way he used to before bedtime. Walks off convinced that everything is bearable.

224

But it's not.

The closer he comes to his destination, while walking through the urban campus of the Fashion Institute of Technology in the middle twenties, with its curiously shaped suburban-looking dormitories, and its big metal slice-of-geometry sculptures, the full moon reflected in its entirety in almost every classroom window, the more he realizes that he has a brushfire of anger flaring inside. So he turns around on his toes and walks right back to Frank's building. Pushes down on the buzzer button with his index finger as if poking someone in the chest accusatorily.

Lucy: (through intercom) Who's there?

Todd: (gruff) It's me.

Lucy: (suspiciously) It doesn't sound like you.

When Todd arrives at the apartment his anger is doubled. Frank and Lucy have already slipped into their night clothes. His, a black vest, bare chest, black piratical tights, a lasso lying exposed like a stain on the couch. Hers, just baby-blue dancer's tights, no top, her breasts seeming to speak spookily in some other language. They stand there looking dumbly at Todd like two grotesques in a Diane Arbus photograph.

Todd loses it. No one else says zip. He clears his throat, rearranges his muscles and bones, like a singer in a spotlight about to dive into a song. He is walking on a fine line, like the line drawn on a highway by patrolmen for the inebriation test, liable to stumble off any minute into humor one way or melodrama the other.

Todd: (quavering) This isn't right. I feel like we're living in the Dark Ages and you two have an arranged marriage or something. That you have to live in it. But that the real love is between me and Lucy. I feel that. And it isn't right.

Frank jumps out of the couch, grabs Todd and pushes him chaotically out the front door toward the wall by the elevator, then shuts the door. Rumbles past Lucy. Is more a natural force than a person right now, a thunderclap, or a river run.

Frank: (on his heaving way into the bedroom) I made him. Why doesn't he go back where he came from?

Lucy stands there like the main character in the riddle story "The Lady or the Tiger?" but with neither door opening.

Lucy: (shouting in to Frank, trying to get a rise, completely confused) Where's Mahatma Gandhi when you need him?

When Todd had been standing there, his words an oil geyser, Lucy felt a creepy kinship. Not intimacy or anything as airy as that. She felt sweat of his sweat, breath of his breath. He was talking for her freedom as well as his. He was recomposing *Fidelio.* She felt toward him as toward a political liberator, a Bolívar. Not liberating her from Frank, but from herself. Her feminism had to be given her from the outside, as everyone's identity must finally be, but only after they have worked to prepare themselves, like an instrument, to play the song of myself.

Lucy is rubbing her index finger pensively over her oily thumb.

THE SHOOT

Todd works today at a photographer's studio in the twenties on the East Side. They're shooting an ad for Power, a SoHo store that sells clothes that look like costumes for a Japanese remake of an old Flash Gordon movie: ichthyornis-wing shoulders, knee-length squire tunics, belts as chain weapons, tights stuffed in bolero boots.

Todd is walking across the polished wood floors of the loft dressed in Japanese samurai gear, no shoes. His expression as disgruntled as one of Picasso's split faces. Rimini, the owner of the cutting-edge boutique, in a black parachute-jumper suit, wearing black oriental slippers and an imitation black belt waltzes smack into him.

Rimini: (tall, balding, feathery) Todd. You're the dream face for what our store is trying to be.

Todd: Uh boy.

A cluster of Puerto Rican and Chinese girl models on the shoot are in the dressing room to be painted by a Mexican lady makeup artist, her own hair piled way up on her head with painted purple streaks exaggerating her eyes.

The two other guys are Richard, young, dark-skinned, unselfconscious, bound to go far, and Patrick, a curly-haired blond French boy from Antigua in the Caribbean. Todd toys with these newcomers.

Richard: Gee. It had been raining for days. And just yesterday, when I had my first outside shoot, editorial, it was beautiful out.

Todd: Great. How'd it go?

Richard: (his eyes go deep and bright) Wonderful. They gave me the best clothes. And I did all the single shots. When they put me and the other guy in a shot they always put me in front.

Todd: A star.

Richard: (reflecting, changing tone) Well no. I'm just glad to get some tear sheets for my book.

Todd has a Xerox of this same dialogue with Patrick.

Patrick: (stopping lungfully singing a vaguely familiar pop song) I have an audition tomorrow so I have to practice.

Todd: Really? An audition for what?

Patrick: I'm a singer. And just look at this face. Can't you see me as a singer?

Todd: You'd look great on a record cover. I can see it.

Patrick: You'll be asking me for my autograph in a couple years.

Todd: A star.

Patrick: (same readjustment) Well. You never know what's going to happen.

Klaus, the German photographer, has a bald shaved head,

pointy ears, bony body. He's dressed in a Power concoction too—gray baggy golf pants, white padded T-shirt, red designer sneakers with a lipstick logo on the ankles. Klaus is sadistically bossy toward men, ravenous toward women. Some chemical imbalance makes him pick nittily all afternoon at Todd.

The drop for the photograph is a painted map of Japan on a dropcloth, like a painter's canvas that drapes down over the wall and across the floor. The models file tiptoedly on as onto a temple slab or into a geisha house.

Klaus: (shouts) Todd. Wipe your feet before you walk on the set.

The action shot requires that the American boys jump up in the air with the Puerto Rican and Chinese girls, holding hands and arms, screaming and smiling with Yankee glee.

Klaus: (all through the gymnastics) Todd. Higher. Todd. Higher.

Klaus then carries the test Polaroid over to Todd to show him that he doesn't know how to walk in a walking-forward scene, one of the oldest modeling tricks, rocking forward and back to simulate a stroll.

Klaus: (generic Euro accent) Man. You probably thought you were walking. (laughs) No. You must go way forward and up on your toes. Even if you fall flat on your face.

Todd: (threateningly) Don't book on it.

Todd joins his partner for a close-up. She's a Japanese-looking Chinese model with an East Village haircut wearing a silver-and-black dress from the fifties with pink tennis shoes.

Klaus's assistant is Johnny, an effeminate Korean boy, thin, long greasy black hair, dressed in a white button-down shirt, white painters' pants, white socks. All through the shot Klaus bears down on Johnny, stoking Todd's own sense of injustice.

Klaus: (all screech) I have some direction. Now you put your arm in hers. Johnny. I told you to flick on that fan. (Johnny runs over to fix the fan) Johnny. Hold this reflector. (Johnny embraces the golden reflector) No. Not like that. Up. Up. How many times do I have to show you?

When Klaus takes a Polaroid, he waits annoyed as Johnny runs over to grab the developing print from his rigidly outstretched arm. When he finishes a roll of film he holds out the camera for Johnny to change the film. When Johnny, unplugging some bright lights, doesn't snap to in time, Klaus, in a sneeze of nastiness, simply throws the thousand-dollar camera across the floor at Johnny's small feet.

Johnny starts to whimper. His unsuccessful swallowings make Todd berserk. He steps forward, readying for one of his outbursts.

Todd: (not quavering) You are every dumb two-dimensional tyrant there ever was. And I'm not gonna stand in your firing line for one more second. . . . (drawling out a last insult) Poindexter. . . .

Todd stamps off the Japan floor. Klaus laughs and laughs and laughs. His assistant bows down to the floor to pick up the Leica. Todd's partner girlishly eats her fists. Surprise. Soupy is standing at the door, watching, talking with a huffy Rimini. Todd feels caught in the act, but only slightly.

Todd: What you doing here?

Soupy: (dryly) Negotiating.

Soupy walks Todd into the dressing room, sits him down on a pale watermelon-red director's chair, presses down on his shoulders to keep him from popping up again.

Todd: (fierce, direct) I quit. Everything in this business has turned to dirt for me. . . . You can be as hot a calendar man as ever walked the earth and that doesn't guarantee you'll have love in your life. . . . It's not a business of air . . . heads . . . exactly. But air something. I'm an air something. And I wanna change. . . . There I said it.

Soupy: (the bright lights showing up his crow's feet, age lines, dark circles, sagging skin) To tell you the truth, Todd, I wouldn't respect you if you decided to stay in it.

Suddenly all the lights go out. Local brownout. Todd changes clothes in the dark and scuds down the stairs before anyone else.

THREE PROPHECIES

Todd arrives home fifteen minutes later, after perversely loitering in front of the show windows of the fur salons on his block, gaping at all the ice-princess white furs, and then trying to decipher the different services listed at the Fur Synagogue a few doors up.

When he walks into his late-afternoon apartment, the ruby red digital counter on his answering machine is lighting up a "3." He tosses his sack, slips off his sneaks, and unthinkingly assumes a lotus position, his legs in a pretzel, in front of the machine. Plays back his messages.

Message #1: Todd. This is your mother. Your aunt and uncle, Ray and Bette, are separating. I think his job in the factory is a spirit killer myself. The two older children are fine, almost married. But Robbie is in trouble. I've done some homework and there's a special prep program at NYU that might be good for him. I wonder if he can come live with you.

Message #2: Todd. This is Rosa Prauheim at the Rosa Prauheim Gallery. I want to follow up on our talk about showing and selling your scrapbook pages in our, my, gallery. I'll be out of town until next Wednesday.

Message #3: Todd Eamon? This is Joe Martell, the director. I saw the article on you in *GQ*, and I saw your *People* commercial. I have a part in a movie I have a hunch you might be right for. I'll try you at your agency.

Todd can't believe these messages in one series. They are like the three prophecies of the future by the witches in *Macbeth*. He pushes down the button on his machine that allows him to preserve them, so they are not washed over by the teletides.

SISTER RUTH THERESA

Lucy has joined an evening therapy group. It's run by Sister Ruth Theresa, a licensed psychotherapist, in the basement of a Roman Catholic church near Gramercy Park. The theme is "Love and Intimacy: Let's Find a Way of Forgiving."

The basement is damp and chilly, with vanilla stucco walls, white-speckled tile floor, exposed pipes. The eight members sit around in a circle on folding chairs. Sister Ruth Theresa presides at the tip of the circle in a big plump Agatha Christie armchair. She has an extremely angular and intelligent face, curiously close to the faces of the unapelike apes in *Planet of the Apes*. Auburn hair, cut short, rough. Her eyes look out with some understanding, some accusation, from set-back sockets. Even though she's a nun, she isn't wearing black and white, but rather a dress of warm Scottish plaid, a yellow cashmere scarf wrapped around her neck, dickey style, manila stockings, comfortable brown canvas earth shoes.

Each of the members speaks in turn, trying to formulate some pain in sensible words. Over and over they are saying that something is wrong. Whenever they try to mythologize, to blame the weather, or fate, Sister Ruth Theresa brings them back, forces them to demythologize, like a commonsense crackerbarrel Maine wise woman, trying to discover a practical solution to the wrong, perhaps so her group members will then be more open to that true pain, which has no answer, only expression in myth.

The Professor: (short, chubby, wearing a conservative blue suit, brown tie oxfords as shiny as vinyl, a metal watch with an accordion metal band around his wrist) My wife says that I'm the man in the bubble.

Stationery Store Owner: (long, languorous, in cheap brown suit with cream stripes, draped in his chair as if he were an abandoned coat, has visited Sister Ruth Theresa for ten years, speaks her language) I found that my wife, well we're not even married, that she would say she would call and then she wouldn't call. At first that drove me nuts. But then I just learned not to expect her to call. We have low expectations of each other.

Sister Ruth Theresa: (soothing) Low expectations can help a relationship.

Journalist: (black dress, round horn-rimmed Harvard-style glasses, one black-stockinged leg tucked up under the other) My alcoholic boyfriend is brilliant and funny but he uses women.

Architecture Draftsperson: (her brown hair flowing loose, dressed in a purple wool dress, pretty blue curved legs, efficient white nurse's shoes, to Stationery Store Owner) You're the luckiest man in the room. You have someone who you love and who loves you. You should be happy. That's what I want more than all the tea in China.

Sister Ruth Theresa: (evenly) I think that you're projecting like crazy onto this relationship. Watch out.

Dentist: (mid-forties, small, thin, mouse-faced, Southern-accented, in yellow Dacron shirt, green polyester pants, fake argyle socks, black go-go boots with zippers on the sides) I think the reason I'm so stuck on Dondi—that's what I call him, his real name is Donny—is that he's the same age I was, sixteen, when I left South Carolina. It was so green there. It was the happiest time of my life. People up North are too cold and cruel.

Sister Ruth Theresa: (sarcastically) Then why don't you move back if it was so wonderful?

Lucy is drained from listening. She is a folded person on a folding chair, her arms clapped around herself, her legs crossed over. She is all in black: black cashmere sweater, black blouse under, black denim skirt, gray stockings, black pumps. Her black leather jacket is hanging on the back of her chair, its zipper clinking every so often against the metal. She holds her fingers flat against her mouth, yawn fashion, to draw in on her slim cigarette.

Sister Ruth Theresa: Lucy. You're the church mouse tonight. Don't you have anything to share?

Lucy: I guess I have everything to share. My story. But I feel so dead serious. I have cramps in my stomach. My back aches. I don't feel pretty tonight. I need to be touched.

Sister Ruth Theresa: (reciting) Love cures. Both those who give it and those who receive it.

Lucy: I think I really need physical therapy. I need a massage.

Sister Ruth Theresa: I can give you a referral when you leave tonight. But first tell us your story.

Before she begins, Lucy tosses her mostly smoked Benson & Hedges onto the bald floor, smudging it out with her toe so that all that remains is the blotch, like a squashed bug.

Lucy: (so soberly) I thought that young women ought to be explorers. So when I left Paris to move in with Frank I imagined I was willing to leap without a safety net. Bravery never goes out of fashion. But now I find I was just being my own stunt-woman. Easy was hard, and hard easy.

Sister Ruth Theresa: (concentrating) Then move out of Frank's apartment. (to the circle-at-large) We need to prove our independence before we can prove that infinitely more valuable birthright, our interdependence. Good-night group. Until next week. (chuckles) Don't forget to dress warmly.

After the session, Lucy puts on her leather jacket, draws an alligator-skin-covered checkbook from an inside pocket, and writes a lilac check to Sister Ruth Theresa for twenty-five dollars.

Lucy: Now for real, do you have a masseur?

The sister hands her a gray parchment oversized business card with the name ERIC, the rubric SWEDISH MASSAGE, and line drawings of exotic birds and flowers. The card has a sixties feel. The sister suggests that Lucy travel to the East Village tonight for a rubdown. She explains that Eric is trustworthy, safe and gay. Lucy pushes the buttons on the nearby wall phone.

THE SIXTIES

Lucy arrives at the apartment building on Sixth Street between Second and Third. She rings the buzzer. Pushes open the wood door with a Confederate flag as curtain over its pane of glass. Climbs up the spiral stairs of uneven lengths. Up to a third floor.

Eric is homely. He's tall, blond-almost-white hair, bony-shouldered, witch-nosed. Is wearing a yellow T-shirt, black boxy pants, black nylon socks, and black corduroy slippers. His skin is smooth, his hello grip is strong.

Eric: (to ease Lucy) I know Sister Ruth Theresa because we were both in the same body-sensitivity workshop last summer on the Hudson.

Eric then hands Lucy a plain white wraparound towel from the Y, points her toward his bathroom. It's a tiny water closet crammed with a porcelain bathtub on four lion's-claw legs, a toilet with pulley chain, a sink. There's one prison-cell window up above head height. Stashed here and there are herbal shampoos, healthy oils and gels, elixirs to drink, tablets to drop in the bath, bottles and bottles of vitamins, as well as vials of vitamin drops. A hanging spider plant endures.

Lucy wraps a towel around her body like a Dorothy Lamour sarong and returns to take her place lying out flat on the massage board, an oversized ironing board for ironing humans.

Eric begins to work. No music. But Lucy feels as if she's listening to a radio. Eric kneads into her body. Rubbing in the thighs and calves. Smacking around her upper arm muscles. Pressing on her stomach. Then he flips her over and pushes down on pressure points in her back so that she feels her body heating. Lucy is moaning.

Lucy: (in a wail) I've been so unhappy. And I didn't even know it.

Eric: You need to luxuriate, Lucy.

Lucy: I know. I know.

After a forty-five-minute massage, Eric lets Lucy take a bath for a half hour in his tub. He prepares a steaming bath and pours in a soothing gel. She falls asleep in the tub, her head on a clip-on pillow Eric designed especially for the backs of tubs. She breathes in the finely puncturing steam.

When Lucy wakes, her skin is pink. She stands, dries herself, puts on her skimpy peach lace bra and matching peach panties, and tiptoes into the living room. The steam heat is blasting.

Eric is sitting cross-legged on his couch. His shoes and socks piled neatly next to the television, socks tucked in shoes. His yellow T-shirt draped over a globe on a desk. Eric's chest is flat, with plenty of black hairs making a nebula swirl design. Lucy curls her one leg under the other as she sits down next to him.

Lucy: It's so comfy here. Warm as a jungle.

Eric: (nostalgic) This is the first room I ever dropped acid in. I was seventeen then. Now I'm thirty-two. I was taking a bath with the guy whose apartment it was. He later became my lover. But in the tub he started to look like a Spanish pirate. The floor of the bathroom became soft rubber, engraved with fossil designs. I made it from the bathroom toward the light coming in the kitchen window, above the plates there, see, but the window steamed up. I crawled like a baboon out of the primeval past.

Lucy: (chatty) They've discovered that many of the baboons and apes were actually much larger than prehistoric men. But the cavemen killed them off somehow. Maybe that's where the King Kong story came from.

Eric: (continuing on the subject of origins) I'm from Sweden. The son of a Swedish diplomat to the UN. He and my mother went home years ago. But I stayed to be lovers with the guy whose apartment this was, even though he had a lover, so we were three.

Lucy: Two men. I sympathize.

Eric: The first few nights we slept together I slept between them. A's cock in my ass. And B's cock in my mouth, my cock in his mouth. It was totally satisfying.

Lucy: I love that story. But why did you tell it to me? I guess maybe after you massage someone, and you have to shut up the whole time, you want to spill something out.

Eric: Maybe. But why did you come walking out here in your underwear? Why did you fall asleep in my bathtub?

Lucy: Maybe I felt comfortable because you're a gay guy. Once I went home with an ape-man lawyer, real drunk, and I fell into snoring in his bed. I hadn't put in my diaphragm or anything. And I woke up and he was there over me with a raging dick all ready to put in me. I was so upset.

Eric: Hadn't you taken the pill?

Lucy: No one takes the pill anymore. Not like when you were young.

Eric: (corrected) Oh.

Lucy: But maybe I shouldn't treat you like, like another woman, a girlfriend. I don't know your mysteries.

Eric: You're safe with me. If that's the answer to your questions.

Lucy rests her limp hand on Eric's forearm. She rubs up and down so the hairs tickle.

Eric: You can even spend the night if you want. I can sleep on the floor on my inflatable mattress. I'd like that. I don't like to be alone. And I'd like to sleep on my inflatable mattress. Reminds me of being out in the woods in nature.

Lucy: Why did you ask me to stay overnight?

Eric: I just told you.

Lucy: Because I'd love to. I decided tonight to leave my present situation. And this would help me settle my mind.

Eric walks to the deep dark sink and washes out a cloudy glass with a sponge that has soap still dried in its pores so he doesn't have to add any new. He rinses the glass in warm water from the tap. Fills it with ice cubes and adds cold water. Carries the glass to Lucy. Then returns to a stove to heat up some tea.

Lucy: (decisively) Now I'm going to make the call I've been thinking and thinking to make. And say the words that have only been going through my head.

Lucy tucks the telephone receiver under her jawbone on one side, pushes the buttons deliberately.

Lucy: Frank? I decided tonight under the auspices of my group to move back to the Bowery. . . . I still might want to be your love slave. . . . I'm with a masseur but not to worry he's gay. . . . Hmmmm. . . .

Lucy hangs up, her face distorted into a bluish face of Peter Lorre.

Eric: (screwing round from the boiling tea water) Wud he say?

Lucy: He just said you could be Jack the Ripper's sex-ed instructor for all he cared. But it'll pass. He's insecure and prideful. And a male beauty. That's all.

Eric removes the inflatable mattress from his closet and blows it up, heaving, puffing his thin face. Then he opens the couch into a bed. Lucy sits back down on it while Eric pours two hot herbal teas in cups, adding honey with a wooden implement that traps the sticky honey until the contact with the hot liquid causes it to melt. He hands one fragile cup to Lucy. Sits on the bed with her. They drink. He turns on the tiny black-white television, an antique, to watch a rerun of *The Honeymooners*. In tonight's episode, Ralph, an early prototype of Archie Bunker in *All in the Family*, instructs his future brother-in-law how to be a macho "king of the castle."

Eric turns off the television. The two fall asleep by the light of a kerosene night lamp, Lucy on the couch-bed, Eric on the inflatable mattress.

Lucy: (muskily) I feel as if I'm in the woods of Vermont.

Eric: (from below, drifting off) Or Maine.

WAILING ARABIC LOVE SONGS

Both Todd and Lucy are showing signs of spring starting. It's March, the month that looks like May, but feels like February. Todd's wearing Scottish-plaid pants, a canary-yellow T-shirt, white deck shoes. Lucy's in white pants, a light-blue hospital orderly's shirt, straw slipper-shoes.

Lucy is settled back on the Bowery, but today is visiting Todd. They are down at the Arab grocery store near Todd's building. In the back is a flower rack. Lucy grabs one bunch and pays at the counter. A cassette of wailing Arabic love songs is playing on the counterboy's box. He is young, wearing an Arabic-letter necklace, his hair a tumbleweed of brown wires, his big-collared pattern shirt mostly hidden under a thin plain dirty white cashmere sweater. Ali leers at Lucy, and winks. While he is ringing up the purchase, a beggar in Cairo-green felt pants approaches Todd with a Polaroid of his brother who is sick and needs money for the doctor. Todd donates a quarter.

Outside, Lucy hands Todd the flowers, fondly.

Lucy: (kissing him on the cheek) Here's a house gift. I have to catch a cab.

Todd: Walk me to the corner.

They walk up Eighth the half block to the corner where Todd will turn to get to his doorway on the side street. On the way they hear sounds that are definitely not winter sounds: kids yelling in a playground, the roll of truck treads over roads free of ice, helicopter choppers. The view up the boulevard—Eighth Avenue is as extra-large-size as any boulevard in Paris—climaxes at a brick wall of a tall office building painted with a cigarette-pack advertisement. The cylinders of cigarettes rise at different heights like organ pipes.

Lucy: (walking) I'm glad I got out of that S & M trip before the spring. It's definitely a winter sport.

Todd: It's like modeling, S & M. Constricting. Life's constricting enough at it is. Money. Life span.

Lucy: Okay, thinker.

Todd: (in a lyrical mood) I'm gonna pick up my cousin Robbie in a month. If you help me with him, then the three of us could be a family, of partners, a loose one.

Lucy: (noncommittedly) Is he cute?

Back in the apartment, after Todd sticks the bouquet in a gray cylinder vase and balances it on the fold-over ledge at the top of his drafting table, the flowers immediately turn into a visionary variegation as his attention zooms into the pastel roughage with total absorption: purple violet accretions, white hankies of flowers with violet edges, dark-green leaves in tourniquet twists, girlie yellow zinnias bursting out of their pale-green girdles, stolid white carnations, puckered buds. It's a mescal mix, deepened in significance and, therefore, beauty, perhaps, for Todd, by all this talk about home.

THE NUCLEAR FAMILY

At the beginning of May, Todd is ready to pick up Robbie in Allentown. It's a Saturday. Robbie's room now has a mattress. A black touch-tone phone with long cord on the floor. And a couple of clip-on lights on window ledge and closet door. Todd is leaving the rest up to him.

The car that Todd rented is beige, automatic. He plays the Top Forty stations on AM at maximum volume, contorting to the music within the restraints of his harness seatbelt. Drives through Lincoln Tunnel, connects to the New Jersey Turnpike, then Interstate 78, curves along blue mountainsides cascading

239

down into green-gray waters, the reverse of nature's expected color scheme, then makes his way into the green-brown center of Pennsylvania, passing through the little city of Bethlehem, known for its electrical Christmas decorations, and finally to Allentown, old-world Allentown.

Todd stands on his aunt's street, taking a breather. Dressed all in white: white sweatshirt, white chinos, white sneaks. The houses are all cranberry shingles with single doors and one-step stoops. They resemble rowhouses in Welsh coal-mining towns. Parked in front of Todd's car is his parents': a generic too-big Cadillac-y sedan, tan, waxed, polished. The sky is slate gray. Todd waits for ten seconds in front of the green wooden front door. Hesitant. Then he pushes the buzzer. His own mother, not his Aunt Bette, answers. Todd first sees his mother through the scrim of the screen door.

Todd: It's me. Back from the wars.

She opens the light door as if it were heavy.

Todd's mother, Elaine, has a pudgy sorrowful face, with just a trace of bathing beauty left. Her skin sags some around the neck. Her brown tinted hair is contoured into a swirl that resembles a fancy bun, a hot-cross bun. She is wearing two white oval earrings. Is dressed in a tasteful brown dress, with a thin mauve leather belt tied uselessly around the waist, its tassels hanging down her right side. She is shorter than usual because she's changed into her red Korvettes, or rather hasn't changed out of them. The red Korvettes are a kind of flat-bottomed sneaker for car travel. Elaine only comes up to Todd's chest when they hug.

Elaine: (still in hug, but angry and embarrassed) There's so much screaming and cursing going on, and so much dirt in this house. I offered to come down and clean it myself. (even more whispered) And your Aunt Bette has a new friend now, a sixty-year-old friend, here, wait till you see him.

Todd: She's probably getting it more than I am.

Elaine: Not that kind of friend.

They saunter down the entrance hall, decorated in a wallpaper of dirty-white carnations on a dark-green background. Todd's Aunt Bette steps right out from a door that leads into a side room. She doesn't look like Elaine's sister. She has dyed-red Lucille Ball hair, thinning. Her teeth aren't fixed straight. She uses turquoise-blue eyeliner. Is wearing a blue cotton dress, brown stockings with runs, no shoes. When she sees Todd her face scrambles from an easy grin into an alcoholic-looking pathos. She grabs Todd then pulls him to her. Her breath smells strongly of toothpaste. Although she is aggressively mothering Todd, she also seems to be falling into him for support. She is meatier than Elaine but less able to stand on her own feet. Elaine is cool, snobby, sounding like a Jacqueline Onassis on pills. Bette is always spilling her feelings, some more sincere than others.

Todd: (braying his head back from the gusts of her Colgate breath) That's powerful perfume Aunt Bette.

Aunt Bette: Todd. I haven't seen my baby in so many years, such a long long time. Ever since you became famous you forgot all about me. But I have all your pictures. Your mother sends me the magazines, trying to gloat it over me. But I love them in spite of her, in spite of you almost. You never call. (lowering her tone) We have to talk about Robbie.

Todd: (feeling as if he has just been asked five questions in a row) Where is he?

Aunt Bette: Come in. Take off your shoes and stay awhile.

Todd leans onto the hallway wall for a second. Every room is like walking into a new generation, or a new saga. Then he imperceptibly catches up.

They push into the cramped side room, its only window onto the street muted by a lace curtain. The dominant piece of furniture is a green old-fashioned couch with fuzzy-ball upholstery, napkinlike arm protectors, and bones-of-brown-wood legs. The big green chairs that match the couch fill up most of the rest of the room. A large cherrywood console TV with a big round antenna flickers with an old movie, *Du Barry Was a Lady*. The floor is cluttered with space-age toys manipulated by Tammy's two-year-old boy.

Tammy, Bette's only daughter, the middle child, is sitting in one of the big chairs. She's twenty-one, kind of beautiful, has dirty blond hair that darkens a shade every year, is wearing a soft daisy-yellow pants suit and black Capezio dance shoes. She is chewing a wad of pink gum, and every so often gives a kick to one of her son's toys. She has just sent a G.I. Joe doll knocking backward into the faded rug. Tammy used to be a tomboy. Her husband is sitting in the other green chair. He has a pockmarked face and greasy black hair. Has on a short-sleeved gray shirt with his name stitched in red, *Ed*, blue starched pants, black round boots with at least a dozen eyelets for the laces to pass through. His yellow socks match Tammy's pants suit. Ed works in a garage with Clark, Bette's first son. No one else is in the room right now.

Tammy: (Todd bending over to kiss her on her cheek) I can't believe you're getting stuck with my kook brother.

Ed: (stands up and walks over to shake Todd's hand) Don't listen to her. Robbie's a good guy. He's good people.

Todd: (kidding, staring into the sluices of Ed's blue eyes) Might not be if he hangs too much with me.

Ed sits down again. Todd settles onto the prickly couch, his aunt on one side, his mother on the other. He flings his left hand up behind his neck, flaps right hand down on lap, churns one way, then grinds the other way, constantly altering his posture in a confining spot.

Aunt Bette: He is a good kid. But a bad apple. He spent too much time around his parents.

Elaine: He reminds me of friends of yours, Todd. The ones who were in the drug crowd in high school. I still applaud you for having friends who were in the drug crowd and yet your not being in the drug crowd.

Todd: (broadcasting old news) Tina wasn't on drugs. She had frizzed hair.

Ed: I walked out of the game last night into the street and there was black guys everywhere selling dope and doing dope. Disgustink!

242

Tammy: Don't talk about dope in front of your son.

The son crawls over, right after Tammy's remark, and sticks his head cautiously between his young father's legs, as if he were sticking his head into an oven. Then he slips down and starts to fall asleep with his tiny head resting on his father's warm mucky work boots.

Ed: See? Doesn't bother him none.

Aunt Bette: Everyone's in the other room. And I have to get the instant mashed potatoes ready for dinner.

Elaine: Instant? Real potatoes are easy and nutritious. I don't know why anyone would make instant.

Aunt Bette: (to Todd) Your father is in the other room.

Todd: (knowingly) Keeping a low profile.

They stand up and walk through a short hall, or extended archway, toward the living room, a big public space crammed with everyone else. Clark and Tammy and their sleeping son rest in the side room for a few minutes more, pretending to watch the costume film, but really just taking a break from all the visitors.

Robbie is standing at the end of the short hall. Elaine and Aunt Bette pass around him like stream water curving around an abrupt upstarting rock. Todd stops in front of him.

Robbie: (simply) I was just coming in to get you.

Robbie is about the same height as Todd. Has long silky black hair. Is wearing a Grateful Dead T-shirt, two-tone jeans (fronts are silver, backs are black), low white tennis shoes, no socks, a silver ID bracelet uninscribed.

Todd: (decisively) Let's go to your room first. Before wading in there.

Robbie breaks off. Todd follows him through the side room and up to his second-floor dark-pink bedroom. Faded squares and rectangles mark the sites of removed posters, with some of the patches of tape still sticking. Three beat-up green ultrasuede suitcases rest on the bare linoleum floor.

Todd automatically checks out the window. On the street below a couple of guys, two white, one black, are lugging bags of groceries and a few six-packs. Probably for a party later on. An imperceptible rain is falling, turning the stiff bags into loose messes and making the guys' heads glisten. Robbie is sitting on the bed, his legs out resting on his ankles' backs. He kicks off his sneaks and draws one foot up on one knee, starting biting off a toenail. Todd sits down next to him, watching him closely, if casually.

Robbie: (testing) You ever met Lauren Hutton?

Todd: She's too old for me.

Robbie: (rolling forward) Cause I saw her in *American Gigolo*. She used to be a model. She has this space between her teeth. That's what I want. Some older woman to take me around the world on a boat like that. And me just stay in my cabin and do isometrics all day while she's out working the deck. That'd be cool.

Todd: (going along) I thought you wanted to be a singer in a band.

Robbie: I'm through with that. Bands was yesterday.

Todd: What's today? Gigolo?

Robbie: (gesturing profusely) Well I have a lot of ideas, about society, and about relationships between people. I have a lot inside me, and I notice these things, but I don't know how to express myself, or what to do with it. I want to go to school so I can learn the right terminology and shit.

Todd: (hand on Robbie's thigh) I like you. I'm glad you're coming to be my roommate.

Robbie: (inching out from under the hand) I'm impressed with you too. I've seen all your pictures in the magazines.

Robbie walks over to the windowsill and picks up a red rubber band, ties his hair back into a ponytail, and snaps the band around to keep the tail fixed. Then he reaches into a navy-blue backpack on steel poles, pulls out a magazine, *Heavy Rock*, with pictures of some howling young men on its cover. He tosses the magazine to Todd.

Robbie: Look on page seventeen.

Todd turns to page seventeen.

Robbie: That's me in the crowd. See?

Page seventeen features a live concert photograph of a boy band, with shaved heads, dressed in motorcycle outfits. The crowd in the front, by the stage, is a blurred youthquake. Robbie's head is circled in red pencil, otherwise unidentifiable.

Robbie: (shrugging earnestly) It's a start.

Todd grunts.

Robbie: (ultrasensitive to the unspoken) I hear you.

Robbie reaches into the bag again. This time he brings out a bottle of orange California Cooler. White wine, water, carbon dioxide, fructose, natural orange flavor, citric acid, artificial color, sodium benzoate preservatives. In its cloudy phosphorescence the bottle appears to be concealing a genie.

Robbie drinks down the bottle, talking most of the time. Then he slips into his sneakers again, without tying the laces, and the two return downstairs. Todd makes a right into the living room, but Robbie makes a left.

Robbie: (explaining without turning around) I have some goodbyes to say. Outside.

The big room is filled with smells: cigarettes, beer, whiskey, meat and potatoes, lemon air freshener. And noises: baseball game on television, rock radio station, lots of talking and shouting. Clark, the oldest son, is sitting talking with his work buddy, Ed. Clark is tall and spindly. His black hair sprouts. His wife, Barbara, is sitting next to him, with big breasts and a big body. She is joining in the talk about baseball players. She and Clark know all the statistics. Tammy is asleep on a couch with her son wrapped in her tummy in a papoose fur-lined tote bag.

Todd's father is sitting in a big brown armchair, drawn close to another big brown armchair, where Al, Aunt Bette's new friend, is slumped. Todd's father is drinking a diet soda. When he was younger he didn't drink because of his ulcer, and now he doesn't drink because of his heart condition. His name is Harry. He has on a Perry Como sweater, light blue, with three ivory buttons, a polo shirt with a horse stitched on, gray wool pants, nylon socks, and penny Loafers that look too small, copper pennies stuck in. His face looks remarkably like his wife's.

Al is thin. He is a Jack Sprat. She eats no lean. Together they are the blueprint for Bette's son and daughter-in-law, Clark and Barbara. Harry is president of a successful carpet-cleaning company, and Al is always trying to wangle his first wife's brother a job there. Aunt Bette is in the kitchen dumping a sealed packet of French butter beans in a pot of boiling water.

Todd approaches. His short father stands and they shake hands. Todd stares at the blue veins in his hand as they grip. His father sits down again, and Todd draws up a wooden desk chair to sit next to him, crossing one leg over by grabbing on the ankle.

Harry: Is everything okay?

Todd: (unaware of modulating to his father's monotone) Okay. My *People* commercial is out. Did you see it?

Aunt Bette walks in from the kitchen with a stack of magazines that have Todd's picture: *GQ, Men's Wear, L'uomo Vogue, L'Officiel, New York Times Magazine, International Male catalog, Sears Roebuck catalog, Pizza Hut uniform catalog, Interview, Esquire fall men's clothing issue.* No one is much interested, except Clark's wife, Barbara. But her interest is enough to start Elaine going.

Elaine: (the most expensively dressed woman in the room) So the next step is to be a movie star. Joe Martell called him out of the blue. (nervous laugh, then, as if atoning for the laugh) Of course life doesn't work like that, probably won't happen. But it's always nice to be considered.

Harry: (inappropriately livid) Don't discourage him. I don't think acting is as hard as we think it is.

Robbie walks back in the room, uneven dots of rain splashed on his clothes. He sits on the edge of Al's chair.

Robbie: (across to Todd) Al is the quiet one. He goes perfect with my mom. Speak Al.

Al: (softly) I was just talking to Mr. Eamon. I was telling him about my operation.

Robbie: I feel real bad about that Al. I'm glad Mom stayed with you, even if my dad did practically burn down the house he was so angry.

Al: (announcing to no one) Robbie's a good kid. (to Todd) New York will be a good place for him. He's too big for Allentown. He's not bad, he's just smart.

Dinner is a rolling two-hour fiesta. Eleven people sit around two tables pushed together in the steamy kitchen. A tiny window with a geranium on its sill is left open so the rainy breezes blow in. Todd reverts, antisocially, to irrigating his dry hills of mashed potatoes with rivers of gravy, over and over again. Tammy's little boy is stuck on a light wood highchair with a decal of a rooster on its back. He has a blue bib about him, and his great-aunt Elaine is spooning apricot paste into his mouth. After every silver spoonful he sticks his tongue around outside his mouth bitterly.

Aunt Bette: I remember when he was a baby his little thing used to get hard as a nail. And if he was bawling and I wanted to get him to shut up I'd have to play with it until he gurgled himself back to sleep. My own boys were that way too.

Clark: I'm still that way. Right Barbara? (laughs in her face)

Barbara: (congenial, after chewing away some corn kernels) He still needs a pacifier.

While Robbie is upstairs gathering his bags, Todd says good-bye to his parents.

Todd: (hugging his mother) Whatever you do, don't get fat.

Todd: (shaking hands with his father) I hope you flower when you retire.

Then he waits outside behind the driver's wheel. Aunt Bette walks Robbie to the car. She stands in the rain crying. Robbie stands by nobly, waiting for her to give him the push-off.

Aunt Bette: (weepy) I hope you don't blame me for not providing you with the proper home life.

Robbie: (remonstrating) Mom! You gave me a great home. It was neat here. I can relate to a mom with a boyfriend. The others seemed like old prunes. The other mothers.

Aunt Bette: Thanks. I love you. And I know that you're my special son. (leaning in the car, to Todd) Todd. Show him the way. I know it's not your place to take care of him. But open up his horizons so that he goes beyond his parents. Okay hon?

Todd: (his throat bunching up all the way down toward his chest) I promise Aunt Bette.

GREASER HOOD

In high school Robbie was sort of a greaser hood. Or a punk. Smart, though. But in the new setting of Manhattan he instantly loses that heavy black outline. He fits right in. Is just another restless hungry statistic. Is normal.

On Saturday night, the night after Robbie's arrival, Todd still has not returned his rental. Robbie notices it parked below, while standing up in his window, dressed in the same Grateful Dead outfit as yesterday, going crazy. The moon is glaring in his window like a hocker that spreads out when spit on a flat glass surface.

Robbie walks out in the main room. Todd is working at his drafting table on his collages.

Robbie: (flatly) Todd I'm outta here for a bit.

Todd: (not turning around) Cool.

So Robbie sticks his new key in his right sneaker, along with the car key he slides off the see-through glass kitchen table with high-tech black metal legs on his way out.

The anonymous beige car is parked right downstairs at the corner. Robbie slips in. Revs up. Goes for a drive. Down the erratically elevated West Side Highway, the closest Manhattan has to a freeway, in the direction of the silver stereo speaker of the World Trade Center, disco architecture. In a smoke of traffic he rushes past billboards and through factory-lined stretches of road. Seems as if the car, all the cars, are driving themselves automatically, on their way to a preprogrammed destination. Near the Holland Tunnel, Robbie swerves, U-turns, travels back up the grittier West Street.

By now has his wet palm down the silver front of his duotone pants. Is hard. Turns, magically, at Twenty-eighth Street heading east. The street is lined with a phantasmagoria of whores, walkers, transvestites, transsexuals, pimps. They brazenly primp right in the road, soliciting at car windows with all the elbow greasiness of the rangy guys who force window washes on out-of-state drivers during the daytime hours. The girls' masculine other half.

Robbie cruises once for overview through this stretch of illegal amusements. Metal trucks from New Jersey are pulled over at the curbs. Limos steer up and suck painted ladies into their black-cloud posteriors. In the basketball court young guys lean up against hoop poles while girls kneel down in front of them in the puddles of shadows lapping away at that one most urgent muscle.

On the second time around Robbie honks at a girl. She has a chiseled young still-pretty Joan Crawford face, brown hair to shoulders, blue pinstriped shirt open on cleavage, in tight light cloudy blue jeans, red heels, like in Oz. She comes up to the window so close that Robbie can smell the cinnamon flavoring in her red lipstick.

Robbie: (leaning out window) I want a free BJ.

Teri: I'm Teri. Why free?

Robbie: You think I can't get it here from one of your sisters?

Teri: (dropping eyelids in a caricature of seduction) Let me in.

So Teri hurries around to the other side, her speedy ministeps caught in relief by the pop-up headlights of the rental. Robby leans over to pull at the metal lock handle. She slides in all the way over to his manic body.

Robbie: (she's so close he can't turn his head all the way right) Where should we go?

Teri: (a voice of stripped gears) Over by the wire fence.

She's referring to the wire fence of the basketball court, its wires tied off at their tips like barb.

Robbie turns off the car. Silence as big as any wilderness when the engine noise stops. Without looking at her places her hand on his crotch. She scratches up and down with her long red nails. Then Robbie puts his hand on her crotch. Feels a long hard roll of flesh in there. The adrenaline starts to pound in his head. He can hear his own heart.

Robbie: You're not a girl you're a guy.

Teri: (putting his hand on her warm breasts) Feel these. Don't tell me that.

Robbie: You're a transvestite.

Teri: (dropping back for a minute into the car seat, over by her own window) It was the voice wasn't it? It's cause I stopped taking the hormones and the voice goes first.

Robbie: (eyes glinting) No it was the dick.

Teri: You mind? (as desperate as he for some point to all this) You ever get fucked by a girl? You ever suck off a girl? It was the voice wasn't it?

Robbie: (his breath sulfurous because coming from down deep) No I never did. And I don't want to.

Teri: You want anything?

Robbie: I could dry-hump you in the backseat. That's it.

Teri: Dry-hump me. Mmmmm.

So they both climb over into the back. Robbie turns her over and unbuttons her shirt while she's on her belly, takes it off, exposing her white fishy skin to the car air.

Teri: (trying to screw her head around) You got anything to take?

Robbie covers his sweaty palm over her moving mouth. With the other hand pulls down the skin tight jeans. Lets his own roll of flesh out like a rifle through a hole in an old-fashioned fort. Sticks it between her legs. They both dance up and down, spastically, in some kind of happy hurt.

Teri: (while he's dry-humping her) I get businessmen. I get

truck drivers. I get goombahs. I get Hasids with the hats and the beards. But I never got you.

By now Robbie is waxing smoothly between her legs. He spits to make himself wetter. Then he just rivets on.

Robbie: What am I?

Teri: (syncopated with his thrusts) You're an . . . all-American . . . you're an all . . . American.

Robbie sprays a concentrated spray between her legs. She comes all over the leather seats of the rental.

Teri: (never satisfied) I'll lick it up for you. I'll lick it up for you.

She does. She crouches down in the floor space and licks the mess on the backseat. Robbie sits back and watches her, just amused.

Robbie: I like you. I wish everyone was like you.

Teri: You wanna be my boyfriend?

Robbie: No.

Teri: Don't even answer. I've had them for months. Then they always end up saying what they really want is the real thing.

Robbie: Don't let it get you down.

Teri: (crawling up to kiss him on his chin) You puppy. You're adorable and soft.

Robbie agrees to give Teri a lift down the street to Fifth Avenue. Teri talks all the way.

Teri: You don't know what I went through. In my head mostly. But I wanted to be a woman so bad I felt so guilty I used to take blood thinner that I had hid in my purse to give myself bleeding. I don't know what it meant. Most people live dreamy lives I think. They're not handed a bowl of blood to drink every fucking day.

Robbie slows to a stop next to a Citibank branch that looks so invitingly lit up from inside with its blues and whites that it's positively musical.

Robbie: (adolescently croaking voice) Better luck next life.

THE CULTURE OF NARCISSISM

It's Michael Ives's birthday party at the Underground, a basement-upon-basement club at Union Square. Ives, a former Yale crew team member, with hair as blond as wood, teeth as thick as bones, a torso stretched perhaps from rowing, making his legs seem short by some perspectival trick, is walking through regular disco scenery, trailed by less famous guys (in waiting) from the agency, hit up regularly by girls who want to play swans to his Zeus. The men's division's biggest money-maker this year, Ives is always vaguely tan, evidence of bookings points south.

Todd is here. Soupy called him to invite him as his picture is still in the agency book. So he stops by, dressed in a quiet dark-blue Gap sweatshirt, white jeans, black Loafers, no socks. Soupy is greeting everyone at the door. In a powder-blue zoot suit, red carnation.

Soupy: (to Todd) Don't stay too long or you'll want back in.

Todd: (relieved at not having to project anymore) Like an alcoholic at a cocktail party?

He's only staying ten minutes. Walks through the two-story disco with catwalks crossing overhead, small rooms lit red like the bedrooms of pashas, so much human confetti blown about by a transmitted wind of Barry White and Michael Jackson.

Todd climbs metal fire-escape stairs to a separated glass box of a VIP birthday-cake quadrant. Opposite of expected, the most elite and guarded room is the most crowded. The faces of models, would-be models, model hags, photographers, bookers shine in a kind of moonlight. They are all like Cervantes' Knights of Mirrors, reflections not only of each other, but reflecting too the personalities projected in their most famous ads. Print models are like silent-screen stars, all presence, no voice, so more mystery.

Marlo Thomas Model: (popping up in front of Todd in her genie jewelry) I worked with you in Düsseldorf. Remember?

Todd: (lying) Yeah.

Todd turns around to Ives who has a girl on either side, both of whom are using words the equivalent of throwing their hotel keys onstage at Las Vegas.

Todd: (to Ives) I always wanted to ask you. Are you related to Charles Ives, the composer?

Ives: (stuffing mouth with chocolate cake, putting on a forced dumb-jock voice) No. Burl Ives.

Suddenly Paul is there, rematerialized in one of his red-check flannel barbecue shirts, emanating warmth. Todd and Paul grab each other around their ribs, hug, to the artificial treble of Diana Ross's "Upside Down".

Todd: (shouting) This song was popular when we were.

Paul, after a few sentimental and heartfelt riffs of "how are you," relocates to the bar.

Todd gazes down past a metal pipe of a railing to the citric dance floor below (acidy yellows and oranges) transected by white *Star Wars* laser beams. A harlequinade is transpiring. Soupy has dressed Richard, the healthy dark-skinned muscular new-comer model from the Power shoot, in a coat of mail made of Scotch-taped-together composites of everyone in the agency, men and women. He blindfolds him with a long strip of stickers advertising the name ROXANNE normally used for mailing pack-ages. Then he leads him through the crowd and pushes him onto the dance floor where he has to dance blind. Doesn't seem to mind. Reggae music is playing. Soon other models begin to rip the composite apart (sympathy? jealousy? fun?) and the boy is freed from the public spell.

Todd feels the powerful hand of Jerry, pro baseball player from Philadelphia, smack on the back of his shoulder. Turns, sees Jerry dressed in black wool zip jacket with white satin ker-chief around neck, tan linen pants, white bucks, hair slicked to side, with part, looking like an out-of-context matinee idol.

Jerry: (regional accent) Todd. I hear you're on your way out.

Todd: Or my way in.

Jerry: (skipping the needle forward) Todd. You like doing it with young girls?

Todd: Maybe.

Jerry: What's the youngest you ever did it with?

Todd: Sixteen.

Jerry: I had two fourteen-year-olds the other day. But the one . . . maybe she was thirteen . . . was too small for me to fit in. Is your dick normal-sized? Maybe you could help me out. Do her. I'll do her friend.

Todd: Pass.

On his way along one of the I-beam overhead walkways Todd passes Joe MacDonald, the classic model with eyes, hair, jaw, skin, all evoking some American aristocracy, vaguely Boston, that probably never was and never will be. Usually in a suit in pictures, MacDonald has on T-shirt and jeans, and around his neck, like a tribal talisman, a necklace made of all his airline baggage-check tickets, stitched together.

In one warm cave-room near the exit on the way out, colored slides are projecting on an overhead screen. Famous magazine pictures of the era. Not just of Roxanne's models. But all of the faces of the entire pulsing fractured world-in-an-eye of that year. Todd walks in during the men's phase.

Slides: Jeff Aquilon, captain of the water polo team at Pepperdine University, lying dazed on a mattress on a loft floor, his stomach rippling, modeling briefs and socks. Michael Ives eating an ice-cream cone. As dark as a Greek in *The Iliad*, Dimitri Boyd, in chamois shorts and nothing else lounging on white tiles. (His *Penthouse* shoots often turned into orgies with him screwing the girls in the bed, art directors watching.) Vern McHale in flowered print shorts and nothing else leaning against a white bike. (He posed for *Rockshots*, the porn greeting cards, nude except for a Santa hat.) Nick Rea, in a forest of women's shadowy legs. (Gym instructor, gave Tantric massages to guys or girls for money when starting out.) Rick Edwards lying back in a lounge chair, his white terrycloth robe open, black Speedos crotch shot, a woman in white lace bikini adoring his chest with her hands and eyes, his face in a joy of self-delight. John Reilly in a tall black tux. (He would do coke all night, rent a room at the St. Mark's gay baths and leave the door open to invite one taker after the next, reviving himself in his home sauna the next morning before work.) Chet Cardine, white sweatband wrapped around his carved head, wet matted hair hanging down, brown eyes a powerful invitation to the void. (Discovered by Roxanne at a tennis match, ended up an alky recluse on a mountain above Malibu, overweight and ghoulish as the later Presley.)

Todd feels good to have been there. It was a pastel moment in history. But he is glad too to be walking straight for the heavy black steel door with the red exit sign gleaming above. He pushes against the horizontal pole that allows the door to open as he presses in with his forearm. A whoosh of chilled blue air rushes in, like an answer to a question.

Slam

AT THE GALLERY

Rosa's gallery is white. Its smooth walls are white. Its recently painted plank-wood floors are white. Its track lights are white metal. Waiters, from the company Todd used to work for, are zigzagging around in white jackets, straightening white table-cloths on bar tables, emptying cans of translucent ice into white porcelain ice bowls, folding white napkins.

Even Rosa is wearing a white dress, and white high heels below. But the rest of her is as colored as cans of paint. Her hair is rusty red, down to her shoulders. Her skin is dark, perpetually tanned dark by a machine, with orange freckles. Her eyes are blue. Her nails are painted blue, too. She is in her forties, as etched as the cameo actress Sylvia Miles.

Rosa: (in her German accent, to Todd) All the revolutions of the world were just PR inventions. Parties that people attended for business reasons. The real revolution is art.

Todd: (in copper linen sportscoat, yellow silk shirt, blue jeans, white deck shoes, no socks) That's interesting Rosa.

Edward Stack: (dressed in a paint-spattered black canvas suit, a late beatnik, the other artist in tonight's show) But the Marxist revolution started in Germany but was then enacted in Russia. How does that fit in?

Rosa: (very *tant pis*) Oh it does. It's just like Danceteria stealing the crowd from Hurrah's, or Mudd Club realizing the space only implied by CBGB's music. The real politics is clubs.

Edward Stack: (shouting back while walking over to be with his wall of paintings) You wanna go out after?

In one Stack canvas, *Neighbors,* two brutes in guinea Ts, with shaved heads, face off in front of their suburban shacks, each with ferocious spike-collared wolf-toothed dogs on leashes ready to rip at each other. In *Burning Limo in Beirut,* a black Cadillac bursts into red-orange flames that lick at a pink sky. Looks like a *New York Times* photo come to life, revealing its colored essences.

Todd then files off to stand by his wall of collages. Holding a plastic half-cup filled with green-colored white wine. Soon the cube of a room fills up. A wave of sound keeps gathering force then smashing against a far wall. Lots of blacks and whites, clothing, make a graphic threshing floor. Pointed shoes, rounded boots. Hair glossed with different waxes, gels. Cigarettes smoked outside. Todd's eyes take a snapshot of every red dot thumbed by Rosa (sold!) on one of his collages, pressed now in Plexiglas like colored leaves preserved in wax paper.

Lucy, in a peach laboratory smock, buttoned, is recording the opening on a hand-held video camera she borrowed for the night from the production company where she now works. Moves about like a creature from a technological lagoon with a mechanical eye for a head. When she turns on the lights, the milky stream brings to life whomever it falls on, as faces searching for recognition are recorded.

Lucy: (passing by Todd, whispers romantically) I plan to swallow you later.

Robbie, hair down to shoulders tonight, stays out of the way. He sits most of the time in a window ledge, the glass blanked out by a sheet of black cardboard. Then he sees a guy and a girl snorting coke in a hallway leading to a toilet in the rear of the gallery. He moves right in, like a wolf, predatory. They agree to go in with him on a twenty-five-dollar score. The guy is black, wearing a square military cap, earring in right ear, Clash T-shirt, fatigues and boots. The girl with him is Spanish, has on a red velvet bunch of cloth. While he disappears to find his dealer, she talks garrulously to Robbie. Robbie keeps smoking in deep on the joint he lit.

Spanish Girl: A new pizza palace opened on Seventh Avenue in the Village. So we went to try a slice. In two days Carlos has an appointment with the police department. He took the test two years ago. They're looking for a few good men.

Robbie: (quick breath) I'd rather be a Guardian Angel than a cop.

A cub reporter from a downtown newspaper is asking Todd about the relation between fashion and art, like one of the caricature paparazzi in *La Dolce Vita.* He is thin, with shiny black hair, like an ant. Todd, though, is happy to talk this way.

Todd: (liking the feel of his own voice) The Mannerist period in painting, after the High Renaissance, was high fashion. Bronzino's portraits of handsome courtiers. Parmigianino's portraits in mirrors.

Just then Frank walks in. As bold an entrance as that of a gunslinger in a Western saloon. He is wearing an elegant black suit, black Brooks Brothers tie shoes, a red tie with little yellow polka dots the color of his pushed-back hair, and wire glasses. Is holding himself arrogantly, obviously steeled, with his new girlfriend, her arm wrapped around his crooked arm. She looks almost exactly like Sharon—short, blond, sharp, fulsome.

Lucy stands back behind the fencing mask of her camera.

Todd feels an invisible, if clunky, dredger scooping out a big pile of his most visceral feelings.

Frank: (blocking any palpitations, to Todd) How much is that?

He points to the collage that includes Todd, Frank, Lucy, in playing-card-suit shapes, with street love tattoos drawn in, cut out by Todd in his Perry Street apartment.

Todd: (feeling falling, tied to a parachute of sadness) It says on the sheet.

Frank: I wanna buy it from you. Let me buy it directly from you.

Todd: (hard to talk) I can't.

Frank: (testingly) Then I don't buy it.

Todd: (almost meaning it) Good.

A change of position implies so many other changes. When Todd moved the rose closer to the skull on the one page, the skull became less stark and horrific, and more kitsch and baroque, a solemn warning changed into a joke on taste. By moving closer to his new girlfriend, Frank has moved a possibly forever distance away from Todd and Lucy. And yet no one has changed less than Frank.

It's like working out a geometry problem. That's why Goethe's *Elective Affinities* is the best-named novel. First Todd and Lucy and Frank were in a triangle. And the triangle was not just a configuration but also a meaning. Now Todd and Lucy and Robbie are in a kind of triangle. Maybe isosceles, instead of equilateral. But a triangle nevertheless. Same configuration, different meaning.

Lucy, who has only watched, films Frank and his new girlfriend (her scimitar earrings glinting) as they turn backs and walk out through the confusing front glass door.

L.A.

Los Angeles (where Todd is flying to screen-test for a part in a Joe Martell movie) extends farther out beyond the frame of his curvilinear airplane window, gleaming amber. His rental is almost demolished by a shovel-truck on a detour through suburban turf with lots of Mexican-tile ranch houses with slanted drive-in-food-stand roofs. Is staying at Chateau Marmont, a big movie set of a chateau built in the early part of the century, where Billy Idol stayed the time he paid to have his bicep tattooed. The next day Todd reads lines in an office overlooking a parking lot for an executive who resembles a cigar wrapped in a suit. Takes a lunch break, drives down Sunset Boulevard where one billboard features a wire cage attached below that runs its length, where marathoners inside in pajamas eat and sleep and sit cross-legged, the winner earning a contract with a talent agency. Todd returns in the afternoon to read the same lines opposite a young woman stand-in, on a soundstage, with technicians the only audience. That night drives past all the motels on Santa Monica with their Las Vegas colors: turquoise, pink, gold, white.

At the hotel later, drinking rusty cognac in teeny bottles, scouring the bowl of chef's salad, he revives. Jerks off in his white cotton robe, like a class of kids let out of school, like a Queen song, then falls asleep in the eerie light of the Johnny Carson show.

Todd: (to TV) Take me. I'm yours.

That night Todd has his unsettling, borderline dream, a dream that makes him even more decisive. While he is screening the nightmare for himself on the inside of himself, on the outside he looks as placid as a nude.

TODD'S DREAM

The Russians have launched missiles that are on their way, unstoppable. Todd is dressed in the striped pajamas prisoners wear, his hair white with ashes, cigarette ashes. Is standing in a bomb shelter cluttered with double beds, mattresses on rusty springs, which are all collected together in a big square in the center of the cavernous room, a converted subway station. The atmosphere as gaslit as a black-white photograph that's been sepia-tinted. Todd's partner is a good-looking girl he doesn't know well, but knows some. A brown-haired girl in a white canvas dress. She stands next to him. News is broadcast in a hollow voice from a silver portable radio set up on a stand in the center of the room with its antenna pointing up to the ceiling that the missiles are about to hit. The dozens of fellow citizens in the hall all file up to a cafeteria-style counter to collect their ration of baby corns soaked in formaldehyde. They sniff in to get drugged, subdued, narcotized, numbed. Then file back. Todd tries to find a comfortable loving position with his partner—his head on her chest—but they don't quite fit. She tries his chest but that doesn't work either. They can't quite relax. No one to turn to. A crackling comes on the radio. The announcer flatly announces the arrival of the bomb. Then he finally shrieks in an emotional voice, "Mercy!" The wire burns out. The glow of the heat begins to light up the room meltingly as death begins.

POSTNUCLEAR FAMILY

The summer cabin is modern: angled roof, wall of windows, knotty-pine paneling. A hammock hangs outside like a distended belly between two trees. Cabin is set on a cliff of Baiting Hollow, a dirt-road community on the north shore of Long Island, along a series of cliffs that extends for hundreds of miles, like the cliffs of Crete, over the grainy beaches of the Sound. On the other side of the Sound is low-lying Connecticut.

Todd and Lucy sleep on the first floor, on a couch-bed. At night, prone, they can descry a natural silkscreen of brown trees and platinum sky through the windows. Robbie snores downstairs in a musky room with bunk beds, noisy mosquitoes working their way through unravelings in the screen. They've nicknamed the cabin "The Bomb Shelter." A carved shingle with the name hangs out front.

This morning Todd wakes up first. At six. Slips on green Army shorts, white T-shirt, sneakers with tractor treads. Pads outside into the yellow glare. His hair is cut short, as short as at Panarea, revealing all the bumps of his skull. Looks older than two years ago at Skunk Hollow, more angular. The beach below, where lobster fishermen are busy assembling floating traps, looks older, too, than the smoother beaches of the south shore, more prehistoric, with big boulders scattered across as if dropped in a meteor shower. Todd leans back on one boulder, his back chilled by the moisture compressed there during the night, his front warmed by the sun's heat lamp.

Lucy: (at screen) Cooooo. Cooooo.

Todd turns and makes out Lucy, a pastel smudge in her peach slip, through the pointillism of the screen.

Todd: (full and deep, like a Labrador or setter) Arrf. Arrf.

This is a satisfying dawn break for both of them. In the restless up and down. Of the central human endeavor of creating intimacy.

When Todd returns Lucy is back under the rose-design sheets, making her usual baby gurgles. Todd undresses, joins her. Together they perform a flat-out ballet of sleeping moves.

Lucy: (laying her head on Todd's chest) Give me chest space.

Todd: (positioning his stomach behind her back) Let's spoon.

Lucy: I love snuggling you.

Todd: (throwing a curve) Did you and Frank used to do spoons?

Lucy: (slamming it back) No. We had different positions.

Todd has a morning hard-on, and Lucy feels wet, but they don't tear into each other. They save it, to propel them with a little extra wind through the day.

Not Robbie. Cigarettes burning in two different ashtrays, he is down on the floor in his dark room downstairs. No clothes over his bony, gray, skinny, smooth body. He looks always somewhat like a black-white image in the middle of a Kodachrome world. His face absolutely smooth and unbroken. Body odor astringently sweet, emitting heavily as he sits on the floor with a *Playboy* magazine propped up on the far wall, open to a rosy nude actress with breasts as plushly buoyant as Astroturf. He wears Mona Lisa's smile as he zooms in on the stapled icon.

Fifteen minutes later Robbie showers at the top of his voice. It's eleven o'clock and Todd and Lucy still aren't out of bed. So he just slams upstairs, barges through the screen door in plaid swim trunks.

Robbie: (gesticulating) You guys need wake-up music.

He squeezes through a clutter of tables, chairs, pillows, benches, unpacked suitcases, tied garbage bags, *Time* magazines, *Philadelphia Inquirers*, lamps, past the bed, to the record bin. Picks out an album by Bruce Springsteen, that troubadour. The speakers are soon full of saxophone and piano and drum.

Robbie: (singing along in the Boss's hoarse voice) Everybody's got a hungry heart / Everybody's got a hungry heart / Lay down your money and you play your part / Everybody's got a hu-hu-hungry heart.

Lucy: (during the diminuendo) You trying to tell us you're hungry?

So the three start moving around the busy room in curves and arcs and straight lines and epicycles. Todd folds up the bed to make room to dress. Lucy boils hot water for three instant coffees. Robbie twitches and hums to the electrical prods of the big ballad.

Lucy: (to Todd, while rubbing behind Robbie's swim trunks) Nice buns. You ever harbor secret fantasies about your cousin?

Todd: (appraising the boy straight on) If he weren't my cousin I wouldn't mind sniffing his shorts. But I control myself.

Robbie: (big grin) Faggot.

Robbie drives the used station wagon that Todd bought from an Italian man down the road for $175. Only one door works so they all have to climb through this door on the passenger's side, front. The unhinged rearview mirror rests on the front ledge, propped up like a vanity mirror. Todd lies in the back, his feet pressed on a stuck-shut window. Lucy, wearing a striped jersey that hangs down to her knees, insists on listening only to news on the car radio; when one broadcast ends she switches to the next. Robbie is sporting his red-gold marine cap that overpowers his own face by its heavy, though pretty, physicality.

They are driving to Susie's fresh-produce stand. Through fields that stretch to the left and right with rows and rows of poking vegetables and corn, sprayed by a hose on wheels that stretches a hundred yards, looking like a skeleton of a plane taxiing. In the haze of one forest-green field rises a tiny barn with a water tower on its top, surrounded by a brim of wood, looking like a top hat. A tarn halfway up a hillside of berries is as yellow as yellow watermelon. The north shore is one of the last regions in the country to continue a tradition of family farming, though there are plenty of migrant workers along the roadside, staring at each car, cruising, like Sicilian boys ogling any car passing through their forgotten villages.

Susie, the daughter of the owner of the roadside stand, fancies Robbie. She's almost eighteen, overweight, her thumb bandaged from the time she sliced it off a few weeks back, her face a cratered lake of acne. She always wears the same dirty white button-down shirt (her father's) and blue jeans that hug her wide hips and puffing behind. Todd and Lucy knowingly search the bins, passing fresh goods to Robbie, letting him do the talking. He builds up a pyramid on the counter between him and Susie of zucchini, sweet corn, spaghetti squash, pink potatoes, yellow tomatoes, beets on stems.

Robbie: (rubbing his shirtless chest and tummy) You party last night?

Susie: (opening her big mouth) I went to the races. When you gonna come?

Robbie: (explaining to Todd and Lucy) Hot-rod races.

Susie: But I stayed out past curfew. So m'Mom's not letting me out tonight. I have to watch (sticks an unbandaged finger in mouth in gagging gesture) television.

Robbie: (adjusting the visor of his shadow-casting cap) At least you got a chance to be bad. I haven't gotten into trouble once out here.

Susie: (lowering voice, conspiratorially) Cookout on the beach tonight. Under you. Bring your own poison.

Robbie flashes her his armpit, a raunchy sign of affection this summer in these parts. Then she weighs the food groups on a digital scale. Todd pays. On the way back Robbie cruises in a cloud of gray-pebble dirty exhaust past his favorite landmark eyesore, the ranch house where the motor-heads live. Where they pile cars up on bricks all over the front yard, and in the driveway, to work on them. Dismantled engines sit like monuments along the curbside.

Robbie: (laughs and laughs) Those clowns.

Lucy: I'm hungry.

Todd: Step on it.

The three eat lunch on a picnic table that teeters on the ridge of the cliff, in the full midday heat of the sun, sweat dripping onto their white paper plates. Today they are eating Lucy's skilleted fresh corn kernels mixed with cottage cheese and chutney bottled at Susie's. Drinking sun-heated iced tea.

Robbie: (fresh) So how was the screen test? Was acting like modeling?

Todd: Could be. The difference is in modeling if you get stuck on your image you just mess up your life. In acting if you get stuck on your image you can't act very good.

Lucy: (made more buxom by the sun and wind and rain, correcting) Not very *good*.

Lucy likes to lie in the hammock after lunch, its movement as subtle as the rocking of an ocean liner on a calm day in the Atlantic. She is listening to the different whistles of the birds. They are as busy in those trees as bureaucrats in their offices. Their calls as organized as the patterned sounds of Teletype machines. Lucy whistles back, convinced she is breaking the code.

Todd sits at his drafting table in Robbie's room. He uses it as his studio during the afternoons. Is trying to ignore the *Pin Downs* calendar Robbie tacked up with Todd's picture as the August man, posed as a lifeguard with white warpath makeup on his nose and under his eyes. Todd is working on a spread he has titled "The Très Riches Heures of Todd Eamon" after the medieval illustrations he saw in Janson's *History of Art*. He is making an ideal landscape from the scenery of Baiting Hollow, with a photo of The Bomb Shelter at the apex, under a blue starry Ptolemaic sky. He's looking for bits and pieces of scenery— trees, bushes, fishes, hot rods—in local magazines. His head is as clear as a crystal in an old radio. Doesn't mind the flies swatting their wings all over his clammy skin.

Robbie is back at the stereo upstairs. When he sticks onto a song he just plays it over and over. Today it's "Hungry Heart."

Robbie lies for twenty minutes on a Y towel spread outside on top of the picnic table to work on his tan. Then returns inside to sing along to the song.

Robbie: (singing and gyrating to the second chorus) Everybody needs a place to rest / Everybody wants to have a home / Don't make no difference what nobody says / Ain't nobody like to be alone.

As shadows begin, late afternoon, to soften from black to purple, this odd family goes for a walk along the beach. They pass by the skeletons of a few harmless fish, not predatory. Then reach a stretch of beach polka-dotted with the round blubbery bodies of purple-and-white viscous jellyfish.

Robbie: Those are dangerous. No wonder no one's swimming.

Lucy: They're just Frisbees. Underwater Frisbees.

Farther along they meet friends of Robbie's, a gang of three surfers, standing in front of a sheer slab of tan rock. The three are all dressed in surfers' uniforms even though there is no surfing possible here. The first is wearing a black uniform with the words RIP CURL listed a few times down a stripe on his sleeve, the second an orange uniform with a PIPING badge on the shoulder, the third a decal on his chest of a curving wave. All three are blond, have immaculate nails.

Robbie: How'd you squids get here?

Surfer #1: We're casing it for a party.

Robbie: Susie said.

So Robbie hangs with the three. Todd and Lucy continue to comb the beach, eventually climbing the cliff. In an hour they will barbecue fresh tuna, the smoke of the coals whirling upward like a curving rococo pillar.

As afternoon is flipped over into evening, Robbie, flushed and rough around the edges, sits with his three friends above a blazing fire they've built from stones and wood, sucking on bottles of hot gin to keep warm, then smashing the bottles against the big rocks. Soon the moon is directly above them, full and white. It is a lamppost and they are the drunks leaning against it.

Surfer #2: I hope the girls get here soon.

Surfer #3: They're probably all lesbians.

Robbie: I like lesbians the best. They're a real challenge. They're all virgins.

Surfer #1: Some of the bars in the city have all-lesbian nights. You wanna go cruise together Robbie?

Robbie: A lesbian I know in Allentown took a Polaroid of my stiff dick once.

Surfer #1: You got to second base.

The girls eventually do arrive in their one-piece bathing suits. Even Susie, spilling from the seams, who snuck out the back screen door of her farmhouse. All party in the glowering. Drink firewater. Their voices clicking like the voices of birds, or animals that live in the wild. For a minute Susie has Robbie held down splayed while her friends pour gin down his throat, then extinguish their fiery tongues in his steamy mouth. He makes a roaring sound from all the way down in his lungs.

Todd, sitting on the bench on the cliff, spots the orange Dionysiac flames reverberating like drumbeats off the rocks below. Decides to reconnoiter. Feels a rose of responsibility toward Robbie growing in the rich black soil of his heart. The road down is a hollow dark funnel, an arbor covered by trees that block moonlight. Not much to see. Todd's inside feelings are magnified for him as outside stimuli wane. But these aren't complicated feelings, feelings with names. They are like planks of wood, concrete bricks, wet buckets of cement, ladders. His insides are a construction site. The beach opens up in front of him as unindividuated as a setting for a myth.

Meanwhile Robbie takes a breather, sweating from dancing so hard and watching his own reflections, and those of his partners, like cavemen paintings on the walls.

Robbie: (no one hears) I feel sick.

So Robbie shuffles through the orange-black phantasmagoria of the outside toward the unbroken water. Wrapped now in a black beach towel. Reaches the big shore, sand and water indistinguishable, except by moving and nonmoving, felt on the soles of his teenage feet.

Robbie: (like a red Indian praying) Oh Spirit of the Waters. Please make me a stud. Like my cousin Todd.

Three minutes later Todd grabs two hands on the back of Robbie's shivering shoulders, as if they were the handlebars of a bicycle.

Robbie: (turning around, squinting) God.

Todd: (faceless) The day's almost over. I want you to come back upstairs with me.

Robbie: There's no upstairs here. There's a cliff.

Todd: You know what I mean.

Robbie: You don't seem like you anymore.

Todd: Do you know what you're talking about, alcohol breath?

Robbie: (tentatively) No . . .

After they climb the crag for the last time of the day, Robbie slowly, Todd bolstering him, they split. Robbie descends down the wood stairs to crash on his bunk in a vapor of nitroglycerin smell. Todd ascends to the main room of the cabin where he sits for a while with Lucy on the couch.

Lucy: (curled up in oversized white sweatshirt, no other clothes, explaining) Home movies.

Lucy is playing her videotape of the gallery opening on the TV screen. She plays the shot of Frank's back disappearing over and over again, sometimes at slow speed, sometimes at hilariously fast speed. Then she looks up at Todd like someone who's waiting for feedback. She looks as white-haired as Betsy Ross in the reflected electronic light.

Lucy: You like? Sweetie?

Todd: (unresponsive) I feel like we used to live in two. And now we live in three. Dimensions.

Lucy: (teasing) You would.

After touching Lucy on her rather high forehead, Todd changes into a red hooded sweatshirt to walk around outside. The sky is shedding falling stars. Todd angles over to a flower bed. Bends down and pushes his right hand way down into the soil as if it were a trowel. He unearths a goosh of mud in his palm and pulls the lump out. A segmented worm works its way out of the warm, slides along Todd's palm, then along a finger, then drops back on the ground. The organism gone, Todd squeezes the oozing excess mud through his fist.

Todd: (yelling in through screened window-wall) It must have been August two years ago I was out on Skunk Hollow. There were falling stars then too.

Todd stands and looks over the cliff into the deep perspective of an infinite box of water, land and sky. The moon is striking down in a vertical chute that is as direct as lightning, though continuous rather than suddenly broken, and is as gold-yellow as the sun, though cold not hot. It is striking down into the purplish waters of the murmuring Sound and splintering on contact into an Aztec print of zigzags and wavy lines. It is vivisecting.

Todd, emptied out, turns and walks quietly back into the cabin. Lucy looks up cattily, with an understanding face, as he kills the light by the switch by the door. One tall yellow candle is burning its tallow on top of the TV. Lucy stands up as if part of a procession, Todd walks toward her, they meet in the center of the room. He busily undresses while she just slips from her oversized white sweatshirt.

They do it standing up. In the buff. Todd's hands cupped on Lucy's behind, guiding himself into port. Her hands holding on the backs of the wooden posts of his thighs, her neck thrown way back and unusual noises coming out of it, foghorns.

Lucy: (shriek) Do it to me.

Todd: (in a tight little voice, not his) I like sweet young pussy.

Lucy: (in her own voice) I like long thick meat.

The cock is a rock, as at Stonehenge, erect to the earth, but passive to the sky where the rockets came from that once landed on its clock dial of a face. The cunt is a furrow, the burn in the earth left by the rockets taking off from its surface, but also the calligraphic writing on the earth to guide them back home later.

Fucking is like the ditches they make marines dig in boot camp that they then fill in again at the end of the day with the same dirt they've uselessly shoveled.

Todd and Lucy both moan as they both contract the shivers, and then the release, a natural fix. They are holding on to each other, bones sticking out, flab hanging loose, hearts pumping about 160 beats per minute, way above average.

Falling stars are flaming cigarette butts darted down into the Sound by climaxing gods and goddesses upstairs.

Pretty soon Todd and Lucy open up the couch-bed and crawl onto its creaking springs for the night. They are two lumps lying there. Cured like hams by the night air.

Lucy: (a voice in the dark, hoarse) Do you think the marinade works on the swordfish as well as on the barbecued tuna steak?

Todd: (loose, easy, get down) Tuna.